Murder in Gutenthal

NEIL BERGEN
INVESTIGATOR
427-6610

"WE STOOP TO SNOOP"

Murder
in
Gutenthal

A Schneppa Kjnals Mystery

— by Armin Wiebe —

Turnstone Press

Turnstone Press
607-100 Arthur Street
Winnipeg, Manitoba
Canada   R3B 1H3

Turnstone Press gratefully acknowledges the assistance of
the Canada Council and the Manitoba Arts Council.

Cover illustration and design: David Morrow Illustration

This book was printed and bound in Canada by
Hignell Printing Limited for Turnstone Press.

Canadian Cataloguing in Publication Data

Wiebe, Armin
Murder in Gutenthal

ISBN 0-88801-158-X

I. Title.

PS8595.I5311M87 1991   C813/.54   C91-097158-7
PR9199.3.W543M87 1991

Portions of this novel have been previously published in slightly different form in *Good Humour Man.* (Queenston House) and *Prairie Fire.*

I would like to thank John Parr, for making me an offer I couldn't refuse, and Sandra Birdsell, Wayne Tefs and Millie, my wife, for reading various drafts and pointing out the loose ends.

For Millie and Jenny

1

THE Bible lay on the corner of Nobah Naze Needarp's grave. The grave is only two plots away from my father's grave so I had to see it even if I wasn't looking for anything. But I am always looking for something, and listening, too. Listening to my blood. My father was Beluira Bergen, listening still on that great party line in the sky. I have sometimes thought, though a person wouldn't say such a thing, that God must have taken my father because he needed a special set of ears. I come to his grave almost every day. It helps me feel who I am. And I find things at the graveyard.

The Bible was a black zipper Bible so I had to zip it open to see whose it was. Some Bibles around here I know without looking inside. Like Zamp Pickle Peters always carries a German Bible with bevelled page ends and Hingst Heinrichs has carried that little Gideon Testament we all got in grade five ever since he saw a show in Neche one time where a soldier had his life saved because the bullet hit the Testament in the pocket over his heart. I maybe know some people who would want to shoot Hingst Heinrichs, but this is Gutenthal and people don't shoot each other here even if it is only a mile to the ditch that cuts us off from the States. But I do know the Bibles around here and, if nobody is listening, I do think there have been murders in Gutenthal, too, but I wouldn't say such a thing to anybody.

So I zipped open the Bible because how else would I know who to give it back to and I was quite surprised. I had never seen Oata Siemens carry such a Bible. I had never seen Oata carry any Bible to church at all because she always carried the baby and Yasch carried the Bible, and it wasn't a zipper Bible. But right there inside this Bible it said:

> Presented to Oata Needarp
> for Perfect Attendance in 1961
> by her Sunday School teacher,
> Mr. Lawrence U. Dyck.

And then when I was going to zipper it shut again a piece of paper dropped out. I picked it up from the grass beside the grave. It was white letter paper with a blue flower in the bottom corner and it smelled a little like the shaving lotion the Watkins man sells. The writing looked the same as in the Bible.

> Dear Oata,
>
> Thank you for listening to me in my hour of need. I will be forever grateful for your sympathy and understanding. If only things could be as we desire. But we must let the Lord's will be done.
>
> As always,
> Lawrence

Well holem de gruel, what was that supposed to mean? There was no date on the letter and I couldn't figure it out but it could mean so many things that I really didn't want to think about such things here in Gutenthal. I mean this isn't B.C.! Still, who would have thought that L.U.Dyck ever had anything more in his head except to argue with his brother A.Dyck about which was better to use to clean the barn, a shovel or a fork? So, I followed my nose over to the second row of the graveyard to the Suaromp Dycks' double grave. Then for sure I thought something must have blown over from the States because lying there between a wild rose bush and a sowthistle was a little magazine that said on the front: "How about an Affair with an Older Man?" And people think nothing ever happens in Gutenthal. For sure if anything happens in Gutenthal I know about it. I am not Beluira Bergen's son for nothing.

In school they called me Boy-o-Boy Bergen and Corny Mountain, and I bloodied a few noses when they called me Beluirakje and Corn Ears. I tried to deny my heritage and wished I was a Heinrichs or a Friesen or a Warkentin, and I used Alexander Graham Bell as a swear word. I once even cultivatored up the buried cable and put all of Gutenthal out of earshot and I didn't tell anybody about it until I went in for faspa. But when I saw Mama sitting there rattling with those little buttons on the dial phone and trying to connect dead batteries to the farmer phone, I just couldn't hold out. So I drove all the way to Puggefeld to phone the telephone office about what had happened and I even gave them heck for not burying the cable deeper in the first place. Last year for Mother's Day I gave Mama one of those touch-tone speaker-phones so now she can listen in even when she has her arms up to the elbows in bread dough. I even disconnected the microphone part so the neighbours can't hear Mama talking back to them.

For years I tried to be different from my father. I wouldn't even answer the phone when it rang *our* number. I read Peter Funk in the *Reader's Digest* at the barber shop while my ears picked up what was said around me. I studied the correspondence lessons that Koadel Kehler, the teacher's kid, would lend me. I built my muscles with the American Body Building Club. I learned judo and karate and Chinese foot fighting long before they got kung fu on TV. Koadel only ordered the lessons. I learned them. I would strip naked in the hayloft to do push-ups and kick the straw out of the bales. Koadel only practised for a day or two after he got the lessons in the mail, then he ordered something else he saw in the ads in *Mechanics Illustrated.* Play guitar in seven days. Earn money writing short paragraphs. Be a ventriloquist. Make money drawing cartoons. Be a lawyer. Investigate accidents with a shapely woman at your side. Import and export a fortune from other lands. Grow rich raising earthworms. Be a chiropractor. Be your own boss. Be a private detective.

When I was seventeen Koadel Kehler passed on a booklet about phrenology. I studied my face in the mirror, saw the oversized grey eyes, turned to see the profile of my long, slightly down-turned, perfect drip nose, then turned back full visage, my hair cut like a wheatfield in August, my narrow face doubled in width by those satellite dish ears, and I knew there was nothing I could do to change what I was—not even if I paid Funk to increase my word power.

They say Koadel Kehler is writing books now. I'm a private detective. I specialize in lost cattle, stolen grain and forgotten Bibles. I see the holes in the fences. Strange combines in familiar fields. I leave the funny plants growing between the sunflowers for the RCMP. I have to be realistic. Solving murders in Gutenthal would bushel about as much as shipbuilding in Rosenfeld.

My business card reads Neil Bergen, Investigator. The effective detective. Some call me Corny Pee-Eye. But mostly people call me Schneppa Kjnals. Corny the snoop. I would like it better if they called me Neil, but in my business pride is the deadly sin.

Divorce is the bread and butter of the private detective. So said the lessons from the Hollywood School of Detection, run by ex-NYPD, ex-FBI, ex-CIA, ex-KGB, and ex-Winkler police officers willing to share their vast knowledge and experience with you for a fee. Thank God it was Koadel's fee, not mine. So what if the certificate of honour suitable for framing came in his name? I did the work. I answered the questions on how to follow a husband or a wife or a dog or a cat. But divorce is still mostly a sin in Gutenthal, so the bread and butter is more like a hollow bun without a crust.

But Oata Siemens's forgotten Bible was in my hand, or was it forgotten? And the "Affair with an Older Man" magazine? Both looked clean. They hadn't been out in the rain. Then I shrugged it all off. I mean, Yasch Siemens's Oata making somma borsch with A.Dyck's brother, L.U.Dyck, was about as likely as having those vinegar and sourdock brothers sell the farm and move to town. Only as I put Oata's Bible on the seat beside me in the grey Volkswagen and drove away from the graveyard to make my rounds of Gutenthal I noticed a dark car stopped about a mile away. Someone was putting something up on a telephone pole. When I got there the car was gone but the yellow auction sale notice made me wonder if maybe I was turning into a prophet. A.Dyck and L.U.Dyck were selling the farm!

Many little things happened that day. Dola Dyck's Angus bull got out through the fence and almost made it into the green alfalfa, but I had him back in place and was twisting the broken strands of barbed wire together by the time Dola pulled up in his green pickup truck. He managed to find five dollars in his coveralls, then drove away, leaving behind a cloud of oily smoke.

Next, Laups Leeven's two-year-old boy was driving his tricycle on the post road almost three-quarters of a mile from home. Shups Leeven nearly paid me with a handful of wooden clothespins after she hugged her son, then she laughed apologetically and reached back into her clothespin apron and pulled out two dollar bills that had gone through the wash in Laups's pants. And ten haybales fell off Hingst Heinrichs's truck and he didn't notice until I waved him down and told him about it. Hingst prides himself on not being a cheap bugger so I scored a ten.

I was about to turn into Yasch Siemens's driveway when I saw trouble on the bridge over the double dike by Penzel Panna's flax field. I forgot about Oata's Bible and drove on. My heartbeat quickened as I recognized the rig and then the driver.

"Hutz Drot 'n Drasha Bulchi!" Rosmack Rampel muttered as I got out of my car. The back wheel of the disker hung over one edge of the bridge while the dual tire of the Versatile four-wheel-drive tractor hung over the other. The disks had scratched the rough planks like claws before coming to rest halfway across the narrow bridge. Rosmack flashed her black eyes at me and said, "How come all the councillors get new bridges to their fields and we have to use old ones too small for even a horse 'n buggy?" She talked in Flat German, pure field and manure pile Flat German. It was amazing for a teenage girl to speak Flat German at all, let alone like a threshing-gang foreman, even more amazing for Rosmack with her raven-black hair, black eyes and deeply tanned face. In her jeans and plaid shirt she looked like the perfect CBC Indian.

Rosmack Rampel, Rape Rampel's adopted daughter, always holding rosmack at home and at school, settling disputes and keeping order. Talking Flat German like she had just come from Russia or Mexico, she came home from school in grade three and said that she had had to 'hold rosmack' while the teacher was out of the room. So her brothers started calling her 'Rosmack' and the name stuck and spread so only Rape Rampel himself still calls her Rosie.

Her real mother was one of the Indian beetweeders who worked for Rape Rampel for a few summers. When this baby girl was born, Rape and his wife adopted her because they had three boys already then and Rosmack's mother was too young and poor to look after the child. So they said. Some said it was only half an adoption because according to the willow leaves Rape may have brought more to the situation than a generous heart.

Anyway, Rosmack grew up a happy kid keeping order among her brothers and shocking strangers who heard this dark-eyed girl spitting out Flat German. But children learn from adults, and as Rosmack entered her teens Gutenthal was no longer the safe place for her it had been before.

Certainly, the situation on the bridge was unsafe. Rosmack is usually pretty good with machinery but I could see that a few more wrong moves would put the disker and tractor into a tangled pile in the ditch. Still, sometimes all that is needed to get out of a situation is a second set of eyes. So with some study of angles, sharp twisting of the steering wheel, and careful hand signals from me, Rosmack manoeuvred the outfit off the bridge and onto solid ground. When she leaned down out of the cab to wave goodbye I noticed the flash of her high school ring on her long brown finger, and her nose was covered with beads of sweat.

I was sweating, and itchy, too, and as she drove away I felt like my soul was filled with barley dust.

It was Saturday and on Saturday nights I help out at Barbara Ball Bearing's place. That is my charity work. The rest of the week I am a good neighbour for a fee, but Saturday nights at Barbara's is strictly charity. Charity without a tax receipt. And whether it comes to a tenth of anything doesn't matter. Just to breathe the same air as Barbara is enough—well, of course I want more, but just to be there in the same house watching the lines of her panties through her slim jims when she bends over to put a beer bottle into the case, or seeing the way her long toes kind of grip the floor like a bird's claws, or getting a glance of a strap through the neck of her soft full baby blue sweater is enough to keep me coming back every Saturday night even though I don't drink beer.

Barbara knelt beside the flower bed, which looked like a giant whitewall tire. That is usually where she is before the kids arrive. I like to watch her pulling the weeds, though I know she is the farthest away from me then, the farthest away from anyone. A '57 Chev is buried under that flower bed, the Chev that turned Barbara Ball Bearing into the youngest widow Gutenthal ever had. Six weeks after the wedding Memphis Toews smashed his '57 Chev into the little green Renault Lucy Lamoureux had received for her sixteenth birthday. The steering column punctured his chest, but the bottle of States beer was unspilled in his left hand, the Zippo lighter in his right flicked open, the unlit Black Cat filter cigarette still stuck in the gap of a missing front tooth. The day after we attended Lucy Lamoureux's funeral in the cathedral in Letellier, Barbara buried her husband, wreck and all, at the foot of the yardlight pole and became a missionary to youth.

I got out of my Volkswagen as quietly as I could, but the old door squeaked and Barbara looked up. She dropped the handful of weeds into the rusty pail beside her, grabbed the handle as she stood up, flicked her ponytail with her whole body and wiped all the words from my mind. I walked up to her and when I got within reach she held out the pail and put out her other hand, palm up. For a second I could make out the fortune lines, lines that formed an M. I put my hand on the handle and she released it. I didn't move. She looked me in the eye.

"Neil," she said. I couldn't resist. I placed my car keys into her hand. My fingers touched hers. I kept them there for a moment, let her fingers stroke mine as she clasped my keys, then shoved them into her pocket.

"They're starting to come," she said, and I could hear the sound of an approaching car. I kept my eyes fixed on Barbara as she turned away. "I have to wash my hands," she said. I stood there holding the pail of weeds as she ran through the gate of the picket fence but in my head I followed Barbara up the veranda steps and through the screen door. I could hear the radio playing in the kitchen. I saw myself open the door, slip inside, then hook the screen behind me. On the radio Brenda Lee sang in a whispery voice. Barbara sat at the kitchen table in her well-filled sleeveless blouse. She raised a filtered cigarette to her red lips and spoke to me with her big blue eyes. Without any words to trip over we embraced in a cloud of smoke.

"Wake up, horny Corny!" I turned. Fuchtich Froese's son, Shtreedich, clasped the top of his car window frame with his middle finger as he idled past me. His brother, Yachtich, showed me a mouthful of black and white teeth, and I was happy this was Barbara's place and not mine. The Froese brothers had tried out for a wrestling team last year, only they didn't know the fighting was not for real. The WWF couldn't afford body slams from these fellows, who tossed four bottom ploughs around on Hallowe'en. And they weren't eighteen yet.

But it was Barbara's place and she was in control. The yard was soon filled with cars and pickup trucks and as the boys carried their twelves and twenty-fours of Club and White Seal to the veranda or into the kitchen, they dropped their keys into Barbara's hand. Their girls, if they had some, followed them shyly if they were new, or more boldly if they had been around for a while. It was a warm summer evening with just enough breeze to keep the mosquitoes away. Barbara brought the record player outside and after the brown empties had begun their march along the veranda rail, the girls and some of the braver boys started to dance. As it got darker some couples slipped away into the house or out into the shadows of the barnyard but they soon returned to the light. This was Barbara's place and though Barbara wasn't against hugging and kissing and even petting under her roof, she also wasn't against dumping a pail of cold well water on passions threatening to go out of control.

I was restless as I gathered empty beer bottles into their cases and carried them to the summer kitchen. I have a yeast allergy so I couldn't drink beer. Maybe it was a good thing. Barbara, too, seemed a little distracted, putting her old records on the record player more often—Richie Valens,

Buddy Holly, Eddie Cochrane—and as she leaned on the veranda railing staring at the whitewall tire flower bed under the yardlight I wished I could make all the kids disappear. But instead, more kids came. A young guy in a baby blue Ford brought two twenty-fours and Sadie Nickel's little sister. I hadn't seen him before. He looked kind of out of place with his short Sunday School haircut and his thin moustache, and after a couple of beers he seemed to get a bit noisier than the others and he tried to dance with all the girls. Two Harley Davidson motorcycles showed up about midnight—Rosmack Rampel, dressed in her black leather jacket and white crash helmet, and a guy dressed in black—black boots, black denim trousers, studded black leather vest over a black T-shirt, black scarf tied around his head. His black hair, cropped short at the sides, gradually tapered to a ridge from front to back along the centre of his scalp so his head looked like a cold chisel. Mirrored shades covered his eyes in spite of the dark and he was chewing on a match. As he and Rosmack got to the veranda and handed Barbara their keys I saw he was carrying a zipper Bible. Funny thing for a biker to carry on a Saturday night. I didn't know this jerk, but he was with Rosmack, and that didn't put any cream in my coffee. I didn't even get blue milk in my coffee when I heard some of the kids whispering that the guy had just been released from Headingley Jail and his name was Beitelkopp Blatz.

For nine months I was a Pinkerton man. Nine months of graveyard shifts, patrolling the aisles of the assembly lines at the Versatile plant. Nobody tried to take a combine home in his lunch pail. I got a transfer to a mining camp in the north. One winter was enough to drive me back to Gutenthal. I went independent.

For a few weeks I did nothing except the few chores in the

barn now that Papa was gone. Mama had rented the land to Hingst Heinrichs and I had saved some money from my Pinkerton job so I didn't feel like a lazy bum living off his mother. I just let Gutenthal soak back into my skin and brooded about how I could be a pee-eye without leaving home.

Now I watched Rosmack Rampel leaning against Beitelkopp Blatz's shoulder as he pointed out something in the zipper Bible to Wilbert Fehr, who was opening a beer bottle with his teeth. I thought back to when I had first met Rosmack at the fair a year ago. A bunch of Puggefeld punks had been giving her a hard time. I intervened.

It was a small incident but it gave me a vision of what a private investigator could be in a place like Gutenthal. The detective as a good neighbour. Sure everyone should be a good neighbour, but who has time nowadays? And it costs too much. Charity is easier if it is tax deductible. I'll be a good neighbour for a fee, I thought.

A few days after the fair I was riding Marie, the black mare, along a field road when Rosmack came up behind me on her motorcycle. She stopped the Harley beside the horse and we looked at each other for a few moments. Then she smiled and said, "Thanks for helping me with those jerks!"

"Any time," I said. "That's what I'm here for." She gave me a questioning look, then said, "Guess I better go. See you." She roared off, leaving me wishing I was ten years younger.

She is seventeen now, still rides her motorcycle, still has trouble with punks, still thanks me. We are connected. When I need help she appears out of nowhere. When she needs help I am there.

But at Barbara's party Rosmack didn't need my help. She never had a beer and neither did Beitelkopp Blatz. With his arm around Rosmack, I heard him say to Shtreedich Froese,

"A merry heart doeth good like medicine: but a broken spirit drieth the bones."

"Is that a Bible verse?" Shtreedich asked as he stuck his empty beer bottle into the case I was carrying.

"Yeah sure," Beitelkopp said, "Proverbs 17:22," and then that bugger turned his head and kissed Rosmack smack on the lips like there was nothing to it, but before my broken spirit could dry my bones Barbara touched me on the shoulder and whispered, "Have you seen Sadie Nickel's little sister?" I hadn't and I couldn't see the guy with the moustache either. Barbara's face had a dark and worried look on it.

Of course we checked the baby blue Ford first, and Barbara didn't knock before she yanked the back door open. She gave a sharp whistle which brought Shtreedich and Yachtich running to the car. The moustache boy was pretty drunk, and showing us his underwear with the yellow stripe down the sides didn't help him either. He blubbered about being a peace officer and that he'd get us all for this but when Barbara gave orders to Shtreedich and Yachtich you didn't have much of a chance, and on top of that, the little Nickel girl was only fifteen and the beer and the excitement didn't go down so well and the moustache boy was lucky we had pulled him out before the girl gave a heave ho all over the powder blue back seat.

"Kids play, but don't play with kids!" Barbara said. "Take him to the barn and give him a cold shower."

I was happy Shtreedich and Yachtich were on my side in this and after the spray of well water had soaked him for a few minutes the young Mountie stopped threatening us with charges and was hoping I think that nobody would report his behaviour.

I heard the motorcycles start up while we were in the

barn and both Rosmack and Beitelkopp were gone when I came out.

I ended up driving some of the kids home, though none of the regulars had drunk very much and there was quite a stockpile of beer for a future party. Barbara cleaned up the Nickel girl and I took her home. The wet RCMP boy had been sitting on the veranda steps, but he was gone when I returned about fifteen minutes later. Barbara's house was in darkness, only the yardlight over the flower bed still on. I drove home, more restless and frustrated than ever, thinking one minute about Barbara and the next minute about Rosmack, worrying about what trouble Beitelkopp Blatz could get her into.

Mama was waiting up for me with freshly baked bread, so I tore a soft slice into a bowl and poured milk over the pieces. But my heart was so heavy that I hardly tasted the fresh bread and the hint of dandelion in the milk. I was too old for a Harley Davidson and my grey Volkswagen was just no match for the ghost of the '57 Chev.

2

Y UNGES Yeeatze phoned at 6:30 on Sunday morning just when I was dreaming about Barbara Ball Bearing's sleeveless sweater and Rosmack Rampel's long black hair. It took me a little time to figure out what Yunges Yeeatze was trying to tell me because he doesn't just tell you what happened, he always tells you yet what he was thinking about while it was happening. But this was what I figured out when my ear stopped ringing.

When Yunges Yeeatze looked out of the window on Sunday morning and saw six white brassieres hanging from the washline, he thought how lucky he was to have six sons instead of six daughters or there might have been forty-nine brassieres hanging there and the last time his wife, Trudy, had bought a brassiere at the Flatland Mall, it had set him back $12.50 plus tax and still she turned the light out before she undressed so he couldn't even enjoy this expensive cloth.

Yunges Yeeatze's next thought was that the brassieres had been hung in an interesting way, like a set of box end wrenches, the smallest one on the left and the biggest one on the right, and he wondered how come his one Trudy would need so many sizes, but then he was a busy farmer who maybe didn't look his wife on enough so he wouldn't know if a woman's brassiere size changed from day to day with her mood. Who would a person ask about such a thing? For sure, the *Country Guide* never had an article about this. Then Yunges Yeeatze remembered something from the night before and he phoned me.

At first I didn't think he should have phoned me so early over such a thing but when Yunges Yeeatze ended his story by saying he was absolutely, positively sure his Trudy had washed six pairs of shorts and hung them on the line to dry after the boys had their Saturday night bath, my ears lifted. Yunges Yeeatze was absolutely correct. When boys' shorts on a washline change into brassieres overnight something strange is going on. And there had just been too many strange things going on in Gutenthal.

I tried to go back to sleep, but I couldn't even get Barbara and Rosmack focused on the movie screen behind my eyes before Mama started rattling with the pots in the kitchen and then the phone rang again. It was Mrs. Daughters Doerksen and in her voice that always sounds like wind blowing through a flax field she told me her six daughters' white Sunday brassieres had changed into boys' shorts and for sure those shorts weren't white any more. There was just a little bit of barbed wire in her voice that told me if her daughters had to go to church wearing weekday brassieres there would also be hail on somebody's crop. So I was happy to say to Mrs. Daughters Doerksen that I would do everything in my power to bring the brassieres back to her in time for church, but Mama wanted me to eat breakfast first before she would let me go out of the house. Which was true. If Mama didn't make me eat a big breakfast in the morning I would probably be dead, because too often my day gets so busy I don't get a chance to eat until after the sun has gone down.

I got to church on time to watch the Doerksen daughters walk up the steps in a line from eleven to seventeen and Mrs. Daughters Doerksen stopped by my grey Volkswagen to slip a two-dollar bill into my hand. A few minutes later Yunges Yeeatze and his wife led their sons past me in a line from five to twelve but they didn't stop to pay me. I guessed it wasn't that important to the boys to have their shorts back.

Inside the church Klaviera Klassen started playing the piano. Most Sundays I was sitting inside the church, too. It was a restful place after a busy Saturday night helping Barbara at her parties. But this Sunday I had decided to keep an eye on the yard because last Sunday when Yasch Siemens's muttachi went outside during the sermon somebody turned the swivel on the beckhouse door and Yasch's poor muttachi couldn't get out until Rape Rampel heard her hammering on the door when he came out first after church. The Sunday before that Yut Yut Leeven and Eva Enns couldn't open their car doors because somebody had filled the keyholes with Crazy Glue and the Sunday before that when Klaviera Klassen stood up from the piano bench her stockings caught on a shoe tack that had never been sticking out of that bench before. Two Sundays before that a garter snake crawled out from under the pulpit while Preacher Janzen was praying. My theory was these were the pranks of kids, but I hadn't been able to piece any proof together yet.

Rape Rampel's Chrysler drove into the church yard and

parked close to the beckhouses. Rape and his wife and Rosmack climbed out of the front while the boys squeezed out of the back. Rosmack tossed her head so her long raven-black hair spread out over her white blouse down almost to her black skirt. She stood straight, not bent over like so many tall girls, and her dark face frowned at her blond, freckle-faced family.

"We're the last again," Rosmack said in Flat German. At the sound of her words the whole family hurried to the church steps so they could get seated before Klaviera stopped playing. I held my breath. Rosmack passed my car without a glance. She walked tall, her slim legs steady on her three-inch heels, and even in her Sunday best she looked like she belonged on a motorcycle. She gave me no hint that she knew I was sitting there watching her, no hint anything had happened with that shuzzel, Beitelkopp Blatz.

Rosmack disappeared into the church and I let my breath go. I looked at the mail-order handcuffs hanging from the mirror, saw my wheatfield hair, my long, narrow watermelon face doubled in width by those two cabbage leaves, saw the oversized grey eyes, the patches of stubble on my jaw. I took another long breath. If I hadn't had to deal with brassieres and shorts so early I could have had a bath and a shave before church. Inside the church the people shuffled as they sat down after the first prayer. I leaned back and yawned as I looked around the church yard. Preacher Funk started to preach in German and I knew it would be a long one. I closed my eyes to rest them a little bit.

Maybe I dozed off for a few minutes, but only a few because church was still on when I awoke. I could still hear Preacher Funk preaching through the open windows but something else had awakened me—that crackling of tires on gravel that doesn't wake you until it stops and you suddenly know you are hearing something. But before I opened my eyes I heard a car door opening. I lifted my chin from where it was knocking against my chest and looked through the handcuffs hanging from the mirror.

A green Ford LTD was stopped maybe a hundred yards down the road from the graveyard. A woman was trying to put the bumperjack together on the front passenger side. I didn't know the car and I couldn't make out who the woman was but I could see she was having some trouble with the jack.

The woman didn't speak when I offered to help, but her long, dark eyelashes blinked together like a doll's. Her face was almost white, but not really white, more like eggshells with some cracks, and she had dark hair, but not black, with a little bit of grey, and her face was round and it seemed big and her eyes were big and dark and her eyebrows were dark, almost wet, painted like a doll face. Her lips were a dark brown, not red like lipstick, and it was almost like she was a dead person, like a dead person that has been fixed up for the funeral and doesn't look like the live person because the face was crushed in an accident and the undertaker put it all back again but the puzzle wouldn't fit together the same as God made it. Except this woman wasn't dead. She was alive and she wasn't painted, not at all, not even lipstick or powder, and her eyes were a little wet and shiny like eyes should be at a funeral.

Her dress was long, all the way down to her shoes, with lots of lace on it, and it was a black colour, only it seemed like it shouldn't be black. The dress seemed old and new at the same time, almost like the time I looked down through the heating grate from upstairs and saw Mama with her wedding dress on, looking happy and sad at the same time. And as I was loosening the nuts on her wheel I tried to remember where I had seen this woman before, but I couldn't think of it. You know how it is with the brain. It's like a vacuum cleaner the way it sucks in all the dust in this world and sometimes it sucks up a marble, but when you empty the bag not everything will shake loose and you know the marble is in there but it won't come out even if you take the machine apart. And then when you have sucked in lots of new dust all of a sudden the marble falls out and you can't remember why you wanted it in the first place.

When I finished changing the tire I gave her my business card and she held it between white fingers as she looked at it. She almost smiled, I thought, before she said, "Maybe you can help me? You see, last Sunday I was visiting over by Holzyebock Hiebat's place and I picked up Yetta's Bible by mistake. I have exactly the same kind and I usually always carry it along every place and so I just picked it up without thinking. So I phoned Yetta about it and she said I should give it to her by the auction sale tomorrow. Only I just found it out today that I have to go to Steinbach to see my aunt in the hospital where she has gall stones and I just can't promise to go to the auction sale. So do you think maybe you could give this Bible to Yetta when she comes there tomorrow?"

All the time she talked her eyes were so big and brown and looking at me from that face like eggshells, you know the kind that are more brown than white, and I just said, "Sure, I can easy do that for you." She passed me the Bible from her big purse, a black zipper Bible just like Oata's. "Here is something for your trouble," she said and she gave me a twenty folded in half. For sure, I didn't say, "You don't have to pay me," because you can't earn a living that way. "Thank you," she said and I watched her go back to her green LTD. She got in and started the car. Then she rolled down her window, waved at me, put both hands on the wheel and drove away like a woman.

I carried the zipper Bible to my car and whistled along with the people singing in the church. Everything seemed in order on the church yard. I zipped open Yetta Hiebat's Bible. I couldn't help it. It was in my blood.

At first I couldn't see anything strange about it. There was no note, no name written inside to tell me whose it really was. I flipped through it and on the Proverbs page where the ribbon bookmark was, a verse was underlined:

> Thine eyes shall behold strange women,
> and thine heart shall utter perverse things.

Then, on the black end page beside the back cover, I saw a heart drawn with a pencil. Inside the heart it said HH and EE. Right away I figured HH had to be Henrietta Hiebat, but who was EE? The only EE I knew about was Eva Enns and two women inside a heart was more than a person could find room for in Gutenthal. I stood there beside my Volkswagen trying to make something out of this and I remembered Beitelkopp Blatz's strange Bible verse and my heart started uttering perverse things and I guess I got so far into my head I didn't notice the people coming out of the church until I heard Rosmack Rampel say, "What happened to your tires, Kjnals?" I looked down past the front fender. The tire was flat. All my tires were flat. And a red brassiere hung from the mirror where the mail-order handcuffs had been.

3

It was one of those hot Sunday afternoons when Gutenthal farmers sneered at Death Valley. Too hot to return Oata's Bible. Wait till the auction on Monday. Kill three birds with one stone. I was sweating in the willows of Hauns Jaunses' Fraunz's dugout. Rosmack Rampel slipped into the green water and again I didn't know if she was wearing a bathing suit or not. I hadn't even heard her Harley Davidson motorcycle. I hadn't heard her hide it in the willows. She could have stepped on me as she went to the water. She must have been that close.

Rosmack swam with her arms, her head up, her long black hair spread out on the froggy water. I imagined I was in a movie. My blond hair had turned black and my arms and chest were dark like corn syrup and we were both naked in the water and it wasn't green, it was clear, and I had just killed a buffalo. We just let ourselves float together and the mosquitoes left us alone. I was watching out for her. That's what I was doing. I was ready to protect her from punks like the ones at the fair. And in my head I saw again those Puggefeld boys crowding around Rosmack's motorcycle. I still saw that Schellenberg boy's hand trying to slide up the inside of her thigh when she rose to kickstart her bike. My lips formed the words again: "I think it's flooded. Here, let me start it for you." I saw the boys move aside with guilty smirks, and I saw Rosmack step down on the kickstarter and roar off down the street, her raven hair blowing back over her black leather jacket.

"Indiana Futz!"

"Who wants to go squaw hopping anyways?"

The memory of those words ringing in my ears made me angry again, and I thought, yes, it was right for me to be there, watching Rosmack swim, protecting her. For sure I couldn't let that jailbird, Beitelkopp Blatz, get in the water with her. But as I watched her swim in the warm green water I felt a little guilty and I wondered what she would think if she knew I was watching her, and then I wondered if she knew, because she seemed to know so many other things, and a part of my brain said I was only spying on her because she was an Indian, and another part of my brain kicked me and said I shouldn't do such a thing to a friend, a friend who was always giving me hints about how to solve cases, a friend who kept me up to date on what was going on with the young people. Not that she was a tattletale or a gossip. No, it was just that she would drop remarks that startled yet fit into my endless mental movie of Gutenthal so perfectly I would wonder how I hadn't connected it up myself. I didn't discuss my theories or suspicions with her. In fact, we hardly ever met, and then only accidentally on purpose. I mean, when you're twenty-seven you have to be careful when it comes to girls who are seventeen. When we did meet we greeted each other quietly, often with just a glance, and savoured each other's presence. Sometimes I took out my handkerchief and rubbed a splattered grasshopper from her windscreen and gazed at the school ring on her long brown fingers curled around the vibrating handgrips. Rosmack would study my mare, or my bicycle, or my Volkswagen, or my little Farmall tractor as if reading my mind, then say something like, "Schnoots Enns went to Grand Beach with her Puggefeld boyfriend on Sunday and were her old ones ever mad!" Then her long fingers would tighten on the handgrips and she'd rev her engine gently a few times and I'd step aside and watch her roar off. Her remark about Schnoots Enns made me remember that A.Dyck and L.U.Dyck had complained that somebody was stealing their purple gas. On a hunch I got the Dyck brothers to fill their gas tank with water. Sure enough, late the next Saturday night that Puggefeld punk's car stalled only twenty feet from the tank. Nobody pressed charges but it took the kid a week to get his car out of the Dycks' yard and I wondered if Schnoots Enns appreciated that I saved her from the beach.

I became so lost in my thinking I didn't even notice Rosmack leave the water until my eye caught the movement of her red shirt through the branches as she pulled her jeans up and I felt older but none the wiser.

Rosmack revved her Harley up the side of the ditch and stopped. I heard voices, Rosmack's and another woman's voice I didn't recognize. I couldn't make out what they were saying so I tried to get closer without giving myself away. Rosmack revved her machine again and roared off. Before I dared move I heard the clang of a bicycle being pushed through the ditch and a woman I had never seen before stepped through the willows straight toward the spot where I was holding my breath. She turned her back to me, parted the willows at the edge and looked at the pond. She stepped back into the clearing right in front of me and began to undress. I almost went crazy trying not to breathe or slap at mosquitoes, but the woman was wearing a black bathing suit under it all, and she calmly slipped into the water out of my sight. For thirty minutes I listened to her splashing while I fought against my bladder. Suddenly, she stood in the clearing, letting the water drip from her tightly stretched bathing suit, and my heart almost stopped when her hand pushed one strap off her shoulder. Then she mumbled, "Oh what, it will be dry soon anyways." I almost burst from holding my breath as she put her clothes on over her wet bathing suit and disappeared.

I waited until I heard the sound of the bicycle on the road before I let my bladder win. Then I stripped and carefully stepped down to the water's edge. Just before I stepped in I took off my shorts and tossed them back toward my pile of clothes. The water was scummy and I wondered how Rosmack and this woman could swim in this green ooze. I waded in cautiously, exploring with my feet as I lifted them out of the sucking bottom to sink them again into deeper mud. When I reached the middle I was in shoulder-deep, the cool water from the bottom shrivelling my legs and balls while my head sweated in the sun, and I let my thoughts swim without shaming myself. Then I saw—something. Something black. I forced my legs against the water as my eyes stayed on the black spot. Out of the ooze onto the mud into the willows where the sun poked through to the black rectangle. Holy Bible. Holy zipper Bible.

This zipper Bible had nothing hidden inside it. Not even a name. It wasn't new because the edges of the spine were worn off and the gold from the H in 'Holy' was almost washed out. One of the teeth near the bottom end of the zipper was bent so it stuck when I pulled on the handle which had a bit of thread tied to the hole as if there might have been a tag there. I thought about Oata's zipper Bible from the graveyard, and the Bible the doll woman wanted me to give back to Yetta Hiebat at the auction sale, and I was just starting to remember Beitelkopp Blatz's zipper Bible at Barbara's party when a bumblebee buzzed around my bare legs. I slapped at it and the Bible slipped from my hand and landed on its spine open to the place where the ribbon marker was. A verse had been underlined with a ballpoint pen. I picked up the Bible and read:

> Behold, I come as a thief. Blessed is he
> that watcheth, and keepeth his garments,
> lest he walk naked, and they see his
> shame.

I looked down, then whirled around. The shortest way to my clothes was through the water, so I waded back with the zipper Bible held high. On the road a car door slammed and as I pulled my feet out of the ooze on the shore a woman stepped through the willows toward my clothes. I froze, shielding myself with the zipper Bible.

The woman's jeans were cut off between thigh and hip, and snow-capped mountains was about all I could say about her shirt. She wore dark sunglasses and she balanced perfectly in high-heeled sandals like she had been born with them on.

"Have you seen any hoes lying around here?" she asked.

Her pink lips looked like they were made to smoke cigarettes. I couldn't see her eyes but I figured they were looking me up and down. "The kids left them here when they finished the field last week because they were so excited about going to Detroit Lakes and I just haven't had time to come and get them." She turned away from me and climbed up the waterhole hump. I hurried into my clothes without taking my eyes off her legs. At the top of the hump she put her hands on her hips and surveyed the rows of beets. "Kids!" she said. "Now where would they have left them?"

"Let me help you look," I said. I tightened the knot in my shoelace and started up the slope. She waited. When I got to her side, my first thought was how easy it would have been to get caught spying on Rosmack in the pond. My second was that she smelled of cigarettes and perfume. Then something glinted from the rows of beets near the yellow flowers of a huge wild mustard plant a sloppy weeder had missed. The woman strode beside me surefooted as a mountain sheep in her high heels with a slight forward kick to her step. I heard her counting the rows under her breath. When she said thirteen I saw the glint was the sharpened edge of a hoe blade. Then I saw four hoes arranged like a cross, the blades pointed in a clockwise direction, one point of each blade stuck in the earth, the other pointing up hazardously.

"Oh those kids," she said. "Good thing I came before they were completely overgrown. Somebody could have been hurt with those points up like that."

I helped her carry the hoes back to her car, trying not to glance too often at her jiggling breasts. After she put the hoes in the trunk of the car she took off her sunglasses. "Thanks," she said, and I saw that her face seemed older than her body.

Then she moved over to the driver's door in such a way that I would notice every curve she had as she climbed in behind the wheel. She spun her tires on the soft dirt road as she drove off, leaving me feeling like I'd been caught with my pants down.

But if your pants are down you need to know which way to point what's left or maybe follow instincts you don't understand. I was drawn back into the beetfield where the hoes had been. Something was buzzing at the edge of my brain—a memory, a word. When I was eleven years old, I think it was, I found a short piece of carpenter's pencil and I made a swastika on the side of the barn with it. Later Papa found me in the garden and asked, "Wuhrum hast doat hackenkjriets aum schtaul ye moalt? Veits du nicht doat ess Hitla zeen Teekjen? Hast du nee von den Kjrich yehiet?" Papa didn't strap me, but he made me rub it out and promise that I wouldn't do such a thing again.

Hackenkjriets. A cross of hoes. The spot where the hoes had been was still plain, though in a day or two even I would have difficulty finding it. I got down on my hands and knees and studied the ground carefully but I found nothing. Then I lay down on my back and looked up into the afternoon sky. I imagined the woman's legs again and I got a glimpse at a possible connection. There had been a chain on her ankle, like a charm bracelet. The charm had looked like a tiny swastika. Something else fell into my head then. I had seen three strange women in Gutenthal on a hot Sunday and two had been driving green LTDs. That verse in Yetta's Bible had told the truth.

4

A.Dyck and L.U.Dyck's yard was like a tent crusade parking field. I pulled in behind a '51 Ford just as Oata Siemens got out. A chequebook fell to the ground. I waited with my hand on her zipper Bible, but she reached down as she closed the door. Oata grinned at me when she straightened up and put the chequebook into her purse. "Thanks anyways," she called. The woman must have eyes at the back of her head! But that didn't stop me from staring at her figure as she squeezed past Zamp Pickle Peters's muddy fender. She was losing weight, slowly but definitely losing, and I was wondering how come and at the same time I was thinking it was nice.

"Oh yeah, I found your Bible by the graveyard," I called.

Oata stopped and turned. "Bible?"

"Yeah, I found it on your father's grave on Saturday." I held the Bible out to her as she squeezed past Zamp Pickle's fender again and she got a smear of dirt on her wide white pants.

"Oh yeah," she exclaimed. "That's the one from when L.U.Dyck was my Sunday School teacher. But how did it get to the graveyard?"

"Maybe Yasch . . . ?"

"Oh for sure, he was there with his muttachi last week. Thank you." Oata dropped the zipper Bible through the open window of her '51 Ford and squeezed past Zamp Pickle's muddy fender once more, this time getting the round seat of her pants all grey. Again she stopped, turned and rubbed more dirt off the fender.

"Oh Kjnals, I almost forgot to give you something. Do you take loonies?"

"Good as gold," I said, and Oata handed me two dollar coins.

My eyes followed her past a blue Ford Galaxy 500 two-door hardtop with red vinyl interior and bucket seats. Her hip rubbed against the dust of a sand-coloured Dodge. A man with a pipe in his mouth and a pouch of Sail tobacco in his breast pocket crawled out of a dark green LTD four-door hardtop with a broken left taillight. The dealer's crest was "JR Friesen and Son" and there was a faded "Janz Team" bumper sticker on the right side and a new "Mount Rushmore" sticker on the left. The pipe-smoker blocked my view of Oata Siemens and when he turned sideways to slip between the bumpers of a Chev and a Chevelle Oata was nowhere in sight.

I looked around for one of Holzyebock Hiebat's gravel trucks or the green Ford LTD that his wife, Yetta, usually drives and I thought for a minute about how many green Ford LTDs there were around Gutenthal these days. I looked back at the pipe-smoker's bumper stickers and tried to remember if there had been bumper stickers on that woman's car at the beetfield but all I could remember were her legs.

"Neil Bergen?" I turned with a start when I heard the woman's voice behind me. She was wearing the same long black dress, only this time the doll eyes blinked through big round eyeglasses. She was holding my business card in her black-gloved fingers.

"You're the one they call Schneppa Kjnals?" I felt my cheeks get warm, and I couldn't tell from her dark eyes if she was teasing with her question or just finding out. Why was she here when she had told me she needed to go to Steinbach to visit a sick aunt?

"We stoop to snoop," she read out loud from my card and the eggshell cracked a little around the eyes. "Which are you? Schneppa Kjnals, or Neil Bergen, Investigator?"

I had never had the choice before and I didn't know what to say. Then my business head took over and I asked, "Which one do you need today?" The eggshell cracked a little more, then at once it was smooth again and the eyes were a little wet and it seemed like there should be someone beside her, but I couldn't see who.

"I need you—to buy something for me at the auction. I need you to buy the grandfather clock for me. You must not let anyone else buy it. Buy it, pay for it, don't tell anyone you are buying it for me. At 9:00 Tuesday evening bring it to me at the waterhole hump by the old Heinrichs yard a mile north of the Puggefeld dike. Come alone." All the time she talked her big round eyes bored at me and I knew I would do anything for her, anything I could. Then she reached into her dress, pulled out a white envelope and held it out to me. "Here is the money. If you get it for less—you can keep the change."

As soon as the envelope was in my hand she vanished and I stood there shaking, excited and scared. It was like a dream come true. I had a real case! A real case, just like in the books and on TV! I opened the envelope and took out ten brown bills. A thousand dollars!

That bedutzed me a little bit. How could A.Dyck and L.U.Dyck's old grandfather clock be worth so much? I mean it didn't even keep time anymore and a crack in the face made it look like it was always twenty-five after ten.

As I slipped the money back into the envelope I noticed some tiny handwriting on the inside of the flap: "If for any reason I am not there on Tuesday keep the clock safe and meet me at the same place on Thursday at 4:30." Smart woman, I thought. She even had a back-up plan. I raised the envelope to my lips to lick the flap. The envelope and the money smelled smoky, I thought. The doll woman had smelled smoky, too, but I couldn't remember if she had smelled smoky on Sunday at the church.

But money was money and I figured there should be lots of change left over after I bought that old clock. For a second I thought of sniffing Yetta Hiebat's zipper Bible but I shrugged it off. I'd take care of Yetta's zipper Bible yet, but the important thing was to take care of the grandfather clock.

Still, a detective had to keep his eyes open all the time, and right then another green LTD came up the driveway and parked two places to the right of me. It was Yetta Hiebat. I shoved the money envelope into my shirt down behind my belt and stepped back toward my VW to get the zipper Bible, as she opened her door. Yetta Hiebat was one of those women who would always look like a teenager, no matter how old she got. Her grey-streaked brown hair tied back in a ponytail with a red scarf and her blue jeans and sleeveless

Elvis Presley T-shirt looked pretty good to me as she swung her feet out of the car, flashing the gold chain around her left ankle. Her flat, white pointed shoes left the cracks between her toes showing. A good-looking woman always stops the words in my throat. I couldn't say, "Mrs. Hiebat, I have to give you a zipper Bible back." But I saw a gold-capped tooth in her mouth as she smiled and waved at someone in the crowd, and I caught a glimpse of a charm on her ankle chain as she hurried past without seeing me. Yetta scampered between the parked cars toward the crowd watching the Flying Hieberts setting up their microphone.

Hank Hiebert was tuning up his electric guitar; the auction was about to begin. I looked at the two Bibles still on the seat. I had no reason to follow Yetta except lust and the Bible, and I thought, why burden a lady with something to carry around all afternoon? Besides, I had a grandfather clock to buy. So I left Yetta's Bible in my car and headed over to lean on a press drill near the back of the crowd as Herman Hiebert took the mike off the stand to sing the auctioneer song. Not so good as Leroy Van Dyke, but better than Yodelling Abe Wiebe, and the crowd sure listened.

I like auction sales because you can watch so many people. Now I watched L.U.Dyck come out of the house and I saw he had a new moustache and his hair was black and curly when before it was grey and straight. I thought I must be slipping on the job because I didn't know about this before. Hank Hiebert held up a dozen crescent wrenches tied together with wire and Herman called for the first bid. A fat man with a cigarette burning his lips lifted a hand with one finger pointing to heaven. Beside him a woman with sunglasses and pink lipstick smoked a long white cigarette. At first I thought it was Yetta because she was dressed almost the same, except her T-shirt had Tom Jones on the front and she carried a pack of L&M smokes from the States. Then I saw her high-heeled shoes and figured she must be the woman who had picked up the hoes from the beetfield. Her sunglasses turned in my direction and I wondered if she was remembering me without any clothes on the way I was remembering her bare legs in the high-heeled shoes. Someone touched my arm.

"Schmuggle Veens." I turned at the whisper. Rosmack Rampel's dark eyes smiled at me.

"Who?"

"I saw you looking. Schmuggle Veens's States wife."

"Oh," I said, thinking how it was nice not all women thought I was invisible. Suddenly, I wondered if what I was looking at was so easy for other people to see. My stomach pinched me as I remembered that time on the escalator in Polo Park when a little brat called out for everyone to hear: "Mommy, that man is looking at your bum!" And I wondered again if Rosmack knew I had spied on her swimming in Hauns Jaunses' Fraunz's pond on Sunday. "Who is Schmuggle Veens?"

"You know, the guy who got caught smuggling Flat Germans from Mexico across the border."

"I don't remember that."

"Must have been when you were away up north."

"Yeah, I guess so. Schmuggle Veens's States wife?"

"Yeah." Rosmack gave me an elbow in my ribs and the money envelope slipped down into my shorts.

People watched Rosmack as she moved through the crowd carrying her white motorcycle helmet, making Flat German remarks. L.U.Dyck came out of the house again and Oata Siemens followed him carrying a grandfather clock and then Yetta Hiebat walked in front of me and I looked down at her ankles and on the way down my eyes saw a zipper Bible in her hand and when I looked up again I couldn't see Oata and the grandfather clock anywhere, though I saw the man with the pipe in his mouth and a woman wearing a strange dress with orange flowers on it.

But all that didn't help me. My job was to buy the grandfather clock and it had just disappeared in the arms of Oata Siemens without even making it to the auction block. That left me with a thousand in large bills and a rendezvous to keep behind a waterhole hump. My first real case and I was already getting caught behind the manure spreader. I might not even be able to find my client to refund the retainer!

I was just about to chase Oata when L.U.Dyck's brother, A.Dyck, lifted another grandfather clock to the auction wagon. A.Dyck had a grim look on his face as Hank Hiebert took it, but then I couldn't remember him any other way. The clock face had a crack that made it look like twenty-five after ten. I pushed myself toward the front of the crowd as the auctioneer called out, "Who'll give me fifty?"

Something soft bumped into my arm and a woman's voice said, "Excuse me!" and I thought maybe I knew what that soft thing was but at the same time I saw Yetta Hiebat sitting on the seat of a horse rake, holding the zipper Bible between her knees while she retied the red scarf around her ponytail, and on top of all my other thoughts I had room to wonder if she had taken the zipper Bible from my Volkswagen.

"Two-seventy-five!" drawled a man in a black cowboy hat. I came out of my daydream. They were still bidding on the grandfather clock. Somebody bid three hundred and I felt the softness on my arm again and then a warm breath smelling like States cigarettes whispered, "We can't let it go for under a thousand!" I glanced over my shoulder. In the sunglasses, pink lipstick and tight blue jeans Schmuggle Veens's States wife looked like a Coca Cola bottle that had been squeezed in the middle. The chain on her ankle flashed as she stepped on a cigarette butt. Herman called, "Three-fifty!" The woman shouted, "Four hundred!" and I heard, "Five!" and then, "Six!" and I suddenly remembered my job so I shouted, "Seven!" and somebody else called, "Eight!" and then I heard the woman call, "Nine!"

It was quiet for a moment and Schmuggle Veens's States wife pulled a cigarette out of her pack and lit it with a shaky Bic lighter. Herman already saw his luck had run out and he was saying, "Going once . . . going twice . . . ," when a new voice said, "Nine-fifty!" Herman looked directly into the woman's face and asked, "Nine-seventy-five?" She took a long drag on her cigarette, held the breath of the crowd, then shook her head slowly as the smoke drifted from her nose.

"A thousand!" I shouted with my arm in the air. Beside me I heard the woman whisper, "Jeez, that was close." But when I turned to look at her she was gone.

I ducked behind a top buggy and pulled the money envelope out of my shorts. I counted the bills again. A thousand dollars. All was going well. I made my way through the crowd to the granary where the cashier was set up and paid. A.Dyck watched me pick up the clock from the wagon, and his look was so sad I almost felt guilty for buying it.

"Lots money for clock, eh? You pay tousand dollar for broken clock, Kjnals?" I almost didn't recognize Simple Hein in his made-to-measure pinstripe suit complete with vest he had won from Vaumst Voth's men's wear store in the monthly draw after somebody put Hein's name on the ticket for fun. I nodded sadly.

"Too much for clock," said Hein. "For me, pocket watch, good enough. One dollar. Secon' han' store. Wanna see?" Hein reached for the watch pocket on his vest. It was empty. Then he searched through all the rest of his pockets. No pocket watch. He looked at me with alarm. "Schneppa Kjnals, you steal my pocket watch?"

"No Hein, I don't use a watch. I just go by the sun."

"Sun is good. Can't steal sun. Not so good for night. C'mon Kjnals, give me my watch back." Some Gutenthalers said Hein's people moved south of Fargo, across the line, close to the equator, down Mexico way, and they left Hein behind because they thought his fanbelt was slipping, or at least a screw was loose. In summer Hein lived under the bridge on the gravel road half a mile west of town. In winter he lived in the basement of the beer parlour beside the furnace.

"Did you forget your watch at home?"

"Could be I'm crazy, but not me I'm stupid. Leave watch home somebody come steal. Sell auction sale. Tousand dollar. Commennists come steal pocket watch."

"Hein, did you hide the watch someplace so the communists can't steal it?"

Hein looked me up and down, stared me in the eyes, then circled around behind me until he was staring in my eyes again. "Hey, Kjnals, show me the eyes you got in your back head."

I leaned over, shifting the weight of the clock to my other arm, and whispered in his ear, "Hein, don't tell nobody about the eyes in the back of my head. The communists might find out."

Hein chewed on this, then leaned to my ear and whispered, "Don' tell nobody. I hide pocket watch good. Come see." I followed Hein over to his three-wheeled bicycle.

The basket was half-filled with beer bottles. Hein pointed to a black zipper Bible with a bulge in the cover. "Nice Bible. Fin' on road. Good place to hide watch. Commennists scared from Bible."

I hoisted the clock into a more comfortable position and scanned the crowd which was moving on to the first of the machinery sales. I noticed the woman in the orange flowered dress again but she was too far away to identify.

"Come, let's go buy combine," Hein said. "That's why I wear suit."

"Good idea. You have to dress for business."

Hein went to inspect the combine and I saw Yetta Hiebat still sitting on the horse rake. I gazed at her ankle bracelet and when I squinted, the charm on it looked like a swastika, too, and she wasn't carrying the Bible anymore. So many zipper Bibles and I still had to give her one.

As I carried the grandfather clock to my car I saw Rosmack Rampel headed for her motorcycle. I wondered if she was going swimming. Behind me the auctioneer called for the first bid on the combine and Hein's voice called, "Two tousand dollar!" The crowd laughed, then another voice said, "Twenty-five hunnerd!" Hein's voice called again, "Tree tousand dollar!" Herman Hiebert chuckled and said, "Thanks, Hein, but only serious bids now please."

I laid the clock on the back seat of my grey Volkswagen and thought about the thousand dollars I had just paid for it. I figured I'd better protect the doll woman's investment by hiding the clock under the seat next to the battery, so I lifted the clock over the back of the seat into the luggage place under the rear window, pulled the Hudson's Bay blanket off the seat and tossed it on top of the clock. I bumped my head on the doorframe as I lifted the seat off the battery compartment and started wondering if maybe I had lost my head. I mean, my client hadn't told me she wanted the clock with the broken glass. Maybe she wanted the clock that Oata had carried away. How did I know if I had the right clock? My first case and the manure spreader was still letting fly at me!

I had to find Oata but her '51 Ford was gone! I ran to the driveway to see if I could spot it on the road, but before I could see anything a power steering belt squealed and a green LTD came tearing straight at me and as I jumped out of the way I tripped over my feet headfirst into the little grassy ditch. I looked up as quickly as I could. The licence was covered with mud. I only made out the broken taillight and the "Janz Team" bumper sticker as it sped away down the long driveway. I scrambled to my feet. My back seat lay on the ground beside my VW. The hood over the rear engine was up. My clock! I started to run after the LTD.

"Hop on!" Rosmack called from her Harley. I jumped on behind her and held on for dear life as she opened the throttle and my leg almost clipped a grey jeep coming to the auction.

"Where we going?" she asked when we got to the road.

"Gotta catch that green LTD!"

"Four-door hardtop?"

"Yeah."

"Schmuggle Veens."

"Schmuggle Veens?"

"Yeah, Schmuggle Veens and his States wife. Cut him off by the double dike behind Zoop Zack Friesen's rape field. That's how he goes to the spillway that cuts through the ditch at the border."

Well, if there was one thing that Rosmack knew, it was where the shortcuts were. This time the shortcut took us through Ha Ha Nickel's section of wheat to the correction line past Hauns Jaunses' Fraunz behind the snowfence up onto the double dike to Zoop Zack's bridge.

Sure enough, the LTD was there on the dike on the other side of the bridge. The trunk and the back door on the woman's side were open. I started to climb off the motorcycle, then stopped short, almost never to go again. The bumper stickers said "Detroit Lakes" and "Mennonite Village Museum" and on the open trunk lid I saw "Rhineland Car," not "JR Friesen." In the ditch Gnurpel Giesbrecht stepped out from behind a bush pulling his zipper up and a second later his wife rose out of the barley.

"Wrong LTD!"

"If you say so. Your place or mine?"

"Mine," I said.

In minutes we skidded to a stop four inches from Mama's barn door. With Rosmack right behind me I climbed up to the loft, grabbed the army surplus fieldglasses from the nail on the beam, pushed myself up into the ventilator and scanned the landscape. But there was no sign of the other LTD. I climbed back down to the floor and handed the fieldglasses to Rosmack. She didn't spot the vehicles either but when she turned the fieldglasses to the auction sale she said, "Something going on in A.Dyck's pig fence." I squeezed up beside her and took the glasses from her. A crowd was gathered inside the fence and it appeared as if they were looking at something lying on the ground.

We met Simple Hein pedalling furiously away from the auction yard. He shouted something as we passed but I couldn't hear him. When I looked back he was waving his zipper Bible.

The crowd had left the hog pasture when we arrived. Only

A.Dyck and Dola Dyck still crouched over the body. A pool of blood thickened beside the slit throat. Flies settled over the bristled skin. A.Dyck sprang to his feet when he saw me. "What was loose with you, Schneppa Kjnals? How come you didn't see this? You always notice everything. How come you didn't see this?"

Dola Dyck put his hand on A.Dyck's shoulder. "Now Abe, Kjnals can't be every place." But A.Dyck was right. I should have been there. I should have seen it coming and stopped it. But why would anyone murder a prize boar? Murder, that's what it was. Murder in Gutenthal.

5

SOME people have the rooster wake them in the morning. With Mama and me it was the first ring on the party line. Mama would clump out of her bedroom to push the button on her speakerphone. And it was always the same at 6:10. Elsie Elias phoned her mother from the hospital to say if anybody had died during the night, or if there'd been an accident, or a new baby, or that the doctor was on holidays again. Then Elsie's mother always wanted to know what they were having for dinner because Elsie worked in the hospital kitchen.

I would lie in my bed and listen and wait because Elsie's call hardly ever gave me a clue about how to start my day. The second call usually did. You see, Preacher Janzen had a prayer line from 6:15 to 7:15 every morning when he sat by the phone waiting for people to call who wanted him to pray for them. The people thought he had a private line but I was always interested in wires, so his prayer line came through loud and clear in Mama's speakerphone. The callers didn't say who they were but was there a voice in Gutenthal I wouldn't know?

The calls to the prayer line helped me decide my transportation for that day. Would I walk? Go on horseback? Pedal? Drive the Volkswagen? Putter along with the Farmall? Take it to the Lord in prayer.

On Tuesday the first call came at 6:27. "Unburden your heart to the prayer line," said Preacher Janzen in a voice like a radio.

"I have sinned against my man," said a woman's voice. "In my dream I married someone else and was so happy I thought I had passed into Paradise. Now I feel so guilty but I still lust after Paradise."

"Satan sends dreams to trouble us. Trust in the Lord and he will bless you. Do not let your mind dwell on the forces of the night. Pray with me. Lord, help this woman in her time of need. Give her strength to defend against the lustful arrows of Satan. Bring her peace and love to give to her husband. Amen."

"Amen." There were two clicks as the receivers were replaced.

I heard Mama stirring the porridge in the pot and then she called: "You hear that, Kjnals? After all these years Eva Enns still dreams about Holzyebock Hiebat. Huy yuy yuy, what a life she would have had and gone to be with the Sommerfelders yet? Oh, what is it with people now in these times when they have everything and it's not good enough still. Yesterday when you were by the auction sale I heard Schallemboych's Tien say on the phone to Ovenside Wahl's wife that Zamp Pickle Peters's cousin that is a minister sometimes on TV in Winnipeg went apart with his wife so he could better look after a woman that was calling the prayer line there. So o'feschaemt people are nowadays. Stand up and eat."

I dug the last spoonful of porridge from the bowl and it fell into my head what those initials in Yetta Hiebat's Bible must have meant. HH and EE must have meant Holzyebock Hiebat and Eva Enns! And I wondered why Yetta would have such a thing written in her Bible and I thought maybe Yetta didn't know her Bible had such a thing written in it! Maybe the doll woman had written it in Yetta's Bible and was using me to make trouble for Yetta and her man. I still hadn't given Yetta the Bible back. And when I got back to my VW after seeing the murdered pig the grandfather clock was gone and I found a note under my windshield wiper.

I had grabbed the note and spread it open. In very neat woman's writing, like the German writing they used to try to teach us, the note said, "But it stopped, short, never to go again, when the old man died." Then I bumped my head on the doorframe again as I shoved the seat in over the battery and scrambled into the car. There had been only a click when I turned the key. Rosmack helped me put the wires back into the distributor cap and I had driven all over the country looking for a green LTD and you would have thought Henry Ford had never made any cars like that. I drove around so long I had to pull the reserve switch for the gas tank so my VW could make it home.

The speakerphone crackled with another call but it was just:

"Jake around?"

"On the field."

"I drive there."

Then Mama said, "When I came out of the beckhouse I saw Gnurpel Giesbrecht's green car driving on the middle road where Hingst Heinrichs has his flax. What would Gnurpel want there so early in the morning?"

"Was Gnurpel driving? Or was it Forscha Friesen? Forscha sometimes helps his grandfather."

"You think I have telescopes in my eyes? The car was driving away from here so how could I see who was behind the steer?"

"Away from here? Did he drive over the yard?"

"I was in the beckhouse and we had cabbage for supper so I didn't hear nothing."

I hadn't heard anything either but in my head I could only think Schmuggle Veens.

I went on foot past the barn and followed the field road. Suddenly I saw marks in the dust where a car had made a three-point turn. A cigarette butt lay about a foot from the track, flattened with a triangle footprint where the person had stepped on it, and behind the wide end of the triangle was the hole made by a spike heel. I picked up the butt. Pink lipstick rimmed the white filter of the three-quarter-smoked L&M.

Schmuggle Veens's States wife. I flicked away the cigarette butt in disgust as I thought how my chase of that LTD had cost a pig's life at the auction sale. A.Dyck had been so upset with me he wouldn't even let me get close enough to the pig to examine it. And what was important here, the pig or the grandfather clock? I started to think somebody was doing things to mix me up, like the flat tires at the church and the zipper Bibles. It was like somebody was watching me all the time. Then I thought, why should I blame myself? With so many green LTDs around Gutenthal, anybody could get mixed up.

I went back into the kitchen to ask Mama if she knew the doll woman but she was still thinking about Eva Enns and Holzyebock Hiebat because she said, "How come some things that happen when a person is young are so strong they can stay in your head and still boss you around when you are old?" She bent over the baking pan, sprinkled flour over the bread dough, then kneaded it with her fists. Her arms were white with flour to the elbows and a white spot beside her nose showed where she must have scratched an itch. More flour spotted her brown apron and a seam was coming apart under her left arm so her white underskirt showed through the brown and white print dress. Her swollen feet pressed down on her rubber beach sandals and her underskirt waved just a little as she kneaded the dough. The braid over the top of her head made me think of a silver crown and I wondered if she ever put flowers in it when she was a girl. Mama seemed to be daydreaming and I wanted to ask her about what, only before I could open my mouth a brumming started outside and it got louder and louder until it brummed right over the house so the dishes in the glass cupboard rattled.

"Oh but not now when I'm kneading dough!" she exclaimed and the brumming got louder again.

I stepped outside to watch the silver airplane circle again and touch down at the far end of our field and drag a cloud of dust past the barn into the yard. The propeller didn't stop until the plane was only a yard from the picket fence in front of the house, the right wing spread out over the gate like it was going to shelter it from the rain.

Bulchi Wiebe helped his belly out of his first love, his Canadian-built Found FBA-2C airplane. His second love was bulchi brot, freshly baked butter melting white bread. His third love was Mama. Bulchi always knew when Mama was baking bread.

"Well, g'day Kjnals," he said, as he raised his silver "NO, I WOULDN'T RATHER HAVE A CESSNA" cap and wiped his forehead with a brown handkerchief. "Mama t'house?" Before I could answer Bulchi was already knocking on the screen door, calling "Nita, Nita, are you t'house?" He didn't wait for an answer. He just walked in, slamming the screen door behind him, and then I heard Mama cry, "Ach du!" and Bulchi sang, "Bulchi brot, bulchi brot o mein liebes bulchi brot!"

Bulchi Wiebe had been in love with Mama since she was just fourteen when he saw her at the Jugendverein in the Neualtbergfeld Church. He said he never got married because he could only love one woman in his life. Ever since Papa died he had been trying to get Mama to go for an airplane ride with him, but Mama was afraid to fly. I grabbed the strut of the airplane, thinking it might be handy to get a look at Gutenthal from the air. Suddenly, Mama cried, "But I can't leave my dough!"

"But Nita, I want you to bring it along! See, I made this old time bake oven outside with bricks and I want you to bake your bread in it!"

"But Bient, will the dough still be good if you fly with it?"

"For sure it will still be good!" The door opened and Bulchi carried the bread pan down the steps. Mama was right behind. "Oba Bient, I can't go fly in the airplane with just such a sack on for a dress. Somebody could see me!"

"Only the birds and they don't have a party line!" Bulchi laughed as he lifted the bread pan up into the airplane.

"Kjnals, you have to come with." Mama looked like she might cry if I said no.

"For sure, Kjnals," Bulchi laughed. "Come with. Then you can schneppa the whole country at the same time!"

I climbed into the back seat beside the bread pan and put on the seat belt. Bulchi helped Mama up and buckled her in. Then he heaved himself into the pilot's seat and fastened his extra-long belt around his belly.

The propellers started to turn and we sat there for a couple of minutes while Bulchi played with all the knobs and pull-out buttons. He revved up the motor a little more. Slowly he turned the airplane around. I watched the wing on the left side and I thought for sure it was going to hook onto the tree where Mama has her sitting-in-the-shade chair, but it slipped by and the right wing slipped by the corner of the barn, too, and then Mama was holding her hands over her ears because the motor was getting really loud and we bounced along the field road going faster and faster and the wings were shaking up and down like a young crow trying to fly for the first time. Suddenly we lifted and it seemed like we were flying straight up but so slowly like when you drive up a steep hill and you don't know if you're going to make it to the top. When we were almost to the top of this hill in the air, Bulchi started to turn and it felt like he had stopped the airplane altogether and we would fall and I saw that Mama's face was as white as Holstein milk.

Bulchi Wiebe didn't fly straight to his bake oven. Instead he flew back and forth over Gutenthal so Mama could see our place and the church and the store and the credit union. As we flew over Hauns Jaunses' Fraunz's dugout I saw a motorcycle driving on the field road away from the pond and before I could even see if it was Rosmack Rampel I saw two more motorcycles and as we flew farther away I saw the three motorcycles come together at the middle of this cross of roads, only this cross wasn't like the one on the Red Cross pin. At first I couldn't figure out why this section looked so strange. Then I thought, the roads are gravelled funny. How come only half of each mile of the road around this section was gravelled? From the air the field roads that cut the section in quarters and the ungravelled parts of the mile road looked like a big black swastika. That's where those hoes had been.

About a quarter mile from Eva Enns's place I noticed a small house trailer parked next to a huge stockpile of gravel. Bulchi shouted to Mama that Holzyebock Hiebat had the tender for gravelling the roads. I thought I saw Schmuggle Veens's LTD driving along on the double dike, but a minute later I saw another LTD, exactly the same, driving to the store and I was mixed up. Then we were over Bulchi Wiebe's farm, circling over the orange balls on the power line and the red longjohns flapping from the post on top of his barn. I thought I saw a jeep driving along the road just before we bounced like an India rubber ball and I had to grab the baking pan to keep the dough from spilling out. My heart bounced pretty good, too, and Mama's hands covered her face, and the armpits of her dress dripped darkly and I felt a cold trickle down the side of my ribs.

Bulchi Wiebe wrecked his ankle as he helped Mama out of the plane. Mama was okay, a little shaky, but she was okay. I mean, she had a look on her face like I had never seen before, almost like she had flowers in her hair. But Bulchi couldn't walk. Mama and I helped Bulchi into the back seat of his old army jeep to take him to Knibble Thiessen for repairs. I thought of the jeep I had seen from the plane as I started the jeep's engine. It couldn't have been Bulchi's because his engine was cold.

"But the dough!" Bulchi cried as I let out the clutch.

"Ach, just leave it," Mama said.

"Oh nein, take it with!"

"But what?"

"Knibble Thiessen's frau has an oven, not?"

Like always Knibble Thiessen's Holistic Massage Clinic yard was full of cars with States licences. After Mama and I helped Bulchi hobble to the waiting room I carried the dough to the house and put it down on the table before Mrs. Knibble had a chance to tie her kerchief under her chin.

"Vaut vest du met daut?"

"Switch den oven on," I said. "Mama is making bulchi brot."

I fled outside to snoop around the yard and learn licence plates by heart. I was peering into a red Camaro wondering if a ball of brown cloth on the dash was pantyhose when the clinic door opened and Knibble Thiessen helped one of his patients to her car. She was a States woman with a chain around her left ankle, plenty of pink lipstick and blue eyeshadow. She looked like she had enough gesundheit to walk to Paraguay, only her red shoes had such high heels she looked like she needed forelegs to steady herself. Knibble Thiessen didn't see me and after he had settled the woman in her car I heard him say he would make a house call to her house the next evening. I wondered what Mrs. Knibble would think about that. And I wondered if Mrs. Knibble had an ankle bracelet, too.

One of Holzyebock Hiebat's gravel trucks rummeled by and I thought how handy to Eva Enns's place that house trailer was and how handy it was for me, Kjnals, that Knibble's house call was for the next evening and I wondered if I should get my taillights fixed before I went after him across the line.

While I was waiting for Mama and Bulchi, Rosmack Rampel roared up on her Harley. For about a minute she just sat there on her throbbing motorcycle, her straight black hair fanned out over her black leather shoulders, her black eyes watching me.

"Shaftich Shreeda's daughter Fleeda is home from Africa." The words went in one ear and then got lost as I gazed at Rosmack. She seemed different somehow as she sat there on her throbbing machine as if something wonderful had happened to her or she had grown older since the auction when the pig was murdered. And that had been only yesterday. She didn't say anything about meeting two motorcycles at the crossroads of a swastika. She just sat there, idling, and I gazed at her long brown fingers curled around the vibrating handgrip, staring at her school ring. Suddenly, it knocked me on the head that Rosmack's ring was different. She was wearing a boy's ring with a red stone, and she had used white bandage tape to make it fit her finger. I felt old and guilty. Old because that ring was making me jealous. Guilty because I had let a pig get murdered. I was sure I could have prevented this killing if I hadn't had my mouth open over the ankles of a woman at least fifteen years older than me and if I hadn't gone for an imaginary chase with someone ten years younger. But it hadn't been an imaginary chase. I had been chasing a stolen clock!

"Here comes Hein!" Rosmack yelled. She gunned her motor and the front wheel lifted off the ground as she darted away, leaving me dry as barley dust.

Simple Hein looked like a Wiebe, like one of those brush Wiebes from the east side of the telephone line. All the men from that family had stiff hair which stood straight up like a wire brush. They had long faces, wide chins, high foreheads, and black hair streaked with grey before they entered their twenties. Hein looked like them, even though he was not a Wiebe and not connected up with any Wiebes as far as I had been able to figure out. Hein was a Sawatsky, though people just called him Hein and everybody knew who they were talking about. I guess if Hein had stood right beside one of the brush Wiebes he probably wouldn't have looked like any of them at all, but he always reminded me of them. Hein had a face like them, and he walked like them too, you know, swinging his left arm like it was a flywheel helping him keep his speed up once he was started. And his nose, yes, his nose. That was a brush Wiebe nose.

Hein pedalled his three-wheeled bicycle toward me. Usually, the carrier was filled with empty beer bottles, but today it held a small box of almost clean clothes. Hein was wearing his suit again with shiny new shoes. He had had a haircut, and his white shirt sported a red and black tie. I reached in my pocket for some change. I picked out a quarter and three nickels. When Hein stopped I held out the coins. "Which do you want, one or three?" Hein studied the coins carefully, then slowly reached out for the nickels, as he always had. Suddenly, his fingers moved to the quarter and he flipped the quarter in the air. "Gotcha, Schneppa Kjnals!" Then he gave me a look telling me never to play that game with him again.

I pointed to his box of clothes.

"Are you moving?"

Hein nodded his head vigorously. "Too much knowl. Dunnasche big bang. Atomic bomb. Ears hurt. No can sleep."

"By your place?"

"Yeah, close by. Over the creek. Commennists. Commennists from the States. Too much knowl! Go Yasch Siemens.

Oabeida. Shovel shit. Load bales. Eat faspa. No knowl there.
Could be I'm crazy, but not me I'm stupid."

Hein reached back into his basket for the zipper Bible that
was bulging with the pocket watch. He unzipped it far
enough to take the watch out. As he did so, I noticed a stack
of bills showing between the red-edged pages.

"You keep your money in the Bible?"

Hein seemed a little startled, then grinned at me confiden-
tially. "Bad people don't steal Bibles." He gazed at his watch,
then slipped it into his vest pocket. "Got to hurry now. Go
to auction sale with Yasch." He quickly zipped up the Bible
and hid it inside his box of clothes. "Frenchman auction sale.
By St. Joe. Buy combine. No laugh over Hein there." He
pedalled away, calling, "Don't do beside, Schneppa Kjnals."

I chewed on what Hein had said. My investigation of the
murdered pig was like doing beside because A.Dyck
wouldn't let me come near the yard to look for clues. This
left me with only a rerun of my mental movie of the auction
to look for a motive. But so far the movie only showed
zipper Bibles, ankles with charm bracelets, tight jeans and
L&M cigarettes, an over-priced grandfather clock, high bidding by people with no intention to buy, and a prize boar
with a slit throat. I hadn't even had a chance to get a good
look at the pig's injury. I tried to zoom in for a close-up but
the picture just went blurry. In my head I heard the woman's
voice again, "Which are you, Schneppa Kjnals or Neil
Bergen, Investigator?"

I had less than twelve hours before I had to meet the doll
woman at the waterhole hump. I still hadn't delivered the
Bible to Yetta and I had no clock. I didn't even know my
client's name. I thought for a second about the record-
keeping chapter in the correspondence detective course—

the chapter I had left out—but even a guy like me can only feel guilty about so many things at once.

At least one thing I was doing by the book—waiting around—only here at Knibble Thiessen's there weren't even any more ankles with bracelets to distract me. I replayed the scene with Knibble Thiessen's patient in my head and thought about how a chain around the ankle makes a person look at the ankle first instead of other parts, and I remembered the black jet boots with chains I had when I was fifteen that Mama wouldn't let me wear to church and I wondered if back then people saw the boots first before they saw my big ears. I thought about Hein and his zipper Bible with money in it and I wondered again how come I was running into so many zipper Bibles, and ankles with charm bracelets, and I didn't know if any of it had to do with anything, but I couldn't just stand there waiting for the beckhouse door to open. I got into Bulchi's jeep and turned the key just as Mama came out of the house with the pan full of hot loaves. At the same time Bulchi hobbled out of the clinic, eagerly sniffing the air.

6

My answering machine had a message from Oata Siemens. When I got to her house she told me that her zipper Bible had disappeared from the shelf beside the fridge. After a few questions I figured the thief must have entered the house through the unlocked door during the night when Oata and Yasch were sleeping.

"Why would somebody want to steal a Bible?" Oata asked.

"Maybe he was desperate for salvation," I said. I looked around and spotted the grandfather clock hanging in the living room, reminding me again of the rendezvous at the waterhole hump only hours away. A stolen Bible and a stolen clock. Was there a connection?

"Did you buy that clock at the auction yesterday?"

"Oh no. That clock was Grandfather Needarp's and he had it with him from Russia all the way to the olden home where he died last month. I picked it up from there that time when my fanbelt tore and L.U.Dyck drove me around in town and he saw there was a screw or something loose on it and he fixed it for me. L.U.Dyck sure looks funny with that curly black hair and the grey moustache."

"Yeah."

"L.U.Dyck must have a girlfriend or something, not?"

"Have you noticed any strange cars around the yard?" I let my eyes drink in the soft bulges under her loose blouse and for a second I felt like I was breaking the seventh commandment in my head.

"No, I didn't see any but I was visiting Mother at the mental home after the auction. Yasch was home and he didn't say nothing about any visitors. Besides, I didn't put the Bible there till I got home. I mean, you only gave it to me by the sale, and I right aways went to see Mother because the baby was staying with Yasch's muttachi and I didn't want it to take so long. But I'll ask Yasch when he comes back from the auction sale by St. Joe."

"Did Hein go along to the sale?"

"Yeah, he did. He was so excited he had on his suit. He said he couldn't eat, then he filled up his plate three times."

"So Hein is going to be oabeida for you?"

"Yeah, we fixed up a corner in the cellar for him. Come see how Yasch changed the house around this winter."

The only way into the cellar used to be a hatch in the kitchen floor. Now the hatch was closed in and an upright door opened to the stairs. In the dim light of the cellar window I saw Hein's clothes box on a neatly made up camp cot. The zipper Bible lay open on the clothes. There was no money inside. I looked for a name but there was none on the white. It was too dark to see anything on the black end pages, so I pulled the light switch chain on the forty-watt bulb. In its light I could see the letters HH written in pencil in the bottom left corner of the back page. Under the letters, written in numbers only, was the date of A.Dyck and L.U.Dyck's auction sale.

Holzyebock Hiebat was my first thought, or Henrietta. Then I thought Hank Hiebert or Herman Hiebert. But what about Hingst Heinrichs or even Ha Ha Nickel? They had all been at the auction sale.

As I was leaving Oata said something that didn't make any sense to me. "You know L.U.Dyck, he never talked to me except in the Sunday School class . . . no wait, there was one Sunday when I forgot my Sunday School book, so I went back to the church after dinner to get it and L.U.Dyck was sitting in the chair there under the basement window against the cement wall and the light from the window was shining a box on the floor beside him. I said, 'Hello, Mr. Dyck,' and went over to the chair where I had forgotten my book. He looked at me and said something about a woman in a swine's snout and it was like he was all mixed up, I mean, he talked about casting the swine out of his brother's eye because he had cast swine before pearls and he wished Jesus would come and send the devils into the pigs again so they would run over the cliff and die in the sea. Then it seemed like he came back to himself and he stood up and said I was God's good girl. We went out of the church together and he drove in his car away and I went home and I never thought about it again. Till now."

My left front tire was flat when I finished listening to Oata's story. I borrowed a Jack-all from Yasch's tool shed and quickly changed the tire. As I put the flat into the trunk I noticed the reason for the flat. I had parked on a little rubber block with a thin nail stuck through it. It seemed to remind me of something but I couldn't figure out what, so I stuck it in my pocket. I started to drive away when Oata shouted at me from the steps. "Wait, I forgot to tell you the most important thing!" I got out of the car and hurried back to the house. "I forgot to tell you, Kjnals," she said. "You gave me the wrong Bible. It wasn't mine."

"It wasn't yours?"

"No, it didn't have my name in it."

I ran back to my VW. There was only one zipper Bible left, Yetta Hiebat's. I must have given Oata the zipper Bible from the pond. And somebody had stolen Oata's Bible from my car. Maybe the same person who stole the clock.

It was too early to watch Holzyebock Hiebat's trailer, and Knibble Thiessen's house call wasn't till the next evening. Besides, what did those things have to do with finding the grandfather clock or the swine killer? I still had Yetta Hiebat's zipper Bible to return, but that didn't seem urgent, so I stopped at the graveyard to meditate at my father's grave and looked around for clues about Oata's Bible I might have missed before. I didn't find anything solid but as I stood there looking at my father's name written in German letters on the headstone I remembered an argument I had with him when I was twelve. I had told him he should shame himself for always asking people such driest questions about what they were doing. He answered me that a person couldn't find anything out if he didn't ask questions. And if a person didn't find anything out he could only think lies. "Besides," he said, "people like to talk about themselves. If you ask them questions, you give them a chance to talk it out. People that talk things out feel better and then they live a longer time." I brooded on this by the grave. Papa had asked many questions but he hardly ever talked about himself. Maybe that was why he died at fifty. Asking questions was the part of my profession I found hardest to do. I was always thinking, "Would I want my neighbour to ask *me* this?" I found it very hard to talk about myself. And nobody asked me questions. Not even Barbara Ball Bearing.

I drove from the graveyard to the Gutenthal store. After picking up the mail I bought a Pepsi and without thinking about it a can of Player's Navy Cut tobacco and some Vogue papers. While I was leaning on the drink cooler I noticed Store Janzen's Willy had a new trucker's wallet with a chain in his back pocket. "Nice wallet," I said, and Willy took it out and showed me the special features like the secret pocket.

"It even has a little Bible inside," Willy explained. He had bought the wallet from a Bible van in Pracha Darp yesterday. This guy from the States had heard there was a communist government here so he thought he should bring lots of Bibles across before the border was closed with barbed wire. He had specially recommended the trucker's wallet Bibles because they would be easy to hide if the secret police came to look for them. I asked if there had been zipper Bibles for sale, too, and Willy said, "For sure, any kind of Bible you could want." He told me what the van and the salesman looked like. I was about to leave when Rape Rampel's oldest son, Carl, came in.

Carl picked up his mail, then asked Willy if he had seen Beitelkopp Blatz around. Carl said Beitelkopp Blatz was out from Headingley Jail and had been hanging around Rosmack when she was riding her motorcycle. "Rosmack better not let Dad find out," Carl said, "or he'll take that Harley away from her yet." Before I could get my mind around any questions a motorcycle rummeled outside. I glanced out the window and saw a guy about thirty take off his helmet. His hair was getting thin in the front, but to make up for it he had let it grow longer in the back. He zipped open his black leather jacket, hitched up his jeans and entered the store. We watched him in silence as he stood in the doorway. Suddenly, Store Janzen's Willy's face wrinkled and he exclaimed, "Hova Jake!" Hova Jake grinned, and after some small talk Hova said he was working as a "community organizer." Hova asked if Carl was Rosmack's brother and mentioned meeting her on the road that morning. He'd also met a Blatz fellow at the same time who seemed to have some strange ideas about how the world was put together but looked like a good enough fellow at heart. Hova Jake bought a Coke and I followed him out, clutching the tobacco and papers in my hand, thinking at least I knew who the three motorcycles had been.

I stepped across the street and glanced at an auction sale poster in the credit union window. It was the St. Joe auction, the one Simple Hein had gone to. The Flying Hieberts were not the auctioneers. This one was being handled by Delorme and Ducharme. A Cockshutt combine was on the list.

Inside the credit union, Count Floyd Falk, the assistant manager, squinted at my withdrawal slip. "Not ten thousand? There's an auction sale today." He laughed. "Three times now on the day of an auction sale around here somebody has come in and taken out ten thousand cash. I'm trying to guess who it will be today."

"Have you heard what these people bought?"

"No, I haven't, but it must be important, because one guy took out all his shares to make up the ten grand."

"Well, the price of machinery these days, even at auction sales."

"You can say that again." Count Floyd handed me two

tens and a five. "You might be able to buy a bent crowbar with that."

"Yeah, if some States person doesn't bid it up to a hundred."

Outside, I tried to remember who had bought big items at A.Dyck and L.U.Dyck's auction, but of course I had missed most of it. I took a few steps toward Shusta Paul's shoe repair shop, then stopped short as I saw a green LTD roll through the stop sign and then spit gravel as it turned west. I dashed for my VW and turned the key, pressed the accelerator and released the clutch all in the same motion. Yut Yut Leeven's dog almost lost its tail as I tore past the stop sign and turned west. I didn't shift into fourth gear till the thirty-six ponies over the back wheels pushed fifty-five and I started to gain on that dust cloud in front of me. Closer and closer I got and I was only about five car-lengths behind when the car slowed for the village of Pracha Darp and I crept up behind it so close I could see a "MILK" sticker on the bumper. I couldn't see the driver through the dust, so I honked and started to pull alongside when my engine sputtered. I reached down automatically for the reserve tank switch. It was already pulled. I had forgotten to fill up last night when I got home. I didn't even bother to swear at myself as the LTD calmly drove through the village and then speeded up and disappeared.

Pracha Darp was an old-style village of house-and-barn-together farmyards with rail fences and tall cottonwoods lining the street. It used to be a major centre when people still thought twice before driving fifteen miles to town for something. Now a farmer might drive to town three, four times a day, not counting coffee breaks at the Flatland Mall. So while Pracha Darp once had two stores, a service station, a feed mill, two bone setters and three churches, only one store and one church remained in business. One church had been moved to a museum, the other had become a granary during the shortage of grain hopper cars. Pracha Darp was also the home of Pracha Platt, the man who raised funds for the church and other charities. He drove from one yard to the next and asked for donations. He didn't exactly beg for your money, but he had a way of making you feel that if you didn't give that ten or twenty burning in your pocket to his cause you had some moral screws loose and were maybe even downright stingy. Pracha Platt was standing at his mailbox when my car rolled to a stop at his driveway.

"Mr. Bergen from Gutenthal," he said down to me from his six feet two inches. "I am planning to come to your corner on Thursday to give you the Lord's opportunity to give to the hospital fund. I trust I will find you in generous health."

"Well sure," I said. "If I'm not home Mama is always home. We might be able to find something. For sure a chicken or a loaf of bread. Maybe even a jar of mustard pickles."

Pracha Platt almost smiled before he said, "I knew your father well. He always found something to give. He is safe now, done with this troubled world."

"I heard you had visitors from afar here in Pracha Darp yesterday. A Bible van?"

"Yes, there was . . ." He hesitated and I thought I sensed some disapproval in his voice. "A sincere man . . . talked about the desperate need to spread the Word in this time of moral decline. He seemed concerned about our socialist government here in Manitoba. He said he was lucky to cross the border before it was closed to God's Word altogether."

"Did you buy a Bible?"

"No, I didn't, though quite a few others did. Some bought more than one . . . for gifts I guess or maybe . . . like that Blatz boy with the motorcycle . . . he bought three."

"Three Bibles? Were they all the same?"

"Yes, I think so . . . black zipper Bibles. A zipper Bible is good for travelling . . . say, wasn't that Blatz boy in Headingley for a while?"

I nodded.

"It is heart-warming to know our prison ministry is having some effect." Pracha Platt's voice sounded just a little bit hollow. "Still, three Bibles for a boy like that is unusual."

"Did the Bible seller say where he was going today?"

"I thought I heard him say he was going to spend the next few days in the villages on the other side of the highway. I think that's what he said. What's your interest?"

"Oh, nothing much. Store Janzen's Willy showed me this trucker's wallet with the secret Bible inside and I thought it would make a good gift for a trucker friend of mine."

"Well, if you decide to buy, look the Bible over carefully. Mrs. Friesen at the end of the village bought one and when she opened it at home she found there was no Book of Psalms in it. She came out on the street again to exchange it but the van was already gone."

"Interesting."

After I bought five gallons of purple tractor gas from Pracha Platt I checked Yetta's zipper Bible. All the books seemed to be there, at least all the hundred and fifty Psalms. I let my head dream up all kinds of theories as I headed for the other side of the highway, but nothing made sense to me.

The white GMC step van with a large black logo proclaiming "The B-I-B-L-E Yes That's The Book For Me" was parked on the Puggefeld school yard. Funny way to be smuggling Bibles into hostile territory. Or maybe someone was trying to be so obvious he wouldn't be noticed. Outside the back doors of the van a canopy shaded a display table. Behind it a short-haired man held up an illustrated Bible for a group of children. Four adults fingered the Bibles on the table. I sauntered over at a careless angle so I could glance into the vehicle. The cab was cluttered with clothing, pads of sales slips and copies of *Soldier of Fortune.* A small decal on the dashboard read "Support Contra Aid." I passed around the front and saw the South Dakota licence plate.

The salesman, who looked about sixty, was talking to a Dyck woman as I stepped up to the left side of the table. The top Bible in a pyramid of zipper Bibles was opened at the Book of Proverbs. Behind the pyramid lay four more zipper Bibles in a single row. Pocket-sized Bibles were arranged in a cross beside the pyramid, and the illustrated children's Bibles stood up on end in the centre of the table, forming a V. Next a circle of trucker's wallets surrounded an open wallet displaying the secret pocket containing a miniature Bible and a small magnifying glass. The salesman explained the features of the deluxe Bible to the Dyck woman. A gilt-edged edition with the words of the Saviour in gold, it had no less than five ribbons to mark favourite passages. The salesman pointed out the gold-inked pen included free to make entries in the Family Tree section in the middle of the Bible.

"A perfect family treasure," the salesman said. "A perfect foundation for the eternal family reunion in Heaven." Something about the man's voice bothered me. It was like a States voice, but not quite. He used preacher words but he sounded like something else.

"But a hundred and fifty dollars," the Dyck woman said. "My husband, I don't know if . . ."

"A small price for everlasting life," the salesman said, and his way of talking made me think of one of those Custer's last stand kind of movies where John Wayne says a Bible verse over a dead soldier's grave.

"But such an expensive Bible! I would be scared to read it."

A motorcycle roared into the school yard and stopped near the school. Beitelkopp Blatz climbed off the black Harley. Mirrored shades covered his eyes and he chewed on a match as he sauntered over to the stand.

I watched him from the corner of my eye as he picked up one of the pocket Bibles and flipped through it, occasionally stopping to lipread a verse. I saw he had a girl's ring on his little finger and I had to swallow hard to steady myself. Blatz put the small book down and picked up the open zipper Bible, again flipping through the pages, lipreading verses. He raised his face to the sky at one point and I thought I heard him breathe, "Amen." Then he zipped up the Bible before he replaced it and reached into his pocket.

The salesman had stopped trying to sell the deluxe Bible to the Dyck woman and was showing the trucker's wallet to Peter Petkau's wife, who had come to the stand with curlers in her hair. I thought she had had curlers in her hair ever since she was in grade ten. But like the Dyck woman, Mrs. Petkau was just taking a break from shelling peas, and buying Bibles was not a pressing need. Then the salesman noticed the bills in Beitelkopp's hand and he politely moved to the other end of the counter.

"How much for a zipper Bible?" Beitelkopp asked.

"$9.95," the salesman said.

Beitelkopp chewed on his match for a moment, and said softly, "A merry heart doeth good like a medicine."

The salesman raised his eyebrows just a little and whispered, "He sware unto thy fathers to give thee, a land flowing with milk and honey."

Beitelkopp looked at the bills in his hand and said, "I'll take three." The salesman didn't reply and Beitelkopp added, "For my friends in jail. May they find salvation, too."

"God bless you. It will be the best gift in the world," the salesman said as he took the bills from Beitelkopp's hand. He picked up three of the four Bibles from behind the pyramid and slipped them into a white plastic bag with a four-colour picture of Jesus on it. Beitelkopp tucked the bag under his arm and walked away whistling "Onward Christian Soldiers." He stuffed the Bibles into the saddle bag, then vaulted onto the motorcycle. The bike was kickstarted and moving before the seat of his pants hit the saddle. My head was full of questions as he roared off, heading east.

The Dyck woman had decided to buy a trucker's wallet. "For my nephew who drives transport for Triple E," she said. While the salesman made the sale I reached behind the pyramid for the remaining zipper Bible. With an eye on the salesman, I quickly replaced it with the Bible from the top of the pile. Then I reached for my wallet. As far as I could see the Bible seller hadn't noticed the exchange. In fact, he seemed pleased to make the sale.

Back on the road I unzipped the Bible and began to examine the cover. The cover seemed more cushioned than a book cover would be. As I probed the inside of the back cover I felt something moveable inside. I was reaching for my pocket knife when a sudden roar startled me and I saw I was right in the path of a low-flying crop duster.

A dose of chemical brought tears to my eyes and left me coughing until I crossed the highway. I kept driving as I slit open the covers of the zipper Bible, and when I saw the contents my better judgement told me it was time to go to the RCMP.

7

BUT better isn't necessarily best. Especially when it comes to judgement. Besides, as soon as I took what I had to the horsemen it would have been out of my hands and I thought this case was too complicated to let go at this time. Sure, if it had just been a matter of the hidden contents of the zipper Bible I would have gone to the Mounties right away. If I had found the zipper Bible on the street and discovered the contents accidentally, the moustache kids would have been next to know. But it wasn't that simple! I had a hunch that somehow everything was connected, everything that had happened since I found the Bible on Nobah Naze Needarp's grave.

Because I felt that way, I had to try to prove it. If I went to the RCMP I might never get a chance to prove this connection. In fact, if the RCMP got involved the threads tying all this together might not even *exist*! You don't double-cross your hunches. And if Rosmack Rampel was having some kind of thing going with Beitelkopp Blatz, I would have to get her out of the way before anything turned into paperwork. Besides, I was getting hungry. It was time for faspa.

And I had to find out more about Beitelkopp Blatz. His family lived in what used to be the Blarney School District before the schools were consolidated. Before Blarney, the village was called Frommenfeld but the public school system had given it a new name more in keeping with the two foundering peoples of this country. The government also gave the Inuit people free last names as a Centennial gift in 1967. I guess that was better than the numbers they had before. Still Beitelkopp Blatz had bought six zipper Bibles in two days and if the Bible I had bought was anything to go by, each of those Bibles was missing the Book of Psalms and contained cocaine or heroin or smack or crack. It certainly wasn't baby powder. And Rosmack Rampel had been at Barbara Ball Bearing's party with this Blatz from Blarney who liked to say zipper Bible verses about medicine and this morning Rosmack had been heading toward that gravel road swastika I had seen from Bulchi Wiebe's airplane. Even Rosmack's brother had seemed quite concerned about her hanging around with Beitelkopp, so as I buttered a slice of the bread Mama had baked that morning in Mrs. Knibble Thiessen's oven I asked Bulchi Wiebe, who had come back to visit Mama again, what he could tell me about the Blatzes from Blarney. I figured now that Bulchi had gotten Mama into his airplane he would be hanging around the place all the time so I might as well use him for his bird's-eye view of things.

"Russlenda," he said as he tore up another slice of bread into his bowl and soaked it with milk. "Blarney is all Russlenda. People used to call it Moscow. Blatz went through the Revolution when he was just a boy. Such things to see when you are so young. Saw Mahkno's men kill his sister after they all had their way with her. At the beginning of the war Blatz talked a lot about Hitler until it became dangerous to talk such things. Anybody who said 'communism' where Blatz could hear was guaranteed an earful and when Blatz was finished you might not know any more about communism than you did before, but for sure you would know not to say it when Blatz was around." Bulchi cut off a piece of the soggy bread with his spoon and slurped it into his mouth.

"Wasn't there some trouble with his son?" Mama said, as she poured herself some more coffee.

Bulchi scraped a drop of milk off his lower lip with his spoon. "Yeah, that was his second son, Ernst. Ernst disagreed with his father and thought the Germans had to be stopped. Ernst joined the army but it was already late in the war and he never got overseas. Blatz wouldn't let his son enter the house when he returned after the war. Ernst left, walked to town and got on the train. He never came back to this part of the country."

"What about this young Blatz with the motorcycle, the one they call Beitelkopp?"

"Oh, you mean the Blatzes from Blarney! Forgive me, Kjnals. I was telling you about the Blatzes from Birkenhead. The one they call Beitelkopp isn't even a real Blatz at all. His mother was a Bartel and his father was a Koop and she got polio and he got cancer, and when they both died the Blatzes took the boy in and raised him as their own. Somebody someplace called the boy Bartel-Koop and then somebody else said Beitelkopp and you know how it is with such names—you can't get rid of them, right, Schneppa Kjnals?"

"Right, Bulchi Wiebe!"

The phone rang. I answered it with the speaker off. It was A.Dyck and he sounded desperate.

A.Dyck was sitting at the kitchen table in the farmhouse when I walked in. His grey head was bent over an open zipper Bible that lay in front of him and he was holding a picture, a snapshot, in his hand.

"What's loose?" I asked in Flat German. With shaking fingers A.Dyck handed me the photograph. It was a black and white picture of five young men goose-stepping toward the camera. They were not in uniform but two of them looked like they were wearing black armbands with swastikas on them. The youth on the left of the photo had no armband and seemed to be just a step or so behind the rest. He was a very young A.Dyck.

"This came in the mail today," he said hoarsely. "It was in this Bible."

I picked up the Bible and looked at the open pages. "This where the picture was?" A.Dyck nodded. No verses were underlined on the pages, but when I flipped through the rest of the pages a piece of note paper with a blue flower fell out—L.U.Dyck's note to Oata. His inscription to Oata was on the title page. It was Oata Siemens's stolen Bible.

"What was the Bible wrapped in?" A.Dyck looked around the room, then pointed to the brown paper and string on the floor. A.Dyck's name and address were scrawled carelessly on the paper with a thick black marker. The three two-cent stamps near the corner of the folds had no postmark.

"You say this came in the mail today?"

"Yes, it was in the mailbox."

"At the store?"

"No, not at the store! At the road!"

I looked at him quizzically, like people do in books. "But you don't get mail like that at the road anymore. You have to go to the store to get it now!" Gutenthal had lost rural route delivery long ago, though Pracha Darp and other villages close to town still had it. Still some Gutenthalers had kept their mailboxes at the ends of their driveways.

A.Dyck shook his head. "I was walking along the driveway, looking at everything, thinking about everything that had happened on this farm, you know, things like when the old ones were still alive, and Lawrence and me were young and the things we used to do, when I saw the postman's jeep stop at the mailbox. The postman reached out and put mail in, turned the box to show that there was mail inside and drove off. So I went to get the mail the way I always used to do and there was this."

I sat down at the table. "What does it mean? The picture."

"I don't know where it came from. I never saw it before."

"Do you remember anything?"

"Well yeah, I remember now a little bit, but I was only sixteen then, I think, and Blatz was oabeida for Rape Rampel's father and one time on a Saturday evening Blatz comes along with this motorbike he had made himself and he asked if I wanted along to town. I remember now that I had a dollar and thirty-seven cents in my pocket, all the money I had. I had never been on a motorbike before and we drove through Puggefeld and Pracha Darp and the girls ran off the road and looked at us go by from behind the fences, only in Pracha Darp there was one girl that stayed on the road and Blatz hooked on there and neighboured with her a little bit and then we went to town. Blatz drove up and down the Main Street a few times, then we stopped in front by the Commonwealth Store. All of a sudden we heard someone shout, "Sieg Heil!" and there were these shuzzels marching down the street. When they came past us Blatz signalled to me and we got in behind them and aped them after trying not to laugher ourselves but those shuzzels were so serious I don't even think they noticed what we were doing. We stopped after a few minutes and went into the Commonwealth Store and looked at everything and watched some people drinking Orange Crush from brown bottles and then we went home and I remember I still had my dollar and thirty-seven cents when I pulled myself out to go to bed."

"So in this picture you're not really part of the marching bunch at all."

"No, see if you look real close you can see Blatz's head in between those two. Hey look, that one there second from this end, that looks like Blatz's cousin, the one from Blarney. Sure, that's him!"

"The one that has a son called Beitelkopp?"

"Yeah sure, that's him."

"Do you know any of the others?"

"Well, let's see now, that one there next to me, that's Schmuggle Veens, for sure that's Schmuggle Veens, he used to have a schneizat like Hitler. That other one I don't know. Who would have taken such a picture? And why would somebody send it to me? Now?" A.Dyck rubbed his forefinger under his nose, then he scratched his head. "Could it have something to do with this Nazi war criminals business they talk about on the radio all the time?"

"I don't see how," I said. "I mean, you never did nothing wrong. You didn't kill any Jews."

"For sure, I didn't kill any Jews." He sat for a few minutes brooding about it. Something was bothering him. It was as if he was going to say something more. Maybe he was remembering something else. Then he put the picture back in the Bible and zipped it shut. "It's good that you came, Kjnals. I had to talk to somebody. Now that Lawrence is with Hilda it is lonesome. I should maybe get hooked on with a woman, too."

"Hilda?"

"Yeah, Hilda Heinrichs. You know, the ones that used to live a mile north from the Puggefeld dike. There is still a waterhole there."

"And your brother is with her?"

"Yeah, they will get married now after all these years." A.Dyck stopped and looked at the picture. He closed his eyes for a moment, then looked at me. "She said to say thank you if you came around."

"Thank me? Hilda? For what?"

"I don't know. She just said to say thank you." His hands trembled. My father's voice said, "Ask! Ask!" but I didn't know what to make of it. I couldn't think of any questions to ask. But I needed at least one thing to follow up. I scanned over what A.Dyck had said, then I asked, "Who was the postman with the grey jeep?"

"Martens. Martin Martens."

Then my father's spirit pricked me and I asked, "This Hilda Heinrichs, she drives an LTD?"

"Yah, a green one."

I felt like I was on a roll. The doll woman was Hilda Heinrichs and she was marrying L.U.Dyck and maybe she had something to do with the dead pig, only A.Dyck was sitting there with tears running down his cheeks, and even though in my head Papa's voice was whispering, "Ask! Ask!

Ask about the dead pig!" I couldn't make myself torture a crying man.

So I got back into my car and saw the red brassiere on the floor. I picked it up and stared at it as if maybe it could tell me what was going on but all I could see was that some of the holes in the red lace were shaped like little fish so I threw it to the back where it landed on the Hudson's Bay blanket under the rear window. I let the Volkswagen idle toward the swastika of ungravelled roads I had seen from the air that morning and tried to make some sense out of this endless mixed-up movie in my head that was Gutenthal. Hauns Jaunses' Fraunz's pond was at one end of the un-gravelled stretch of road that made up one arm of the swastika. I crawled in first gear to the half-mile point, turned into the field road that cut through the section and drove to the centre. I noticed nothing out of the ordinary. I continued down the field road, then turned left at the mile road, following the ungravelled stretch until I reached the bridge at the corner. I got out of the car here and examined the bridge carefully. I found nothing under the bridge except a beer bottle. I idled back to the centre of the swastika, turned right and followed the dirt road again. This end of the swastika brought me to a dirt-blocked culvert. It had been a dry spring. The end of the opposite arm marked a corner of Hingst Heinrichs's beetfield that had been weeded the week before. I got out of the car and looked over the row of beets which stretched to half a mile from the pond, and thought how lucky Rosmack had been that no overheated beet-weeders had decided to cool off there while she was swimming. Then I thought about Hilda Heinrichs again and I wondered if L.U.Dyck would be with her at the waterhole hump at 9:00 waiting for the clock I didn't have and I wondered how come this woman would pay the man she was marrying a thousand dollars for a clock, when she could have easy had it for nothing if she just blinked her doll eyes at him, and I thought about what Oata had said and I wondered what all this had to do with the murdered pig, when I remembered Yetta Hiebat's zipper Bible and I just got all muddled up. I needed to ask some more questions.

But when I got home Bulchi Wiebe was gone and Mama was sitting in the rocking chair crying her eyes out. "Mama, what's loose?"

"That man, to ask for such a thing!" she sobbed, and my thoughts were full of Bulchi Wiebe kneeding Mama while she was kneeding dough.

"What did he want?"

"He wants me to give him ten thousand dollars."

"Ten thousand dollars!" The man is really twisted crooked, I thought.

"So driest a dog isn't, to ask me for the money from Papa's last good crop. And I was starting to believe him that he liked me for a person. So polietsch he was, all the way to the end after I said no to him, and he looked like he was going to cry, and he said he would have to sell his airplane then, but I wasn't going to let him smear me on anymore and I just told him to go away. So he backed away from me but he looked at me all the way out the door, and jauma me, he even sippled a few tears down his cheek. Koppkrank. That man is in his head sick." And Mama started to sob again. "You know he even had a Bible in his hand when he asked me for the money!"

"A zipper Bible?"

"Yeah sure, a Bible with a zipper." I thought for a second that Mama was going to laugh.

8

I couldn't make myself ask Mama about L.U.Dyck and Hilda Heinrichs and a pig. She was too upset. So I went to town. I parked in front of the post office and saw Yetta Hiebat get out of her LTD and head into the Flatland Mall. I decided to give her the zipper Bible. It seemed like the least I could do.

The Flatland Mall was having a Tax-Free Tuesday Toot—free hot dogs and watermelon, no sales tax, and six-month interest-free loans for big-ticket items. In the crowd I tailed Yetta without being obvious, but I couldn't seem to get close enough to give her the zipper Bible. Whenever I got near she was talking to somebody or looking at something in a store and how do you give a zipper Bible to a woman who is fingering the lace on a black brassiere or buying a box of Woman's Special K? I was starting to shame myself already chasing after this woman with a Bible in my hand. I followed her out of the MacLeod's store, where she had been looking at a pressure cooker, out of the mall to the sidewalk where I made myself speak her name. Yetta turned, bewildered, as I handed her the zipper Bible and said, "I was asked to give you this." For a second she had a scared look in her eyes. It was only for a second, then she smiled and said, "Oh, from Hilda." But I know for that second she was very scared, very scared.

For sure, I was right now. Hilda was the doll woman and I was still missing her clock. I had only an hour to get it to her, and I still had to find it. I didn't know where to start. I wondered if Yetta could help me but she was gone among the people on the sidewalk. A grey jeep drove by and for a moment I thought it was an army jeep, only army jeeps aren't grey. It was a jeep with a roof and so it wasn't that easy to tell who was inside and I thought for a second about the mail jeep A.Dyck had told me about. Then I spotted the RCMP boy in his powder blue Ford followed by Rosmack Rampel and Beitelkopp Blatz on their Harleys and I started toward my Volkswagen when a cream yellow Cockshutt combine idled down the main street.

Well, I stopped so fast I was rear-ended by a baby carriage. I quickly begged pardon, pointed my left hand like an arrow, cut my way through the crowd to the curb and galloped across the street to grab the combine ladder and climb up beside Simple Hein.

"What's going on?"

"I tol' you, Kjnals. Go Frenchman auction, St. Joe. Buy combine." He stopped at the stop sign. "No laugh at Hein there."

"So what you going to do with this combine?"

"Thrash grain. Custom. Make lots money. Take to garage

now to get all fix up before thrash time." Hein pushed his foot down on the variable speed accelerator and turned left to cross the railway track.

"Who you going to thrash for?"

"Yasch Siemens. Ha Ha Nickel. Big shot farmers. Next year go States for early combining. Get rich."

"How much you pay for this corn binder?"

"Combine! Ten tousand. Cash!"

"Ten thousand? Cash? Where you get that kind of money?"

Hein steered the combine into the Consumers' Co-op Garage parking lot. When he stopped, he let the motor idle while he whispered in my ear, "Don' tell nobody, but it's true what Bible say. Lord provide."

I looked at Hein, waiting to hear more, but he had no more time for me. "Got to talk to Consumer 'bout interest-free service. Could be I'm crazy, but not me I'm stupid."

Maybe I was crazy, maybe I was stupid, but I had to get out of town. I needed to think. Something was going on and I couldn't figure it out. At least I had given Yetta Hiebat the zipper Bible. A couple of miles out of town I stopped and went into the ditch behind a bush. I heard the drone of an airplane in the distance as I was zipping up. I glanced over my shoulder and saw the plane's blinking lights off towards Hauns Jaunses' Fraunz's pond. I looked at my watch. It was one minute to nine. I would just have to confess that I had failed. For a second I tried to remember what the Hollywood School of Detection had said about detectives who got sued for incompetence by dissatisfied clients. And yeah, where was I going to get a thousand dollars to replace what I had lost?

There were no buildings left, just six cottonwoods and the overgrown dugout, but I remembered the old Heinrichs yard. The green LTD was parked where the barn door used to be.

The driver's door was open. A snapshot lay on the seat, a snapshot of a young L.U.Dyck, maybe taken when he would have been Oata's Sunday School teacher. I walked over to where the eating tables had been. He had been with her. I was remembering something. L.U.Dyck had been with this Hilda at a funeral, a funeral for a woman and a child killed in an accident. Hilda, this doll woman with the big eyes, had been there with L.U.Dyck, but what did it mean?

I climbed up the slope of the dugout. A woman in a black dress floated face down near the willows hanging over the other side. I dashed down the hill, threw myself into the water and paddled furiously until I reached her. I turned the body · over and dragged it out of the water. Frantically, my mind scrambled through my mail-order life saving course. I cleaned the dark scum off her face and stuck my finger in her mouth. There were no obstructions. I turned her on her side. No water ran out of her mouth. I positioned her on her back, one hand under her neck. I placed the other hand on her forehead, pushed down gently, then pinched her nose shut and placed my wide open mouth over her lips. I had never touched anything so cold. I blew four quick breaths into her mouth to fill up her lungs. Then I took a deep breath and blew into her mouth as hard as I could. I cocked my ear over her mouth and listened. Then I took another deep breath and repeated the procedure. DO NOT STOP UNTIL THE VICTIM IS BREATHING ON HIS OR HER OWN OR UNTIL SOMEONE IS ABLE TO RELIEVE YOU. Don't stop! Don't stop! Don't stop! Don't stop!

I saw stars when I opened my eyes. I had never felt so cold. I raised my head from the still-soaked dress. There was no breath. I must have passed out. No one had come. It was too late now. I got up on my knees and looked at this woman. Her doll eyes were closed and I thought if only I lifted her into an upright position the eyes would open together. I had to get some help. As I stood up I saw a glint at her ankle. I crouched and found the ankle bracelet. With a charm, just like Yetta Hiebat, Schmuggle Veens's States wife, and Knibble Thiessen's patient from the States. I felt the charm with my fingers. It was a tiny swastika.

Hilda Heinrichs was dead and I couldn't help her now. I had failed, maybe in more ways than I could even know. I should have asked more questions maybe, so my thoughts could have been more like the truth. "He will reveal His plan when He is ready," Preacher Janzen had said a few Sundays before when I was in the church basement listening to the sermon on the P.A. system, while I picked up the forgotten combs, jackknives, lipsticks, cigarette papers and other trinkets from the Sunday School rooms for the lost and found box. "You must obey, even if you do not understand His plan! Do not question. Give yourself to His plan. Not my will, but Thine, Lord!" But was there a plan? Was there a plan that had brought me to my knees beside a wet body in the dark grass of a waterhole hump? What kind of plan would put four women with swastikas on their ankle bracelets into my comfortable world of lost and found? I couldn't ask Hilda any questions. I had to go for help, even though it was too late. I had to leave the scene of the accident. Accident?

My next move was no accident. I removed the bracelet from the icy ankle and shoved it into my wet pocket. When I stood up a yardlight came on about a mile away at Barbara Ball Bearing's place. I hoped it was a good omen.

Music bounced from Barbara's house as I stepped out of the VW, shivering in my wet clothes. Two Harley motorcycles stood near the picket fence, the powder blue Ford was parked near the barn.

"You're all wet!" Barbara exclaimed, letting me into the kitchen. Rosmack Rampel and Beitelkopp Blatz sat on a small couch near the window. Beitelkopp had a bottle of beer in one hand, a zipper Bible open in the other. Rosmack's hands fidgeted with her knees. She wasn't drinking anything. The young RCMP who had gotten the hosedown from the Froese brothers sat at the kitchen table, scraping the label off a beer bottle with his thumb.

"Somebody's drowned," I stammered. "I have to use the phone."

"Drowned? Where?" The cop jumped up.

"In the old Heinrichs pond. A woman. I tried to save her."

Things moved quickly then. The cop followed Rosmack and Beitelkopp out the door after he made a call. I started to follow but Barbara pulled me back.

"You have to get out of those wet clothes!"

Next thing I knew I was shivering under a quilt on the couch with a hot cup of coffee in my hands while Barbara pinned all my wet clothes on the line outside. As I tried to drink the scalding coffee I noticed Beitelkopp's Bible on the couch. I picked it up and felt the covers. The back cover had something inside it, just like the one I had bought from the Bible van.

I heard a siren outside on the road and Barbara came back in.

"Ambulance and a cop car," she said. "What happened?" I told her the simple facts as she moved around the kitchen in her tight blue sweater and jeans. Her feet were bare and she wasn't wearing an ankle bracelet. Then I noticed my wet wallet and a pile of things she had emptied out of my pockets before she hung my clothes up. The doll woman's bracelet was part of the pile.

"Beitelkopp forgot his Bible," I said, as I emptied the wet bills and other papers from my wallet.

"Oh, he'll come back. He comes here almost every night. Funny how people can change. Before he went to jail I had lots of trouble with him. Now he is so polite. He only drinks one beer and sits there reading his Bible or he talks to somebody, if they want to listen."

"Does Rosmack always come with him?"

"She was here already before Blatz came, or the Mountie."

"She came to drink?"

"No, she didn't drink."

I spread the papers and money on the table and slipped the ankle bracelet into the change pocket on the wallet. Barbara poured me another cup of coffee. She put the pot back on the stove and left the kitchen. I heard her go up the stairs. A few minutes later she was back with some underwear, a shirt and some pants.

"I don't know if these will fit, but it will be easier to talk to the cops if you're dressed."

"Talk to the cops?"

"You found the body, didn't you? They'll have a thousand questions for you."

"Yeah, I did."

"Who was the woman?" Barbara handed me the shorts.

"I think it was Hilda Heinrichs." I turned away so I could pull the shorts up under the blanket.

"Hilda Heinrichs?" Barbara held out the shirt.

"I think she used to live there." I slipped my arms into the shirt and pulled it over my shoulders. As I buttoned the shirt and put on the pants I told her what happened.

"Do you think she killed herself?"

"I don't know. She could have slipped and fallen in.

Probably she didn't know how to swim. But it wasn't deep where I found her."

Two motorcycles roared into the yard, and a moment later Rosmack and Beitelkopp came into the house.

"The cops want to talk to you," Rosmack said to me, in a funny way. I nodded at her and noticed she was wearing earrings, round leather earrings covered with a design of coloured beads. A leather, beaded clip held back her long black hair.

Beitelkopp grabbed his Bible from the table and the way he held himself it was almost like he was drunk or something, as if he had to think about each movement he made, even how he held his face. "Well, I guess I'd better go. Coming, Rose?" He could hardly keep a straight face as he said this. High on dope, I figured.

"Not yet. I think I'll stay for a while."

"Sure. See you around. Peace," he said, and he held up two fingers.

Beitelkopp's motorcycle roared away and a car pulled up. There was brisk knocking on the door and Barbara let in a uniformed RCMP officer with a moustache. He looked Barbara and Rosmack up and down, then turned to me.

"You the guy that found the victim?"

"Yes."

"I'll need to take a statement from you."

"Sure."

He patted his shirt pocket. "Come out to the car. I left my notebook out there."

"That your bug?" he asked as we settled into the front seat of the cruiser car. He flipped open the notebook he picked off the dash. "Name?"

"Neil Bergen."

"Address?"

"Gutenthal. Box 70."

"Postal code?"

"R0G 3Q5."

"Phone?"

"427-6610."

"Occupation?"

"Investigator."

"What was that again?" I could feel his eyes drilling holes in my head. I cleared my throat.

"Private investigator."

"You mean like a detective?"

"Yeah. I'd give you my card but they got wet. My stuff is still drying on the table inside."

"Is this one of your cards?" He reached to the back seat and brought back a plastic evidence bag. "We found this beside the body." He looked at the card, amused. "We stoop to snoop," he chuckled. "You have a licence?"

"Uh, no. I just started a little while ago."

"What kind of things do you investigate?"

"Uh, little things, like lost wallets, holes in fences. I keep an eye on places when people go on trips."

"People hire you to do this?" He didn't believe me.

"Well, uh, usually I do the work first. Say, if I see a farmer's cows have broken through a fence and are into the green alfalfa, I herd the cows back into the pasture, patch up the hole as best I can on the spot. Then I go inform the farmer. I've probably saved him a couple of thousand, so it's worth twenty to him."

"Interesting. Well, tell me what happened at the pond."

So I told him the story and he scribbled in his notebook. Once in a while he interrupted to ask me what time this had happened. I could only tell him in general terms. When I finished, we sat there in silence for a moment while he read over the notes.

"Had you ever seen this woman before?"

"Yes." I told him about helping her with a flat tire and that I had given her my card then.

"Is that the only time you saw her?"

"Yes."

"Why did you stop at the yard?"

"Well, her car was parked there. The door was open. I thought she might be having car trouble again."

"Do you know the woman's name?"

"I think she is a Heinrichs. I think she used to live there."

"Do you think she committed suicide?"

For the second time that evening I said, "I don't know."

"I guess that about wraps it up. Looks like you did your best to save her. Drop in to the station in a day or two. I'll have the statement typed up and ready for you to sign." He reached for the plastic evidence bag as I reached for the door handle. "Oh, by the way, there wasn't any body."

"Huh?"

"No green LTD either."

"Huh?"

"There was nothing there."

"What?"

"I don't know what kind of game you're playing, but there was nothing on that yard."

I couldn't believe my ears. I didn't know what to say.

"But—but I pulled her out of the water and gave her mouth to mouth. . . ."

"Just cut the crap and don't play games with me or I'll charge you with public mischief!"

I stepped out of the car, shaking. The cop wrote down the licence number of my VW before he spun his tires and drove off.

Inside the house Rosmack and Barbara sat at the table drinking coffee. I tried to figure out if they had been laughing about me. My pile of moist assets was untouched.

"Everything okay?" Barbara wanted to know.

"Is it true what the cop said? There was nothing there?"

Rosmack cleared her throat, then took a sip of coffee. "It's true, Kjnals. There was nothing. All they found was your card."

"But how could that be? I pulled that woman out of the pond! I tried to save her! I did!" I looked from Rosmack to Barbara, pleading with them to believe me. The pants Barbara had given me were too loose and they felt like they were going to slide down. I pulled them up a little.

"You want to keep those clothes till tomorrow? Yours haven't had time to dry yet." I gazed at Barbara's blonde hair and her blue eyes and I let my eyes flicker over her full blue sweater. I couldn't help it.

"I thought you liked me better with just the quilt on."

"Sure, I do, Kjnals," Barbara laughed. "But if you get caught peeking in old ladies' windows with just a quilt on you'll get thrown in the klink!"

Rosmack listened with a faint flicker at the corners of her mouth. I couldn't tell if she was amused. I couldn't tell if she thought there was any truth in what I had said. I stuffed my wallet and the other stuff into the pockets of the borrowed pants and turned to go.

"I think I'll go, too," Rosmack said as she stood up. "Thanks, Barb."

"Any time."

Rosmack picked her white helmet off the couch. I liked the way her hair was drawn back through the beaded leather hairclip, dropping smoothly down the black leather back of her jacket. I liked the beaded earrings, too, white circles with red arrowheads on a background of white hide. I hadn't seen the earrings before; I hadn't ever seen her wear anything "Indian." For a moment I thought I was looking at someone else—someone familiar but someone else—like maybe Buffy Ste. Marie. And there I was, an overgrown kid playing cops and robbers, making up stories in his head.

"Neil, I have to talk to you," she said in English, when we got outside. Her voice sounded different, excited, worried, serious. Usually she talked to me in gossipy Flat German the way men talk in the field or at the store.

"Well sure," I said. "You can always talk to me."

"Uh yeah, but this is different—this is important. Do we have to talk here?"

"Well no, uh, where would you like to go?"

"Well, someplace private, where we can be alone."

I looked around but couldn't see anyone. Rosmack saw my gesture and added, "I mean I don't want to talk here in the yard like this, somebody might hear us, I mean somebody might come along and it would be spoiled, uh, I don't know, I just don't feel comfortable talking here. There's just no privacy anymore."

"I have to go back to the Heinrichs yard," I said.

"I'll come with you."

"Okay."

At the Heinrichs yard the green LTD was gone; so was the doll woman's body. With the light from my flashlight I showed Rosmack where I had dragged the body up the bank and I tried to show her the car tracks in the grass, but the flashlight wasn't very bright and Rosmack didn't seem convinced. The more I searched around the yard the less real it seemed.

"Neil, I have to talk to you."

"Okay." There was nothing I could prove in the dark.

Rosmack sat down in my VW, giving me another glimpse of her earrings in the brief moment the interior light was on.

"So where did you get those earrings?" I asked when I sensed that she didn't know quite where to start.

"Oh these, uh, Jack gave them to me."

"Jack?"

"Yeah, Jack Harder."

"Oh you mean Hova Jake."

"Why can't people be called by their right names for a change? Do you like it when people call you Schneppa Kjnals? You don't really, do you, or why do you have Neil Bergen on your business card?"

"I guess you're right. Nicknames are just a habit we have. So Jack gave you the earrings and that thing in your hair?"

"Yeah, he got them over on the reserve. Jack is helping the Band with their land claim."

"How come he gave you a present? Isn't he a bit old for you?"

"It's not a present from him! A woman at the reserve came to Jack after he had a meeting with Council or Band or something like that and she asked him if he was from Gutenthal. She gave him a package to give to Rose Rempel." Rosmack looked at me and her black eyes were very shiny, but she wasn't crying.

"Did the woman say who she was?"

"No, but I know who she is. She is my mother . . . I mean . . . my real mother."

"Have you told your parents?" I didn't know what else to say but I thought she needed to keep talking.

"Not yet, I mean I will, but, uh, I just want to have this feeling, I don't know but I just feel so . . . so strange, so different, I mean, have you ever smelled a field of blooming flax at 8:00 in the morning and all of a sudden you are part of the field too and the little hairs all over your body are standing up and you think if somebody was looking they would see light shining all around you?" Her eyes were so bright I almost saw this glow. "I guess not," she sighed. "But I just want to have this feeling alone for a while before it gets all muddled up with talking."

I felt like a blooming flax field as I stared at her through the watery windows of my soul and I almost reached out to take her in my arms but every flax field has some sowthistle and I suddenly saw what I must look like to Rosmack, all ears and eyes, with my brush-cut hair, two days of stubble, invader nose, and my breath certainly wasn't flavoured with chlorophyll and retsin.

"Why are you telling me then?" I kept my tone quiet but I hoped it was stable.

"Telling you isn't the same, I mean, you're not my dad. Oh hutz drot, I'm trying to tell you something else. You see, Jack talked about what he is doing on the reserve, how he is helping them put together a land claim, and he said stuff about aboriginal rights, and first peoples, and saving the culture, and rediscovering the past, and self-government, and then Bernie talked . . ."

"Bernie?"

"Bernie Blatz."

"Beitelkopp?"

"Oh there you go again, Horny Corny Peeping Tom!" I

reddened a little at this new nickname, but defended myself.

"Honest, I didn't know Beitelkopp's name was Bernie, honest I didn't!"

"Well okay, but you know, sometimes nicknames really hurt! Especially if you're an Indian! Anyway Bernie talked about all the Indians in Headingley Jail and Jack called them political prisoners and said how ashamed he was that his people, the Flat Germans, had come to Canada to escape religious persecution but hadn't given any consideration to the people whose lands they took away except as people to give old clothes to, and send missionaries to, and to call them lazy people who only liked to drink and get welfare. And I started to get real mad!"

Rosmack talked on and on about how she had never thought much about Indians before, or what it really meant that she was Indian, and how she felt that she needed to do something with her life so she could help her people, like maybe she should go to university and be a lawyer or a doctor or a social worker or an organizer like Hova Jake or maybe she would go into politics and for sure she had to find out more about her people and would I go with her to the reserve to meet her mother?

The sky had turned completely black as she talked. I arm-wrestled with her question in the dark.

"Why not go with your parents or with Jack? I mean, Jack already works there and knows his way around. I don't know anything about the reserve."

"I can't do this with my parents. I have to do it without them . . . and I don't know . . . I just don't quite trust this Hova Jake!"

"How come?"

"I don't know, there's just something about him and Beitelkopp that doesn't sit right. So will you go with me to the reserve? Please Neil?"

"Yeah, I'll go with you. . . ." An explosion cut off my words. We scrambled out of the car and up onto the waterhole hump. Flames were shooting into the sky about two miles away.

"The trailer," I said. "Holzyebock Hiebat's trailer!"

When we got to the fire, Art Enns, Eva Enns's husband, was frantically gripping his screaming daughter to keep her from running to the trailer, now just a box of flames. "Mama is in there! Mama is in there!" The roof of the trailer collapsed. The girl's screams grew louder. "What you mean? What you mean?" Enns cried. "What you mean Mama is in there?"

"Mama is in there! I saw her go in there!"

Enns looked around like a wild man. There was nothing to be done. If someone was in that trailer it was too late.

"Hey get back!" I yelled. "The gas drums!" At the same time I heard a roar and the Payloader at the gravel pile swung into action. Rosmack was at the controls and with the relentless slow motion of heavy equipment she dumped scoop after scoop of gravel on the drums until they were buried and safe from the flames. The child was still screaming and the Payloader was still running when I ran over to talk with Rosmack. Rosmack shut the Payloader off and I felt headlights behind me and a man's voice shouted, "What's going on here?" The child stopped screaming and I saw Eva Enns hugging the sobbing child, saying over and over, "I was picking raspberries. I was picking raspberries." And then Holzyebock Hiebat was swearing at me about how come I wasn't keeping an eye on his trailer like I should do it without being asked. I tried to tell him how Rosmack saved his gas drums, but he spit at me, "Indiana Futz! Probably started it in the first place!"

Well, that made me so mad I hauled my fist back to let him have it right on the chin, but Rosmack yelled, "It's okay, Neil. Don't make it worse!"

Rosmack got on her motorcycle and kicked it into action. I was too angry to stick around so I followed her, trying to catch up. She sped away faster than usual and I worried about the loose gravel, but she stopped and waited for me on the wooden bridge over the double dike. I pulled in on her right side and stuck my head out the window. Before I could say anything, Rosmack leaned over and kissed me on the forehead. "I believe you, Neil," she whispered. Then she roared away and I watched until her taillight vanished in the dark.

I sat there for a few minutes, dazed with love, Rosmack's voice echoing through my head, then interrupted by the explosion. "So will you go with me to the reserve? Please Neil?" Bang. Too much knowl. Dunnasche big bang. Atomic bomb. Commennists. Commennists from the States. Too much knowl. Dunnasche big bang. Hein's voice overpowered Rosmack's in my hollow head.

There was no traffic on the road until I got to the highway and met a cruiser car with flashing lights and the fire truck about a mile behind. In town, I gave the main street a quick glance, crossed the tracks and drove west. I kept to the town speed limit until I got to Hein's bridge. Dunnasche big bang. Over the creek. I stopped, cut the lights, but left the motor running as I got out of the car and let my eyes get used to the dark. There was a farmyard across the creek, about a quarter mile from the bridge. I could make out the drooping petals of sunflowers in the dim light. Bang! I froze against the side of the car as the sound crackled through the sunflower field. Shotgun, I thought. Then silence. A few minutes later another bang. Exactly the same, exactly the same place, somewhere in the sunflower field. I relaxed. I waited to hear it again. Sure enough, after about five minutes the sunflower cannon boomed again. I grinned at how the cannon meant to scare blackbirds away from the sunflowers had scared Hein out of bridge and home.

The cannon boomed again and I shuddered. I had to admit I wouldn't sleep under the bridge with those explosions going off. Especially not after a night like this. My stomach growled then, and I decided to head home to Mama's table, and my bed, so I could sleep with Rosmack's kiss. Okay.

But things were not okay. The phone rang in the middle of the night. A voice that sounded like Holzyebock Hiebat's told me he couldn't find his wife and when I poked through the ashes in the morning I found bones.

9

Don't ask me how I know this, or how I know it's true, or if I know it's true. Of course, you know what comes in through the windows of the soul, but the guy who said the eyes are the windows of the soul left a lot of windows boarded up, I think, at least when it comes to knowing what is true. What is true is what you make of it. If enough people make the same thing of it as you do, then it's true. If you make something different of it than everybody else, then you're crazy. Truth is no use without believers. Of course, it helps if you take the boards off all the windows so as much light as possible comes in. And you can't just sit still. You have to snoop. That's what I do.

My name is Neil Bergen, Investigator. Cornelius Pee-Eye. The Effective Detective. The Gutenthal Gumshoe. Horny Corny Peeping Tom. But mostly they call me Schneppa Kjnals. Corny the Snoop. And Rosmack Rampel leaned from

her motorcycle and kissed me on the cheek and burned my
stubble.

I'm telling you Yetta Hiebat was murdered. That's right,
murdered. I don't know who dunnit, I have no evidence, I
have no motive, but what I make of it is that Yetta Hiebat
was murdered. And Hilda Heinrichs, the doll woman, too.
Murdered. Just like the pig.

So went my head for a whole day and a half after the fire.
I stayed at home, most of the time in bed counting the boards
in the ceiling, letting the voices from the speakerphone walk
from one ear to the other. Mama tried to make me eat, but I
couldn't. I started to roll cigarettes from the tobacco I had
bought for Shusta Paul but I couldn't remember what I
wanted to ask him about and anyway that just didn't seem
important anymore. I had murder on the brain and nothing
would let me forget it.

Never remove evidence from the scene of a crime. So said
the Hollywood School of Detection's lesson on procedures.
How I wished now that I had thrown that lesson out through
the window of my soul and removed just one rib from the
ashes of the trailer—just one charred curved bone and I
would have had some proof—I would have my dead
woman. My nightmare about Rosmack Rampel's kiss and the
doll woman's icy wet body was jangled out of tune by
Holzyebock Hiebat's call that his wife hadn't come home. I
could still hear the voice, a man's scratchy crying voice:
"Kjnals, Yetta isn't come home. Where is she?" And then
before I could say anything, the high, squeaky voice said:
"Where can Yetta be, Kjnals?" The phone clicked. The dial
tone buzzed in my ear. I looked up Holzyebock Hiebat's
number and pushed the buttons. I let the phone ring twenty
times but no one answered.

I sat looking out the dark kitchen window, half-dozing back into my nightmare. I was relieved that Mama hadn't awakened. I didn't know what to think and I had nothing to say.

At first light I drove back to the scene of the fire. I poked through the ashes with a piece of broken fishing rod. I stopped when I found the ribs. I shuddered and looked around. The Enns farm across the road was altogether still. I thought of the screaming child and decided not to bother them. A.Dyck and L.U.Dyck's farm was half a mile away.

A.Dyck was already up when I pounded on his door.

"Got to use your phone," I said. "Found bones in the ashes." I thought I saw A.Dyck's face go white as he jerked his chin toward the phone. I stepped around the Booker stove into the kitchen to the wall phone beside the window. I lifted the receiver and heard a woman talking in Flat German about a gall bladder shaped like a valentine and even when I coughed into the mouthpiece she wouldn't stop talking and she said, "Line busy. We pay phone bill, too." I finally had to say it was a police emergency and then they didn't want to hang up before I told them what it was until I said I would report them to the phone company. At last I dialled the police number and while it was ringing about thirty times I saw A.Dyck's black Monarch driving off the yard and I worried that he was going to the trailer and would mess things up, but when he got to the road he stopped at the mailbox, then turned in the wrong direction. A very sleepy police answered the phone.

"RCMP."

"I found bones in the trailer ashes!"

"Your name, sir?"

"Neil Bergen. I found bones in the trailer ashes!"

"Bergen, is that spelled with a u?"

"B-e-r-g-e-n. I found bones in the trailer ashes!"

"Address?"

"Box 70, Gutenthal. I found bones . . ."

"Postal code?"

"R0G 3Q5. Bones . . ."

"Say, aren't you the guy who said he found a drowned body last night?"

"Yeah."

"Don't call us, we'll call you!" Click. Click. Click. At least two phones hung up after the cop did. The snoop who cried wolf. That's what they thought. But I couldn't give up. I called the RCMP twice more before they finally agreed to come out and investigate. They got me to give them A.Dyck's phone number and told me to wait for their call before I went back to the trailer. I waited for half an hour without a call and then when I phoned again a woman answered and said the cops were on their way. A.Dyck drove back into the yard as I hung up the phone and I saw him carry a rusty ten-gallon cream can into the barn as I ran to my car.

Kowolchuk and McKay, the two RCMPs, were poking through the ashes when I got there. They didn't look happy to see me. I hurried over to the corner of the ruins where I had found the ribs. I kicked through the ashes but there was not a bone. There was a coil of steel tire belting but no bones.

I had found bones in the trailer ashes, I was sure I had, but the bones were gone, just like Hilda Heinrichs's drowned body. That fixed me with the Mounties. They almost arrested me right there. And then my cream went sour for sure when I picked up the zipper Bible from the seat of my car and realized that I had given Yetta the cocaine Bible I had bought from the Bible van. I slit open the cover of Yetta's Bible and found more little envelopes of white powder and my head almost cracked with the implications and ramifications that zipper drug Bible had had for Yetta Hiebat. I tried to sweep it out of my mind.

But I couldn't ignore what I knew I knew. I went home and phoned Holzyebock Hiebat but he told me to stick my nose in my own beckhouse. At first I figured for sure that Holzyebock Hiebat and Eva Enns had conspired to murder Yetta. I wanted to pin it on Hiebat after the way he treated Rosmack. But that just seemed too much like TV. And if Eva Enns had been with Holzyebock that evening her screaming child had plunged enough daggers into her heart already. I didn't rule out Holzyebock and Eva altogether but my head kept reliving that explosion, and the fact that there had been no vehicle to show how Yetta had got to the trailer stuck in my head like a rusty nail. Besides, the cocaine Bibles were probably a more likely motive for both murders. I kept mulling it over and over while the voices jabbered away on the speakerphone, discussing simple theories that seemed wild to me, and I kept rolling cigarettes I would never smoke, yet I tried to make each one as perfect as the ones Sam Spade made in the movies and Rosmack leaned from her motorcycle and kissed me and Mama called me to say Ha Ha Nickel was complaining that I didn't let him know his cows were in the alfalfa but I just said I was not a cowherd and I rolled some more cigarettes thinking murder murder murder and Indiana Futz she probably started it in the first place and I got a raging boar headache as I remembered how Beitelkopp had kissed Rosmack like there was nothing to it and my fire flamed higher and even Hilda Heinrichs's icy cold lips couldn't cool it and Mama called again to tell me Dola Dyck wanted to know if I had found his wallet and a few minutes later Winkle Wieler wanted to know why I hadn't told him he left his mail on the drink cooler at the store and then Barley King Barkman phoned to ask why I didn't tell him that his fly was open before he went in to see the bank manager and my head just throbbed and throbbed and pounded and Mama touched my forehead and said it was burning and she put a bag of ice on my head and said she had heard a Bible verse on the speakerphone and she said it to me as she spread a cold rag on my burning chest, "A merry heart doeth good like medicine: but a broken spirit drieth the bones," and those bones started flying around my head and the phone rang again and Oata Siemens said her grandfather clock was stolen and I rolled more cigarettes and then A.Dyck wanted to know how come there was mail in his mailbox again and Hein wanted to know how come his bike was stolen and Pracha Platt walked into the house to collect money for the hospital and he said somebody had stolen all the Bibles from the Bible van and I just rolled more cigarettes and thought murder murder and bones bones and I saw the ring with the white tape on Rosmack's finger and the girl's ring on Beitelkopp's little finger and the ice was melting on my head and I saw Yetta Hiebat's scared eyes and when Pracha Platt said Hein had bought a combine at the Frenchman's auction with ten thousand dollars cash money it just went in one ear and out the other because it was old news to me and didn't matter because Yetta and Hilda had been murdered and I wondered if the pig had had a swastika on his ankle, too. Then I heard on the speakerphone that Knibble Thiessen had been charged with impaired driving in the States the night before and that Marie had heard from Susch who had heard from Tien who had heard from Bulla Buhr that Knibble had had a States woman in the car with him when he was held up by the State Patrol and you know how those State Patrols always have their hands on their guns right away when they hold your car up and I reached for the last cigarette paper, rolled the last cigarette, put it between my lips. I stood up, bare-chested, faced the mirror with a sneer, reached for the hat on the dresser, put it on, adjusted the angle, reached for my white shirt, buttoned it across my hairless chest, stuffed the tails into Barbara's olive green workpants, knotted the black tie loosely under the open collar, slipped my arms into the hound's-tooth sports jacket, sneered at the mirror again, then draped the raincoat over my arm. I was prepared.

Seeing is believing, and I believe that you see more than your brain has time to deal with. So the brain stores what you take in, even the stuff you don't have time to use. Then if you do it right you can look through this stuff later and find things you didn't know you saw in the first place. I settled back down on the bed, the hat on my head, the rollie cigarette between my lips. I closed my eyes and called up the graveyard the day I found Oata's Bible. Although I ran through the scene forwards and backwards, close-up and wide angle, I just ended up with a zipper Bible and a "How about an Affair with an Older Man?" magazine. Question: Was the magazine still in my car?

I called up the doll woman's flat tire scene. I tried not to look at her eyes. Her long dress covered her ankles at every angle, even while she was trying to put together the bumper-jack when I first approached. I looked in the trunk as I lifted out the spare. Two tire irons, one L-shaped, one cross; an oval shaped rag rug covering the bottom; one jumper cable; a carton of short stubby Coca Cola bottles; an army style camouflage hat; a box of empty quart sealer jars. Everything was dusty.

I ran through the auction sale segment. I studied Yetta Hiebat as she got out of the car, flashing the charm bracelet on her ankle. I looked past her, trying to see what was in the background. I tried to see who Yetta was waving to when she got out of the car. I looked at the legs of the crowd beside Schmuggle Veens's States wife. I saw running shoes, bare feet, Kodiak high tops, Jesus boots, green camouflage pants tucked into big black old-fashioned farmer shoes, Hush Puppies, rolled-down rubber boots, a woman in just her nylon stocking feet stepping on an almost fresh piece of chicken shit, a pure white pair of cowboy boots, sandals with soles made from an old truck tire. Then my brain seemed to catch on fire and as I watched the trailer burning it struck me that somebody had spliced the film in my head. I was getting Yetta mixed up with the States wife and I tried to back up the memory film again but I couldn't get it to focus.

My still damp wallet lay on the dresser. I took the ankle bracelet from the change purse and dangled it from my finger, almost seeing the ankles before me in the dresser mirror. I raised my foot to the seat of the chair. The gold-coloured chain stretched just enough so I could close the tiny clasp around my ankle and pull my sock up over it.

"Kjnals! Kjnals! Rape Rampel wants to know if you have seen Rosmack anyplace. She hasn't come home yet since the fire."

I spit out the cigarette and dropped the coat. I put the hat on Mama's head as I passed through the kitchen. I left the sports jacket on the picket fence gate. I threw the tie on the seat beside me. "Murder can wait," I muttered as I gunned my VW down the road.

First, I drove to the bridge over the double dike at Zoop Zack Friesen's place where Rosmack had leaned from her motorcycle and kissed me on the cheek before she sped off into the dark night. I had watched her taillight for more than a mile, afraid to move my burning stubble. Then I had headed for Hein's bridge. Why hadn't I watched her light until she was home? Why hadn't I followed her?

It was three miles from the double dike bridge to Rape Rampel's yard. Two miles of ungravelled road south, one mile of gravel west. No farmyards. I crawled along at five miles an hour, watching the tracks in the dirt and scanning the ditch. No track heading into the ditch, no skid marks, nothing. When I stopped at the stop sign I got out of the car, thinking motorcycle tracks in the loose gravel after two days of traffic would be nearly impossible to see. I crawled along the edge of the gravel, but I couldn't tell which way Rosmack had turned.

Rape Rampel came running out of his house when I got out of my car. "What took you so long, Schneppa Kjnals? I phoned to you an hour ago and you don't even come." He lifted his finger like he wanted to shake it at me.

"I was checking the road from where I last saw her after the fire."

"Well, you should have come here first." Rape Rampel sounded really worried.

"How come you didn't let me know right away when she didn't come home Tuesday night?" I asked, putting the shoe on his foot.

"Well, Rosie said she was going to Grossmuttachi's place in Pracha Darp and stay there for night. Grossmuttachi doesn't like to stay alone at night and we take turns staying with her."

"Grossmuttachi didn't phone when Rosmack didn't show up?"

"The phone was so busy with people talking about the

fire that she couldn't get through, so we thought everything was okay. Even in the morning when we heard Rosie had been at the fire we didn't think nothing because we figured she would have gone to Grossmuttachi's afterwards."

"So when did you find out Rose was gone?" I noticed Rape wasn't calling her Rosmack, and all things considered, I didn't think I should either, but I couldn't call her Rosie, not anymore.

"Well, we were busy and Rosie sometimes stays with Grossmuttachi for a couple of nights in a row, and I mean, Rosie can look after herself and that damn phone was busy all the time and Grossmuttachi didn't get through to us till just before dinner-time and then your phone was so busy that it took till faspa to get through to you!"

Rampel's wife called from the steps of the house, "Has Kjnals seen Rosmack anyplace?"

"No, he hasn't seen nothing," Rape said, like he was an inner tube losing wind.

"Have the boys come back yet?"

"No, they're still asking the neighbours."

"Canola phoned from Grossmuttachi's place to say the people in Pracha Darp don't know nothing."

"Did Carl say anything to you about Beitelkopp Blatz?"

Rampel seemed surprised. "You mean that Blatz from Blarney that was in Headingley Jail for a while?"

"Yeah, on Tuesday in the store Carl said Rosmack had been hanging around with Blatz and that if you found out you might take her Harley away."

"Carl never said nothing to me. Did Carl say something to you about Beitelkopp Blatz?" he called to his wife, who was still standing on the step.

"Nothing to me. You think she might have gone some-place with him?"

"I don't know," I said. "I'm just trying to figure out a place to start looking." Mrs. Rampel went back into the house and I studied Rape's face as he stared at the horizon. "You ever go to the reserve?"

Rape twitched his head and I could see his eyes change as the question stuck in. "Not for a long time. I haven't used Indians for beetweeding for maybe five years. How come you would ask such a thing?"

"I don't really know. It's just that Hova Jake was at the store on Tuesday. He said he was working for the reserve."

"So?"

"Well, he was driving a motorcycle so I thought maybe they met on the road."

Rape didn't say anything for maybe five minutes, then he turned and ran into the house. He was back outside in a minute with a picture in his hand and his wife was on the step calling after him, "Rape, where you going with that?"

"We have to check something!" he called back, and hurried to the garage where the brown Chrysler was parked. I hurried after him and climbed into the front passenger seat.

"Have you let the RCMP know?" I asked as he started the car.

"They don't like the RCMP much on the reserve," he said as he backed out.

Rape Rampel didn't say anything for the first few miles. He just stared ahead at the gravel disappearing under the car like a swath into a combine. The speedometer was hidden by a Farmer's Union notebook.

Then as we passed out of the Gutenthal district he spoke.

"You know Rosie is my daughter. I mean, my real daughter." I looked at the picture, her school picture in a plastic frame. I couldn't see how she looked like Rape, except maybe that she tilted her head to the side a little the way he did, but I thought she would have learned to do that. I said nothing. "Her mother was weeding beets for us . . . they were living in the granary . . . she liked to talk . . . and well, anyways, such things happened to the Psalmist, too . . . and nine months later I get a letter from her asking if we want a baby girl . . . and I mean, we had three boys already and she was so young, only fifteen and you can't turn away your own flesh and blood . . . so I prayed about it . . . and then told Alma everything . . . she stormed and told me to go live on the reserve and said she would leave me and I stayed in the barn for a few nights . . . and then one afternoon Carl came to tell me Mama said I should come . . . and when I came in the house Alma was knitting with pink wool . . . and she said, 'Go and get her already!' . . . and that's how it happened."

For a while only the rush of the air through the vents and the clink of gravel against the floor of the car rode along with our thoughts. I wanted to ask questions, I wanted to understand the unknowable, I wanted to snoop where the Hollywood School of Detection had never dreamed of snooping, I wanted to climb through the windows of the soul to discover everything between the lines of what Rape Rampel had told me.

"Rosie knows about me and her mother . . . Alma told her when she was twelve . . . Rosie seemed to understand . . . I don't know, sometimes she seems so alone riding around on that motorcycle . . . but she loves it so much . . . I know it's been getting harder for her now that she's older . . . she never complains, but I know some people call her ugly names . . . oh God, I hope we find her soon!"

We crossed the highway that led to the city. I had never been to the reserve before. I didn't know what to expect. The word 'reserve' had always made me think of a huge, walled town full of tarpaper shacks and cars not fit for white people. When I was a boy the Indians sometimes came to Gutenthal to "beg," as we called it. They drove old cars from yard to yard asking for clothing or flour or gasoline. I remembered one old man who used to come to our place maybe two, three times a year, walking alone. He always came across the field, never on the road. There never seemed to be a car waiting for him anywhere, and he always asked for water. Maybe that was the only English word he knew because that's all he ever said. I would go and get him a tumbler of water from the pump in the house and bring it out to him where he sat on a stump beside the car. Once Mama gave me a biscuit with sausage inside to give to him, but he shook his head when I held it out to him. He just said, "Water." After he drank the water he would sit there for a while looking at the buildings and the machinery. But I don't think he was really seeing those things. It was like he was looking at something that wasn't there because the time we had puppies I waved to him with my hand to show that he should follow me into the barn. I was standing right in front of him and he was looking straight through like I wasn't even there. So I ran into the barn and came out with a puppy that still had its eyes closed and he didn't see it until I put the puppy almost in his face. Then he smiled and took it in his hands and stroked it gently. When he handed the puppy back to me he let his gaze wander over the yard again. Suddenly he stood up and walked straight toward the old sugar tree, the one by the side of the garden that Papa always talked about cutting down. The old Indian knelt down and poked around in the grass at the foot of the tree and picked something up in his hand. At first I thought it was just a flat stone but when he put it in my hand I saw it was an arrowhead. I had never seen one before and while I wondered over it he walked away across the field like he was following a path I couldn't even see. I couldn't get over how he knew the arrowhead was there. I clawed in the dirt around that tree many times but I never found anything else. I don't think the old Indian came around again after that. He must have died. The arrowhead was still in my dresser drawer. I should tell Rosmack about it sometime.

I wouldn't have realized we were entering the reserve except for a sagging weather-beaten sign saying Red River Reserve and a green and white Highways Department sign saying Wunnimin. The Cree name for the place, I figured, and I wondered if it meant the same as the English name. The fields were no different from fields anywhere else, the crops were green, the weeds looked mostly under control. There were no buildings at first, then houses began appearing about every quarter mile. Some houses looked new with fresh paint, others looked run-down, one looked like it belonged in a war zone. Huge holes in the siding showed pink insulation and two-by-fours and through one hole I could see a TV inside the house. Rusty car bodies surrounded most of the houses. Like any other place some yards looked taken care of while others looked neglected. They all looked bare somehow, like almost empty shells.

Rape Rampel didn't say anything as he slowed for the intersection at the centre of the community. A false-fronted general store with a single gas pump faced a small school-house flanked by a clutter of small portable units and a baseball field. A Catholic church and a new aluminum siding Wunnimin Band Office occupied the other two corners of the intersection. Rape turned the corner past the church and after passing three or four yards drove into the driveway of a small house that had once been painted government green.

Four children played in a doorless faded blue '59 Dodge resting on its axles in the knee-high grass of the yard. They stopped their play to stare as Rape got out with the picture in his hand. Three dogs circled him as if he seemed familiar. A woman carrying a baby appeared at the screen door. Rape held up the picture. The door opened and the woman stepped outside. She reached for the picture and stared at it without a word. I decided to get out of the car, too. As I neared the house I saw her shake her head and say, "She not come here." But she kept on staring at the picture.

"What about Jack Harder? Has he been around?" I asked. "Jack?"

"Jack Harder, the land claim worker. You gave him some earrings to give to Rose?"

Rape Rampel cleared his throat, but said nothing. The woman looked uncomfortable and glanced at him, then stared at the picture again. Rape watched her for a moment, then asked gently, "Loretta, did you send Rose a present?"

"Yes, I send her present with Jack. I seen Jack at the Band Office and he say he's from Gutenthal, so I ask him if he knows Rose and I make some beading for earrings and hairclip and I give to Jack to take to Rose. Rose get the present okay?"

"Yeah, she got it okay," I said. "Did she come here to see you?"

"No, she never come here. She never come here. Seventeen years she never come here. Are you mad to me, Rape?"

"No, I just want to know where she is."

I asked, "Does Jack work in the Band Office?"

"Yeah, I think so, maybe he is there, or at the sub-chief's house. She smarter than the chief, so she works on land claim with Jack."

I turned back to the car, leaving Rape and Loretta alone for a moment. One of the children walked up to me, holding out his hand. "Gimme money," he said.

"What for?" I laughed.

"To buy milk for the baby," he said.

"You got a baby?"

"Yeah, and he's real sick. Gimme money."

"Tell me something. Are there any motorcycles here?"

"Yeah. Man at Band has one. He come here once to talk to Mum."

"Ever see a big Harley? A big guy with black clothes and real short hair sticking up like this?" I peaked my hands above my head.

"You mean Captain Black?"

"Captain Black?"

"Yeah, by the store, he comes fast with motorcycle. I ast him, 'What's your name?' and he say, 'Captain Black is back.' And he give me a quarter and say, 'Watch my wheels, buddy.' And he goes in the store and buys a root beer and some smokes."

"When was this?"

"Maybe two days ago."

"Where did he go next?"

"He went to the baseball game."

"Did you go to the game?"

"No, I went in the store to buy gum, then I went home."

"Did you see him again?"

"No."

"Did you ever see a girl on a big Harley?"

"Never."

"What's your name?"

"Trevor."

"Thanks, Trevor." I flipped him a quarter and sat down in the car.

"How come you never told me about the earrings?" Rape wanted to know as he got in behind the wheel and started the motor. Loretta was still on the stoop, staring at the picture of her daughter. Then she called, "Wait!" She walked toward the car, still gazing at the photograph. Wordlessly, she passed it through the window. Rape looked at the picture and then at Loretta. "I'll send you another picture and I'll bring Rosie to visit when we find her." Loretta's face didn't tell me what she thought of that.

"I thought you might know about the earrings," I replied, as Rape backed the car out of the yard. "Rose was wearing them on Tuesday when I met her on the road just before the trailer blew up. She told me a woman on the reserve had given them to Hova Jake to give to her."

"No, I never saw them."

The Band Office was closed with no sign of Hova Jake or his motorcycle.

"So where does the sub-chief live?" I asked.

"The chief's house is the one with the Canadian flag."

"Must be that one over there." I pointed past the playing field to an unpainted house with a flagpole holding a limp flag. About a quarter mile further down the road another flag was stretched between two poles so it would never be limp, a white flag with a brilliant orange sun outlined with black lines. In the centre of the sun curled an unborn child. "Bet that's the sub-chief's house," I said.

I don't know what I expected. Maybe a college-type

woman wearing designer glasses and a headband over glistening black braided hair, a bear-claw necklace resting on the front of a tight Red Power T-shirt. Maybe a short chubby woman wearing a blouse and skirt and flat shoes, the kind you might see actually working at a political convention. Since she was smarter than the chief, maybe I expected her to be young, educated, a good talker in English.

The woman was gutting a catfish on a stained piece of plywood with a butcher knife. A baby squirmed in the blanket on her back as she knelt over the guts softly humming a song. The soles of her moccasins were worn thin, the brown stockings covering the ankles sticking out from the hem of the floral print dress were pilled, and a seam had opened up under the arm of the blue jacket she wore with sleeves pushed up to the elbows. A brown cotton kerchief covered her hair. Deep wrinkles flowed like rivers to her eyes. She spoke, but not in English, as she turned to us with eyes that looked young and old.

"Have you seen her?" Rape held the photograph in front of her face but she seemed not to see it. She spoke again, ignoring English, as if it were no more than the wind or the bark of a dog.

"Have you seen Jack?" I asked. "Jack Harder, the land claim worker." The woman shifted her face toward the sound of my voice but her eyes didn't see me. I wondered if she was blind.

Rape walked up the two steps to the open door of the house and saw no one inside the single room. He shook his head as he returned. The baby began to whimper and the woman reached for the knot in the blanket and lowered the child. Then she brought it round to the front, opened a button of the dress, and the baby's face snuggled inside. The woman began to sing softly as the flies buzzed over the catfish. I felt like we were no longer there.

Slowly we drove down every road on the reserve, showing Rosmack's picture to people we met. Most just glanced and shook their heads. Others said, "Sorry, don't know nothin'."

10

THE call came at midnight. At first I could hardly make out the voice over the raucous music in the background.

"Hey, Horny Corny!"

"Hello, who's this?"

"C'mon Schneppa, don't you know me?"

"Rosmack, where are you?"

"Call me Rosie. Cozy Rosie."

"Rosie, where are you?"

"I'm at a party, Corny."

"Where's the party?"

"Wouldn't you like to know?"

"C'mon Rosie, we've been looking for you!"

"How come? Are you horny, Corny?"

"C'mon, stop the joking. Tell me where you are!"

"Oh Neil, I love it when you get desperate for barbed wire and ball bearings. So long, Schneppa Kjnals." Click.

Mama came shuffling out of her bedroom as I opened the door to go outside. "Pauss up that you don't hurt yourself," she said. "In the night you never know what will happen."

My headlights caught the gas tank as I wheeled the car around to face the road. I stopped and backed up to the tank. No use bungling the operation by running out of gas. As I filled up I tried to make sense of Rosmack's call. I had never heard Rosmack talking that way before. Had she been drinking? Or taking drugs? I thought of the powder in Beitelkopp Blatz's zipper Bible. I had to find her soon.

I screwed the gas cap on and slammed down the hood. The windshield was splattered with dead bugs but I had no time to clean it. I raced down the driveway, hardly slowing for the turn, then raced into the buggy night without a thought for my destination. Suddenly, a red reflector appeared in front of the car. A bicycle! I swerved to miss it, almost hit the ditch, and skidded to a stop. When I turned the car around, the cyclist was nowhere in sight. I inched past the spot where the car had begun to swerve. A tiny glint in the grass caught my eye. I stopped, got out of the car and walked down into the ditch. A body lay face down next to the bicycle. I crouched down and touched a shoulder. The body spun away and a woman's voice whimpered, "Please don't hurt me! Please don't hurt me! I'll do what you ask. Please don't hurt me!" I stared in shock. It was the woman who had been swimming in the pond and she was terrified.

"My name is Neil Bergen," I said as soothingly as I could. "Are you hurt?" She murmured something. "Did I hit your bicycle?"

"Don't kill me, please don't kill me! I don't want to die!"

"No one is going to hurt you. Let me help you up." I reached out to her, but she scrambled to her feet and ran up the bank to the road. I didn't follow at first. I didn't want to frighten her even more. Then she dashed for my VW. I had left the motor running and by the time I scrambled close enough to reach for the door handle she found a gear, jerked the car into motion, and I almost lost my hand. I sprinted after my fleeing car, wincing at the gearbox squealing like a hog losing its nuts as she shifted gears. I doubled over, holding my side, and watched the taillights disappear.

The bicycle clanked with each push of the right pedal, clank, clank, clank, like an old grandfather clock. The eastern sky was beginning to redden. Rosmack's words had begun to make sense to me as I pulled the bicycle out of the ditch and thought about getting my bearings. Ball bearings. Barbed wire and ball bearings. Then I had it. The party was at Barbara Ball Bearing's place. That's what Rosmack had been trying to tell me. Barbara Ball Bearing's. I said a prayer for the safety of the terrified woman in my Volkswagen and set off. I hadn't ridden a bicycle for a long time and this old balloon tire CCM was no ten-speed. I figured I had about nine miles to go so I paced myself and just as the sun rose I turned onto Barbara's long driveway.

Only one vehicle was parked on Barbara's yard. At first I felt overjoyed, then I shuddered, wondering if my VW keys were at the bottom of the well. But a quick glance through the open window showed the keys in the ignition. No woman was in the car. Only the red brassiere was draped over the Hudson's Bay blanket neatly spread over the back seat.

My knocking echoed between the house and the barn. For a few minutes there was no response. I knocked again. I heard the old farmhouse stairs creak as someone came down. The inner door opened and Barbara stood there, yawning, barelegged, wearing a man's checked flannel shirt. My twenty-seven-year-old teen angel. She unhooked the screen door and let me into the kitchen. The counter was clean and tidy and only the radio stood on the table beside the window looking out onto the garden. There was not a beer bottle in sight.

I was suddenly very sleepy myself, and I said through a yawn, "I'm looking for Rosmack Rampel."

Barbara yawned again and stretched. Her shirttails lifted just enough to give me a glimpse of her pale blue panties. "She's not here."

"Was she here?"

"No."

"Are you sure? She called me about midnight from a party and I'm sure she called from here."

"No one was here last night. The kids mostly come on weekends."

"No one was here? Then how come my car is here?"

"Your car? Didn't you come here with it?"

"No, I came on a bicycle."

Barbara stretched her arms wide and yawned as if she was bored with my story. Suddenly, she stepped closer and flung her arms around me and started kissing my lips and then her hand was inside the pocket on my green workpants, rummaging around for things that don't go in pockets. Just as suddenly, she stopped and backed away. She looked a little embarrassed.

"Please go now. That's all I can do for you today. I don't know where anybody is." She turned and walked out of the room and I heard her climb up the stairs.

I went outside to my car in a daze, my mouth tasting of Barbara's morning breath and my nose filled with the scent of her night shirt, sweeter than any perfume. Such things only happen in books. As I sat down behind the wheel, something sharp poked my thigh from my pocket. I reached in and pulled out the beaded hairclip Rosmack had been wearing the last time I saw her. Barbara had been lying to me. And now with this hairclip she was telling me that Rosmack had been here. Maybe she was still here. Maybe Barbara wasn't alone. Had she been forced to get rid of me? Was I putting Rosmack and Barbara in danger by hanging around? Without a glance at the farmhouse I decided to leave. The VW started okay. It seemed none the worse for wear after the night. But what about the frightened woman? Why did she think someone was going to kill her? Unconsciously, I shifted through the gears as the VW gathered speed, and I made a vague plan for a stealthy return to Barbara's farm to investigate further. But I had to circle widely first. I had to collect my thoughts. I needed to visit old scenes. There had to be a clue.

If you don't have a car to chase, make a list. What have you got so far? A tip from the Hollywood School of Detection.

1. The explosion and Yetta Hiebat's bones—missing
2. Hilda Heinrichs, the doll woman—drowned, body missing
3. The terrified woman—missing
4. Rosmack Rampel—missing
5. The grandfather clock—missing
6. The Bible van
7. Holzyebock Hiebat and Eva Enns
8. Zipper Bibles
   —Oata Siemens
   —Hilda Heinrichs
   —Yetta Hiebat

—Beitelkopp Blatz
—Bible van
—Simple Hein
—A.Dyck
—Bulchi Wiebe
9. Barbara Ball Bearing
10. Hova Jake
11. Swastikas—ankle bracelets
12. A.Dyck's Nazi picture
13. The murdered pig
14. Schmuggle Veens and his States wife
15. Knibble Thiessen and his States patient
16. Rape Rampel
17. The old woman sub-chief
18. L.U.Dyck and Oata Siemens
19. Auction sales and $10,000 withdrawals
20. Simple Hein's combine

It was a long list and I didn't know what it was about. I let my VW go where it wanted while I played twenty questions in my head, and what stuck out to me were Barbara Ball Bearing's arms throwing themselves around me, and the terrified woman screaming, and Rosmack kissing my cheek.

Suddenly, A.Dyck's black Monarch swerved past me on the loose gravel and I remembered that Mama had said something about A.Dyck's mailbox. I skidded to a stop, wheeled the car around, and followed him. He started to speed up, so I slowed down, but I kept following him until he stopped in front of the credit union. I parked across the road in front of the store and in my mirror watched him enter the credit union. Through the window he appeared to be arguing with Count Floyd, who must have just arrived because it was hardly even 8:00 yet and the credit union didn't open till 8:30. I got out of the car. As I opened the credit union door I heard A.Dyck say, "Then give me the seven hunnerd." Floyd counted out the money and A.Dyck quickly shoved it into his pocket. "Keep your nose out of my business," he mumbled as he pushed past me and out the door.

"I hope you don't want cash," Count Floyd said. "I just gave out the last of it."

"What's going on?"

"Auction. At 6:00 this morning Holzyebock Hiebat phones to ask if I will open the credit union early for him. Fifteen minutes ago he takes out ten thousand dollars. Yesterday, just before closing time, Schmuggle Veens takes out ten thousand. And before that Shaftich Shreeda phones to see if he has that much in his account. And they all want cash. We don't keep that kind of cash on hand."

"And you didn't have enough for A.Dyck?"

"No. The poor guy was shaking when I gave him the money. What could be so scary about an auction sale? For sure around here if they know you they will take a cheque. But he didn't want a certified cheque. It had to be cash."

"The credit union isn't going broke, is it?"

"Oh no, it's just that we can't keep all our assets in cash here. We keep it in the bank."

Now why would Holzyebock Hiebat take out ten thousand cash? I mean, a funeral for his wife wouldn't cost that much. And Schmuggle Veens and Shaftich Shreeda. And now A.Dyck, too. And Bulchi Wiebe had wanted ten thousand from Mama. I had two murders on my hands, Rosmack was missing, and that bicycle woman, too. I suddenly felt very weak. I hadn't eaten breakfast and I had been up all night.

When I got home Mama was sitting in her shade chair under the cottonwood tree. She was holding a plain brown paper package on her lap.

"A young bengel came and brought something for you."

"Who?"

"A young bengel from the post office."

"Post office?"

"Army Post Office. Special delivery, he said. He looked very young but he was wearing an army suit."

I opened the package in my room and found a shiny new zipper Bible just like the one I had bought from the Bible van. Where the Psalms should have been there was a grainy snapshot, black and white with a patterned border, like you see in old photo albums from the forties and fifties. At first I thought it was a joke, a camera trick. Against the background of a Nazi flag was my face. On the back of the picture in that German kind of writing were the words, "Bergen, is this what our pious little CO was doing during the war?" A chill ran through me as I looked at the picture again. It was a picture of Papa! Carefully, I flipped through the Bible. Tucked into Revelations were two photocopies of newspaper articles. One was from the *Free Press*, describing the government inquiry into suspected Nazi war criminals in Canada; the other, clipped so the source was not evident, claimed the government had no intention of bringing war criminals to trial. Instead, suspected Nazis would be secretly turned over to a Jewish revenge group, currently being trained in the latest physical and psychological torture techniques by CIA and CSIS agents. The article claimed only large numbers would appease the Jews and once a German was suspected of being a war criminal by the revenge group, there appeared to be little hope of escaping the terrible torture, whether one was innocent or not, for in order to protect itself the revenge group could not admit to any errors. The article mentioned the case of a Mennonite woman in Paraguay who had been suspected of giving food and shelter to Nazi fugitive Helmut Schichtmeyer. Her mutilated body had suggested a long, lingering, torturous death. The article ended with the recommendation that all persons with German names take steps to protect themselves against this Jewish conspiracy.

My heart hammered as I searched through the Bible for other clues, but I found nothing. I almost showed Mama the picture, then decided it would be too upsetting. Instead, I asked her what kind of vehicle the young army bengel had been driving.

"I think it was grey, like Martens used to use when they still brought mail to the post box on the road."

I looked at the clock and started toward the door. Then I remembered something.

"Did we get the *Echo* yet this week?" Before Mama could answer I saw it lying on the counter by the radio. I quickly found out what I wanted to know. I looked at the clock again. I had about two hours, I figured. I grabbed another bun off the table, broke it open and stuffed it with a thick slice of bologna.

"Pauss up" was all that Mama said as I stepped outside. I needed to drain my radiator so I went into the barn. Then I climbed up to the loft to take a look around the community with my binoculars. As my head rose up through the opening I heard a soft purring sound. I froze, cautiously looked around the loft, and saw the bicycle woman sprawled on a layer of straw bales, snoring. Her sandalled feet faced me and her skirt was pulled up on her slightly parted thighs. It looked like she was wearing the black bathing suit she had worn in

Hauns Jaunses' Fraunz's pond. Her chin was hidden by the rise and fall of her breasts and there were green grass stains on her knees. For a second I thought how lucky I was to see two angels in one morning, then I remembered the woman's terror last night on the road. How could I wake her without frightening her?

Cautiously, I pulled myself up into the loft. Her eyes were pinched shut as if she was determined to sleep. I took the army surplus binoculars from the nail on the beam and climbed up the ladder to the ventilator. For 11:00 in the morning everything seemed too quiet. Nothing moved. I checked A.Dyck's yard. His car wasn't home. On Holzyebock Hiebat's gravel site only the wreckage of the trailer and the gravel pile remained. Nothing moved at Rape Rampel's place. Shaftich Shreeda's yard, all grown around with trees, showed only the tip of the hip-roof barn. I checked the pond and traced the prongs of the swastika road I had seen from Bulchi Wiebe's plane. Only it was no longer there. The road on all four sides of the section had been gravelled, even the half mile never worked up into a proper road.

Before I could puzzle out the meaning of this a crop duster airplane swooped down and skimmed the surface of the beetfield, mist spreading out from its wings. At the end of the field it rose and I expected it to circle and swoop again, but it levelled off and disappeared to the south. Funny, I thought, and I focused my binoculars on the beetfield again. About five minutes later I noticed a motorcycle on the road near the pond. It was too small to identify, even when I adjusted the binoculars to full power. The motorcycle stopped at the corner where Schmuggle Veens's States wife and I had found the hoes. The rider got off and walked into the field. After a few minutes the rider headed off down the road and turned into Rape Rampel's yard. Rosmack?

Behind me the bicycle woman stirred and opened her eyes. Her eyes looked frightened at first, then relaxed as she seemed to recognize me. Something clicked in my mind and I realized who she was. I climbed down from the ventilator.

"You are Neil Bergen?" Fleeda Shreeda said, sitting up, and I thought how beautiful a woman can be when she wakes up.

"Yes," I replied. "This is my mother's barn."

"I know," she said. "That's why I came here. I needed a place that was safe."

"Safe?"

"And I need your help." She stood up shakily and almost lost her balance, but steadied herself before I could reach out to her. She turned away and reached into her blouse. "My father found this yesterday morning," she said, handing me a folded sheet of paper, curved and warm from her body. "It was inside a Bible on the table when he got up."

"A zipper Bible?"

"Yes, a zipper Bible."

I unfolded the paper and stared at the pieces of newspaper taped to the sheet. "Did your father show this to you?"

"Oh no. He didn't say anything to anybody. He was just very quiet and restless like something was bothering him, and then I heard him on the phone asking the credit union if he had ten thousand in his account and when I went into the hall where the phone is he quickly hung up and grabbed the open Bible from the chair there and this paper fell out but he didn't notice, he was in such a hurry to get out to the car. So I picked up the paper and then I was scared."

"Do you know who would send him such a note?"

"No. It's the kind of thing that used to happen in Uganda when I worked there. That's why I was so frightened last night. I thought I was back in Uganda. I thought it was the night my husband was killed." She buried her face in her hands.

Something in what Fleeda said gave me an idea. I put my hand on her shoulder. She didn't flinch. I coaxed her down the ladder, gently grasping her ankle to guide her foot from rung to rung. She stumbled back against me when she touched the floor and she lingered there for a moment before she turned around. There was a bit of a twinkle in her eyes but I didn't let myself think about it. There was work to be done. I took her to the house and told Mama who she was and asked her to feed her. I said I would be back in half an hour to take Fleeda Shreeda to an auction sale.

The phone rang. Rape Rampel wanted to know if I had found Rosie. I had nothing to tell him and said maybe he should phone the police. I didn't know what else we could do. Rape started to stammer a little bit when I said that.

"Ah . . . yeah . . . sure . . . I-I-I should do that . . . when I go to town. I-I-I have to go to the bank." Then he hung up without saying goodbye.

Before I walked out I stepped into my room and picked up the can of cigarettes I had rolled during my delirium.

Shusta Paul's shoe repair shop was in a small lean-to next to the credit union. Leather and glue smells mingled with Player's tobacco smoke in the dusky quiet of the shop. I don't like to smoke myself, but the smell of a roll-your-own Player's cigarette burning alone has a kind of religious quality to it. Tailor-made filter tips just make a stink. Shusta Paul sat at his bench working on a woman's high-heeled shoe positioned on a cobbler's last. A one-inch cigarette smouldered at the end of the black holder stuck between his teeth. He glanced through his rimless glasses at the can of cigarettes I set on the counter, then focused on the heel of the shoe again.

"You want to know about the Nazis in Gutenthal," he said through a cloud of smoke.

I was startled. "How did you know that?"

"I got a picture, too."

"In a zipper Bible?"

"Yes, in a zipper Bible." Shusta Paul pulled the Bible out of a drawer and handed me a snapshot from between its pages. A very young Shusta Paul profiled against a Nazi flag.

"What do these pictures mean?"

Shusta Paul butted out his cigarette in a sardine can ashtray. "In 1939, just before the war started, a German by the name of Henkel came to Gutenthal. He had a meeting in the school and a bunch of us young men went because we had nothing better to do. He hung the Nazi flag over the blackboard and talked in German about the plans the Nazis had for the world. And he told us how the Jews made all the problems in the world. We were young, we listened, we shouted, 'Sieg Heil!' It seemed like fun at the time. We snickered when Henkel shouted, 'Heil Hitler!' We goose-stepped on the way home and forgot about it."

"But who took the pictures? Henkel?"

"Oh no, that was Martens. He had a camera—always taking pictures of everything. Martens must have taken the pictures. We were so used to Martens and his camera already that we didn't even notice it anymore. That's the story of the Nazis in Gutenthal."

"Martens, the postman?" I asked.

"Yes, that's the one. He passed away last year."

"Who is sending us the pictures?"

"I don't know. It must be someone connected with the Martens family. It must be someone very young."

"What do you think will happen next?"

"I think someone will ask us for money."

"Do you remember who was at the meeting?"

"Most of the men my age. Your father, Abe Dyck, Veens, Rampel, Bulchi Wiebe, Hiebat, Shreeda, Heinrichs, just about everybody."

"Where did this Martens live?"

"Just west of town across the creek."

"Close to Hein's bridge?"

Shusta Paul nodded.

I asked, "Who lives there now?"

"I don't know that. Last I heard it was still empty. You must find out before something evil happens."

Evil has already happened, I thought. As an afterthought I asked if I could borrow the zipper Bible. Then I hurried home to pick up Fleeda Shreeda.

11

BOTH sides of the Neualtbergfeld village street were lined with cars and trucks. Fleeda walked toward the auction yard in her Africa dress, all orange and brown and yellow. It seemed almost sinful, how her legs moved like springs. I had never seen a missionary like her before. The only other woman missionary I knew of was missing a leg and hobbled on crutches.

Fleeda quickened her step when she noticed Holzyebock Hiebat climb down from his gravel truck carrying a zipper Bible. By the time he was halfway across the street, Fleeda was right beside him. Suddenly, she stumbled and bumped into him. The next thing I saw was Fleeda kneeling on the street holding a Bible up to him with one hand while her other hand tugged the dress back up over her shoulder. She laughed and Holzyebock wiped the dust off the Bible, begged himself forgiveness and walked away, looking like he was trying not to hurry.

I hoped Simple Hein was already watching the disker. Hein wouldn't let us use his zipper Bible unless we took him along to the auction sale, so I had made him promise not to buy any more combines, but before I finished joking with him I already wanted to take my words back because I desperately needed his help. I wished Rosmack Rampel was with us, but there had been no time to see if she had come home or not. I was gambling with a hunch I had that whoever was behind this didn't know who I was, who Fleeda was or who Hein was, even though Hein had found ten thousand dollars in a zipper Bible and bought a combine with it. I was sure the person who sent the zipper Bible with the picture of Papa standing in front of a Nazi flag didn't realize that Papa was dead. And Shusta Paul had said the pictures must have been sent by someone very young.

I got my plan from the note Fleeda's father had received. Letters and words from newspapers had been pasted around an ad from the *Echo* for the auction of the estate of the late Mrs. Anna J. Friesen, Neualtbergfeld Village. In the ad an eighteen-foot CCIL disker with seeder box was underlined with red ballpoint pen. The rest of the words told Fleeda's father to deliver the zipper Bible with ten thousand dollars cash to the seeder box. There was no threat in the note. The threat must have come earlier. A picture and the newspaper clippings. I figured all the men who had been trying to raise ten thousand cash must have received the same instructions: Shaftich Shreeda, Holzyebock Hiebat, Schmuggle Veens, A.Dyck, Bulchi Wiebe and Rape Rampel. We had managed to collect five zipper Bibles to exchange with them.

Rape Rampel parked his Chrysler on the other side of the

street and when he saw me he waved me over. He ducked back into the car and picked a black zipper Bible off the seat and put it on the car roof.

"Rosmack came home this morning."

"Where was she all this time?" I kept my eyes on the Bible.

"She's home again," he said. "That's all that matters." What he really meant was that it was none of my business.

I didn't give up that easily. "She didn't tell you where she had been?"

"I said it doesn't matter, Kjnals."

A motorcycle rumbled up the street. Rape stiffened and clenched his fists as he watched it turn into the auction yard. The rider was Beitelkopp Blatz. Quicker than an eye my hands made the switch. Rape breathed out slowly, keeping his eyes on Blatz while his fingers groped for the Bible. He said, "I don't want to miss the stuff from the tool shed." He walked off to the auction, leaving me silently thanking Beitelkopp Blatz and patting the Bible in the inside pocket of my jacket. I slipped back to the Volkswagen to check my hunch. Sure enough, when I opened the zipper of Rape Rampel's Bible the queen's picture looked at me from ten crisp one-thousand-dollar bills. My hunch was right.

We were short a Bible so I slipped the bills into the money belt I wore under my shirt and stuffed the Bible into the extra large pocket of the shoplifter's special jacket Koadel Kehler once ordered from the back-page ad of a comic book. I hadn't believed the ad was for real, but Koadel sent away the money for it and sure enough the jacket came six to eight weeks after the three-to-four-week waiting period and it was a marvellous jacket. I wore it when I went north to guard the mine and didn't require any other luggage. Included with the jacket were a pair of purloiner's drawers. Fleeda was wearing those.

I wandered onto the auction yard, looking for zipper Bibles in nervous hands. Fleeda and Shaftich Shreeda were leaning their elbows on the big rear tire of a blue Fordson Major tractor when suddenly they both jumped back as a jet of tire fluid sprayed into the air. I turned away, grinning to myself. I would never have thought of stepping on the valve stem. Quite a nervy woman, too, I thought, to steal a Bible from her own father.

"Hiebat, Holzyebock," Hein whispered to me. "Put Bible in seeder box." He was sitting on the hood of a three-ton sugar beet truck.

"Did anyone take it out?" I whispered back.

"Not yet." Hein pulled a wooden match from his pocket and chewed on it as he whispered through closed teeth, "Young bengel in army suit walk by disker three time already. Bang hand on seeder box each time. Hartsoft big feet."

"Shhh . . . ," I said. Rape Rampel was walking toward the disker. I pretended to concentrate on the auctioneer over by the tool shed, but out of the corner of my eye I watched Rape back up to the disker and sit on the lid of the middle box. He sat there for about a minute, his right hand pressed down on the zipper Bible. Suddenly, he lifted the lid next to him and slipped the Bible in. He wandered back toward the auctioneer, looking like he had dumped a big load.

Schmuggle Veens was shuffling from the street, his pipe stuck between his teeth, so I whispered to Hein, "Watch the disker."

"Look, bengel comes," Hein whispered back.

Sure enough, a skinny kid, blond hair cut even shorter than a brush cut, pants and jacket covered with leaves, shuffled his size thirteen army boots past the disker and thumped each lid of the seeder box with the palm of his hand before he stuffed his hands in his pockets and sauntered over to the auction crowd. "Watch that bengel carefully," I whispered. I had intended to intercept Schmuggle Veens, but now Fleeda was headed in his direction, so I looked around for A.Dyck or Bulchi Wiebe. I didn't see them so I decided to mingle. As I moved through the crowd I noticed the kid moving, too, rarely stopping, as he moved forward toward the tool shed where the auctioneer was working on bids for a ninety-piece socket set. That's when I spotted a grey jeep behind the implement shed.

I scanned the crowd for A.Dyck and Bulchi Wiebe. I didn't see them, just Beitelkopp Blatz studying a dresser with a diamond-shaped mirror, so I slipped behind the implement shed to check the jeep. The licence plate on the back bumper was ten years old. The convertible top was up and a very faded Royal Mail decal was stuck above the front fender. Newer decals decorated the rear fender: "Soldier of Fortune" with a picture of a machine gun, "Visit Lebanon—Help a Syrian Meet Allah," "No Guts—No Glory," and "Gun Control Sucks." I wondered for a moment what had happened to the sixteen-year-old Corny Bergen who wrote to the U.S. Army and volunteered to fight in Viet Nam. I had been in love with Frieda Loeppky, I even took her to the show in Neche once, and then Tank Toews came back from Germany in his army suit and took Frieda out. That was the end of it. No old shoes for me. But I was going to do better than go to Germany to drink beer. I would fight in a real war with shooting and bullets and everything. The U.S. Army sent me some coloured brochures and a list of defects that recruits were screened for. One defect applied to me. No webbed feet considered. Two toes on my right foot are joined. I guess it's hard to pull the trigger with webbed toes after your hands are blown off.

A pistol lay on the passenger seat of the jeep, a submachine gun on the floor behind the driver's seat. My heart thumped until I noticed the brand name on both guns—Daisy.

"Don't move!" hissed a voice behind me. Of course I turned around quickly and the army bengel faced me, ready to break a board in half.

"Hi kid," I said. "Just looking at the old mail jeep. It yours now?"

"What's it to you?" The bengel looked like he had practised hurting his hands in front of a mirror and I also felt like I was looking into a mirror, a back-in-time kind of mirror. Only such a mirror can show webbed feet. Knowing one's own weaknesses can be a weapon. Mail-order kung fu lessons don't teach you that. So I looked him in the eyes.

"Jungkje, pauss up when you drive that jeep. Your licence is ten years old."

The bengel's chopping hands fell to his sides but his eyes said, "I'll get even with you!" I turned my attention back to the auction yard. Something clicked. I glanced over my shoulder. The kid was cleaning his fingernails with a switchblade knife. It wasn't a Daisy. I prayed that the RCMP would stop him on his way home.

The auction had moved from the tool shed to the farmhouse yard where the auctioneer was busy selling a mangle. Fleeda stood next to a Schellenberg woman from Gretna. I wandered over to her side.

"Three," she whispered in Flat German.

"One," I whispered back.

"I need an empty one," she said.

"You still have room?"

"Sure, but hurry. I see A.Dyck over there."

I slipped her an empty zipper Bible, then shuffled over to

check on Hein. He was sitting on the seat of the Massey-Ferguson combine. His elbows rested on his knees, his chin on his fists. He stared at Schmuggle Veens's States wife sitting on the seeder box of the disker as if she was posing for a calendar picture, the kind that gets hung up in the back corner of a garage. Her shorts looked even shorter than they had been on the beetfield, her blouse tighter with fewer buttons, her high heels higher with less leather, and her toenails looked like they had been dipped in fresh red paint.

"What's happening?" I climbed up to the combine platform and took a look inside the empty hopper.

"Lots action, Kjnals. Lots action," Hein whispered.

"Well, tell me." I looked down at the woman. She must have burned her bare hams on the hot tin of the seeder box when she sat down.

"First, Shaftich Shreeda comes and puts Bible in disker box. Then Schmuggle Veens comes. Puts Bible in, too. Then schinkuhbein lady sits down on the seeder box. Red toes, not bad, eh?" Hein elbowed me in the leg. Schmuggle Veens's States wife crossed her legs and tapped her raised foot in the air so the sun caught the ankle bracelet and made it glint.

The main crowd was watching the household articles being sold. Fleeda stood near the front and A.Dyck strolled purposefully toward the disker, a zipper Bible gripped in his hand. He didn't try to hide a thing. He pulled back for only a second when he saw Schmuggle Veens's States wife, then he lifted the lid beside her left thigh, dropped the Bible in, slammed the lid down and walked back toward the auctioneer.

The States wife just sat there, a slight smile on her lips, tapping her toe in the air, watching the crowd move from the house to the machinery yard. The bidding began on a deep-tillage cultivator and people started to glance twice at the woman shifting her legs every few minutes on the disker. Her left ankle was resting on her right knee when Hank Hiebert struck the cultivator three times with his cane to finalize the sale. The army bengel sauntered up to the disker and shamelessly glutzed over the woman's figure. She ignored him, slowly uncrossed and recrossed her legs, and kept her eyes on the auctioneer as he moved toward the combine. Remembering the bengel's switchblade, I climbed down from the combine platform so I could get closer to him. Hein stayed on the combine. Hank Hiebert tapped the combine ladder and asked if Hein wanted to open the bidding. The crowd laughed. Hein shook his head and glanced toward the disker. The army bengel was sitting on the seeder box, inches from the States wife.

I made my way behind the disker so I could watch the bengel's hands. Neither twitched as the combine was auctioned off.

The auctioneer turned to the disker. Schmuggle Veens puffed on his pipe in the crowd. Hank Hiebert glanced from his clipboard to the legs on the disker, cleared his throat, and stared at his clipboard again.

"Excuse me . . . ," he said, then appraised the crowd and decided the ornaments on the seeder box might add to the sale. He became all business. The bidding went quickly and in five minutes Schmuggle Veens had bought the disker. His wife stayed on it and so did the army bengel. The crowd moved to a chemical sprayer. Within minutes Schmuggle Veens was backing his LTD with the "Janz Team" and "Mount Rushmore" bumper stickers up to the disker. The bengel stayed fixed beside the States wife until the disker began to move. Then he jumped off, watched with a wooden face for a moment and ran for his jeep. A motorcycle started up. Beitelkopp Blatz rummeled past to the road. Fleeda nudged me. I felt the bulk of the Bibles under her dress. The States wife lit up an L&M cigarette and blew a cloud of smoke at us as the shuddering disker jiggled her leg and the swastika on the ankle bracelet flashed in the sun.

12

We gloated as the first Holy Book emerged from Fleeda's purloiner's drawers. It had ten thousand dollars in it. So did the next two, which also had a powdery substance in the cover. The fourth Bible was Oata's. There was seven hundred dollars in Ezekial on a page with a verse marked with one of those pink highlighting pens. I tried not to shake when I read it:

> Thus saith the Lord God unto these bones:
> Behold, I will cause breath to enter into
> you, and ye shall live.

To keep Hein and Fleeda from wondering about the seven hundred I pulled out my money belt and added Rape Rampel's ten thousand to the pile.

"Can buy lots combine with that," Hein said.

"Somebody's going to be really surprised," Fleeda giggled.

"Somebody be feemaesich mad," Hein said. "Feemaesich mad!"

Feemaesich mad was right, and Hein didn't really understand how mad that could be. Hein and Fleeda didn't know my thoughts and my suspicions. Nobody knew my thoughts about Yetta Hiebat and Hilda Heinrichs and their connection with zipper Bibles and the swastika charms on their ankles. Fleeda and Hein couldn't see the mental movie running through my head. They didn't know about the shuddering fear I had that Hilda and Yetta might have been murdered because of a switched Bible. Maybe Hein's Bible with ten thousand in it. Here we were sitting with five Bibles and almost fifty thousand. For sure, somebody would be feemaesich mad and somebody was in trouble.

But who? I thought as I arranged the money in the money belt. My exchange theory was just that, a theory. Well, it wasn't a theory anymore. We definitely had an exchange, a major switch. Who would find out about the switch first? It had to be Schmuggle Veens and his States wife. But what did that mean? If they were behind this whole thing then who would they go after? The five men who brought the Bibles? Would they dare? But Schmuggle Veens had put in a Bible, too. Was that camouflage, or a sign of double-cross? If it was a double-cross then who was in the most danger?

Following the disker seemed the most urgent thing to do. I reached for the ignition key.

"Something is happening over there by the fence!" Fleeda called from the back seat. A crowd had gathered at the fence dividing the auction yard from the neighbour's yard.

I jumped out of the car and hurried over to the fence. About halfway across the yard I stopped and started to turn back. "It's okay, I've got the Bibles," Fleeda whispered behind me.

The victim lay on the other side of the fence in the neighbour's yard. Peter Giesbrecht, the neighbour's fourteen-year-old son, knelt beside the boar. The blood had drained from its throat into a congealing pool on the ground. I climbed over the fence to study the slit throat. I reached out and raised the snout of the pig. The blood drained away and the swastika-shaped wound opened slightly like a mocking grin.

"Hackenkrietz!" I heard a woman gasp. But before I could react, or decide what to do next, Bulchi Wiebe's silver Found airplane reverberated over the yard. My thoughts circled as the plane circled and I slipped away from the scene of the crime. My Volkswagen looked like a squawking bird ready to take off; the front trunk lid was raised, both doors were open, and the hood at the back was lifted like a rooster's tailfeathers. The glove compartment was emptied, the floor mats scattered on the grass, and the green and yellow seat covers Mama made for my birthday had been stripped off like combination underwear pulled down in an emergency. The back seat was lifted off the battery compartment but the cables were still in place.

I started to put things back and tried to figure this one out. All my prime suspects had left the scene, but obviously there was still someone else. I listened to the airplane taxi up the field road. Had Bulchi Wiebe come up with ten thousand dollars? Had he sold his plane? Who was flying it then? I laid the rubber mats over the rusty corrugated floor and pulled up the seat covers again. I didn't think a person could sell an airplane so quickly. Then again, who would have thought I would have almost fifty thousand dollars of other people's money at this auction sale? Forty thousand seven hundred in zipper Bibles. Where was Fleeda? I looked up from the hood where I was putting the cables back into the distributor cap. I couldn't see her. The auction had resumed and the crowd had left the fence. Hein was sitting on the combine.

I closed the engine cover and stood up. An ankle bracelet hung on a stalk of grass beside the rear tire. I picked it up and for the first time I really looked at the charm. Each blade of the swastika had a tiny letter on it. An L, a K, an M, and an I. I knelt on one knee to pull down my sock to check drowned Hilda's bracelet on my ankle when Canola Rampel spoke from behind me. "Kjnals, have you seen Rosmack anyplace yet?" His brother, Carl, was kicking at the gravel with his boot.

"You mean she didn't come home yet?"

"No, she hasn't come home yet. You mean you stopped looking?" Canola's voice sounded like he thought I was a low-down snake without a backbone. I started to protest, but wondered why Rape would have told me Rosmack had come home when she hadn't. What was he trying to hide? I needed to ask the brothers some questions. They had to know something that would give me a clue. But I didn't know what to ask. I harrowed through my brain trying to find a stone to throw into the pond.

"Have the RCMP been down yet? Your dad said he was going to talk to them when he went to the bank this morning."

"Dad went to the bank?" Canola looked at Carl. "He never said nothing to us."

"Maybe he wanted to buy something at the sale. He was here."

"Dad was here?"

"Yeah, I can't see him now but he was here." I pointed to the spot on the road where Rape Rampel had parked his car when I had exchanged Bibles with him. His car was gone. A green car was parking in the spot. At first I thought it was Schmuggle Veens's LTD or Gnurpel Giesbrecht's. Then the driver got out, lit a cigarette and leaned against the car roof, blowing smoke rings as she studied the auction. Her long black hair shone in the sunlight glinting from her mirror sunglasses. My heart thumped as I thought I was looking at Rosmack. The rest of the car doors opened and each of the four girls that got out looked like Rosmack Rampel from a distance. Each had long black hair fastened with a beaded leather hairclip. Each wore large round beaded earrings. Together the girls strolled toward the driveway, then spread out when they reached the crowd.

I looked at the Rampel brothers. Their faces told me they had been thinking the same thing I had.

"Did your dad tell you we went to look for her at the reserve?"

"Yeah, he said he went there, but he wouldn't say much about it."

"Have you seen a grey jeep around your place?"

"No, I think I saw one in town yesterday. Yeah, in town. It was going west across the tracks."

"West towards Buffalo Creek?"

"Yeah."

"Did you see who was driving?"

"No."

"The top was up?"

"Yeah."

"Right in town?"

"Yeah, right in town."

"Funny he didn't get stopped," I thought aloud. "The one at the sale here today had a licence ten years old."

"Ten years old licence?" Canola said.

"Yeah, yellow with black numbers. No Autopac sticker even."

Hein pulled on my sleeve and whispered in my ear.

"Schneppa Kjnals, you got blindfold on your behind-the-head eyes? The Bibles gone. Ten tousand dollar gone. Fleeda gone. Gone in car with Yasch Siemens. My boss. What Oata will think? Could be I'm crazy, but not me I'm stupid. This not I can figure it out."

"What did they use?"

" '51 Ford for sure. Green. You know, Nobah Naze Needarp's old car."

"Yeah, for sure." But before I could shift my thinking gears, Bulchi Wiebe came ploughing with his stomach through the auction crowd carrying a brown paper bag in his left hand that looked like it had a book in it. He kept glancing from side to side as if he couldn't find what he was looking for. When he reached the open spot in front of the combine where the disker had stood, he slowly turned himself around, checking all the pieces of machinery against a slip of paper in his hand. When he saw me walking toward him he hurried in my direction.

"Kjnals, what happened to the disker? Did they sell it already?"

"Yeah, Schmuggle Veens bought it and hauled it off right away."

"Schmuggle Veens? With the States wife?"

"Yeah, legs and everything."

"Yellow hair and blue eyes and too young for him?"

"Yeah, I guess so."

"Hoings laeva and butta brot. This isn't sposig anymore. Come, we have to fly!"

For sure it wasn't funny anymore. It hadn't ever been funny, I thought, as Hein and I followed Bulchi Wiebe across the yard to the airplane. I wanted to ask some questions but we were walking too fast to talk and when we were strapped into our seats it got too noisy. I glanced back at Hein as the plane taxied down the middle road. His face looked like a pale watermelon. My own stomach churned a little as the nose lifted, but I concentrated on looking at the roads, trying to spy the vehicles I had under suspicion.

The plane levelled off at an altitude that would allow us to see a man clearly in the open. Bulchi nudged my arm and pointed to a set of headphones with a microphone hanging at the side of the windshield. I put them on.

"Can you hear me?" His voice crackled through the earphones.

"Yes," I said, without thinking, then noticed the mouthpiece in front of me.

"Good. What was Schmuggle Veens driving?"

"Green LTD. Pulling a disker. CCIL. With his States wife sitting on the seeder box."

"Can't go fast when you pull a disker with the car. Which way did they go?"

"West, I think. West would maybe make sense." I wasn't sure why I thought west would make sense except that west led toward Buffalo Creek and the old mail jeep driver's place.

For a few minutes we studied the roads below us. Nothing appeared to move. No green car pulling a disker. No '51 Ford. No grey jeep. No motorcycles. I tried to organize the facts in my head. We had intercepted four ten-thousand-dollar payments before they reached the disker, as well as A.Dyck's seven hundred. Schmuggle Veens had the disker with the empty Bibles. Fleeda Shreeda had the Bibles with the money and had driven off with Yasch Siemens. Beitelkopp Blatz had driven off on his Harley. The army kid had driven away in the grey jeep. Another boar had been killed. Somebody had ransacked my car, somebody who had dropped an ankle bracelet with a swastika. Rape Rampel had lied to me. Rosmack Rampel was still missing. For now I was under the control of Bulchi Wiebe and his airplane. Could I trust him? He hadn't volunteered any information about himself. "Ask! Ask!" I heard my father's voice from deep in my brain. I decided to come straight to the point.

"Did you find ten thousand to put in the Bible?" I asked.

Bulchi cleared his throat into the mike and almost pierced my ears.

"No. I decided to call the bluff. My Bible has only ten ones in it."

"The others didn't think it was a bluff."

"How do you know . . . ?" He stopped. "What others?"

Briefly, I explained what we had done. Bulchi Wiebe grunted and clucked into his mike as he listened. When I finished I asked, "Why is everybody so afraid? Why did they deliver the money? Why didn't they go to the police?"

"I-I don't know it for sure, except that when we got the letter and the pictures we got them alone. I thought I was the only one. That newspaper thing about the woman who was killed, that is scary stuff." Bulchi paused. "You see, that woman used to live here in Gutenthal. She went to school with us. Lena Bergen she was then, before her family moved to Paraguay."

"Bergen?"

"Yes, she was your father's second cousin. Barbara

Buhler's mother got a letter from Paraguay that told this gruelich story, so when we got this blackmail stuff it was so much scarier. Another thing maybe you should know is that Schmuggle Veens's States wife isn't from the States at all. She's from Paraguay, too, only I don't recognize her. I only saw her for a second in town one day and she looked like I should know her but I couldn't think who." Before I could grip onto these things Hein pounded me on the back. I pulled off my headphones.

"Kjnals, look there! See by the double dike!" I looked down and saw the green LTD and disker stopped near the bridge. I turned to Bulchi but he had already spotted the vehicle. The plane banked and circled. As we descended I saw the open car doors and the raised seeder box lids. There didn't seem to be any people around.

"What are you going to do?" I asked Bulchi, but he still had his headphones on and was concentrating on bringing the plane down. A minute later we bounced down on the dike and Bulchi taxied up behind the disker. He switched off the engine and when the propeller stopped I jumped down and ran toward the disker. The seeder boxes were empty. The car was empty, too. But the keys were still in the ignition. Bulchi Wiebe and Hein hurried up behind me.

"Somebody must have picked them up," I said. I examined the tire tracks. Two streaks about ten feet long suggested that a car had spun its tires. More streaks suggested that a car had made a hurried three-point turn. A shotgun shell lay in the dust near one of the streaks. I stepped over the tracks to pick it up. It was a spent shell stuffed with paper. CIL with a red casing. I held it up for the others to see.

"Yasch Siemens!" Hein exclaimed immediately. " '51 Ford." Both Bulchi and I stared at him.

"What you mean?" Bulchi said.

" '51 Ford. Door handle. Push in thing broken. Woman's side. Oata put in shotgun shell. Work like bran' new. Sometimes only it fall out." Hein took the shell from my hand and walked over to the door of the LTD to demonstrate what he meant. My head started to spin with thinking. I tried to see a connection between Fleeda and Yasch and Schmuggle Veens and his States wife.

"Hey Kjnals," Bulchi said. "What do you think about this?" He stood in the grass at the side of the dike holding up a high-heeled open-toe shoe.

"Schinkuhbein lady shoe," Hein said. "Dat's shinkuhbein lady shoe."

It sure looked like the shoe the States wife had worn.

Something clunked inside the LTD and there was banging on the inside of the trunk lid. A muffled voice shouted, "Let me out! Let me out!" I grabbed the ignition keys through the window and dashed around to the back. In my hurry I jammed the wrong key into the lock but managed to get it back out. I got the right key in and turned. The lid lifted. Yasch Siemens blinked in the light and scrambled out so quickly he almost knocked me down.

"Dunna vatta! How did I get into there?" Then he put his hand to the back of his head. "Dievel my head hurts!"

"I got some water in the plane!" Bulchi said and he lumbered off to get it. I helped Yasch sit down on the front passenger seat of the LTD with the door open. Bulchi brought back an old canvas canteen, the kind I hadn't seen since I was maybe six years old. Yasch took a mouthful, spat it out, tried again and swallowed some.

"What happened?" I wanted to know.

"You tell it to me," Yasch said. He took another gulp of

water. "Ouch!" He put his hand to the back of his head again. "Some schinda must have hit me on the head and knocked me out. Dievel that's a big bump!"

"Can you remember anything?"

"I-I was by the auction sale, yeah, and then . . . then . . . yeah . . . then this woman in a funny dress comes to me . . . and it's Shaftich Shreeda's daughter Fleeda who is a missionary in Africa . . . and she asks if I will give her a ride home because her foda still wants maybe to buy something at the outcall and she isn't feeling so good . . . and I mean, I didn't have money to buy nothing anyways so I said, 'Sure' and we're driving along . . . and Fleeda is neighbouring steady like a threshing machine and I hold still by the stop sign at the post road and next I am in this dark place and I start to bang with my shoe and you open the trunk."

"Do you think Fleeda knocked you out?" I asked.

"Could be, I mean, I don't know . . . she was me beside in the front seat so I think I would have seen it if she was trying to do me something. I mean I used to think she was a knock-out, but this is crazy." Yasch drank some more water. "Whose car is this anyways?"

"Schmuggle Veens," I said. "He bought the disker at the sale."

"Schmuggle Veens? How did I get into his trunk?"

"I guess whoever knocked you out must have put you in the trunk," I said. "Could there have been somebody in your car, hiding in the back?"

"Could be, but I mean, it's not dark in the daytime . . . no, wait, there was a pelz diack in the back that we used for a picnic blanket last Sunday when we went to Morden Dam with the baby after we visited Oata's mutta in the mental home. Some badel could have verstecked himself under there and then klotzed me one on the head. You think maybe that's what happened?"

I thought that was probably it, but Yasch wanted to know what was going on. I told him as much as I thought was necessary. Then we decided to steal the car.

13

IT always bothers me when a detective has to break
the law to do his job. I wouldn't say that I don't have any
sins but when I read a story or watch a show on TV and the
detective breaks into a house, or steals a car and goes the
wrong way down a one-way street, or if the detective shoots
somebody it bothers me. In some stories so many people die
because of the detective that it would have been better if he
had stayed in bed. Sure, those are just stories and if they were
really true and that many people were getting killed all the
time McDonald's would switch from the hamburger business
to the undertaker business. Still it often seems to me that
living in the world is like living in a story because if you do
one thing then something else happens and if you hadn't
done that thing then the other thing wouldn't have happened.
It is not good enough, after you drive your car a hundred
and twenty miles an hour on a gravel road and have a

smash-up with the neighbour's wife and her car full of
children, to say, it was *His* will. No sir, that isn't good enough
for me.

But like I said, I had some sins myself, so here I was driving
a stolen car faster than the speed limit along a gravel road.
It bothered me, but not too much. I had reasons and excuses.
Yasch Siemens was sitting beside me and he had reasons,
too. His car had been stolen and we thought we were driving
the thieves' car. Above us to our left Bulchi Wiebe and Hein
were surveying Gutenthal from the air. Still kind of bedutzed
from being knocked out, Yasch neighboured on about how
he used to think Fleeda Shreeda was a knock-out, and she
was in his head all the time, only she went to be a missionary
in Africa and married herself with somebody there. I listened
with only half my ears, trying to figure out what was going
on, so I wasn't thinking about what Yasch was really saying
when I told him that Fleeda's husband was killed in Uganda.
It got embarrassing because Yasch with his sore head wasn't
thinking straight, or curved even, more like he was swerving
on a muddy dirt road. He started to yammer about how
Fleeda was back and she was free, but he had himself all tied
together with Oata and how he was always going down the
wrong road in his life and I was thinking I should drive him
to the hospital because maybe he was brain damaged from
the klutz on the head the way he was talking. I mean, the
way I saw it, Fleeda could just as soon be against us as for
us. Of course, I wanted her to be for us, but I had to try to
keep my eyes and ears open to all the signals and that is hard
to do when there is somebody yammering beside you about
things you shouldn't really talk about to other people. Once
you say something out loud you never know what will
happen with those words. They aren't yours to boss around

anymore and you can get caught with the beckhouse door open. Then I was yammering, too, inside my head, about Barbara Ball Bearing and her full sweater and about Rosmack Rampel who was still missing and I was seeing myself in the mirror, this overgrown bengel playing police, and I started to wonder if I had just left that zipper Bible on the corner of the grave without looking in it, maybe Hilda Heinrichs would still be alive and Yetta Hiebat wouldn't have burned to death. Rosmack would still be riding her motorcycle around, and I would just have to worry about brassieres turning into shorts on the washline. I was no better than that bengel with the jeep, playing games, and I tried to shove all this out of my head because I was losing the thread of things. But it was hard to clear the head and my mental movie started again and I was helping Hilda change the flat tire and in the trunk I saw the camouflage army cap and there was something else, I didn't know right away what it was, but I kept looking and when I thought I had it figured out I took my foot off the gas and let the car roll till it stopped.

Suddenly I wished I didn't have Yasch along because in my line of work it didn't help if you always had to explain it to somebody what you were doing, especially when you didn't know yourself for sure why you were doing it. Yasch already said, "What want you here?" when I got close to the old Heinrichs place and he was coming out of his bedutzheit and waking up to the real world so it would only get worse to have him along.

Then something else hit me in the head and I said, "Have you heard anything about when Yetta Hiebat's funeral is going to be?"

I had been thinking it was funny how Holzyebock Hiebat would be at an auction sale so soon after the fire, only the

Nazi blackmail thing was maybe scarier than a burned-up wife.

Yasch pinched his chin where he hadn't shaved for a few days. "Yetta Hiebat is dead? I never heard about that."

Before I could explain I saw it again, the green LTD on the Heinrichs yard. A woman in a long black dress stood on the waterhole hump. When she saw us she hurried down the hill into the car and with dirt flying from her back wheels she drove through the long grass across the yard to the field road. I stepped on the gas and went after her, but she got to the mile road with a quarter mile to spare and turned onto the gravel in a cloud of dust. A blue car with white doors cut me off. I slammed on the brakes and skidded to a stop.

"What do the stripey gophers want?" Yasch asked. Kowolchuk, the cop who had questioned me about Hilda Heinrichs's drowning, got out of the car and walked towards us.

"Just a spot check," he said as he leaned over to peer inside the car. "Say, aren't you the guy who said he found a woman in this pond?"

"Yeah," I said.

"Come back to the scene of the crime?"

"Not really," I said. I didn't know what I could tell him.

"Still playing detective, are you?"

"Guess so."

"Different car, I see. Could I see your registration, please?"

It only took about ten minutes to follow Constable Kowolchuk to the police station. I wondered how much of this story I could tell him. I had to convince him we had stolen the car in order to recover another stolen car. But could I convince him about any of the other things? I couldn't even produce one of the cocaine zipper Bibles. At least that might have been believable.

Constable Kowolchuk held out his hand for the keys when Yasch and I got out of the car. I let Yasch tell his story first, I mean, he had a bump on his head, some hard evidence. The cop wrote it all down on a long pad of paper with a ballpoint pen that didn't want to write very good. When Yasch finished, Kowolchuk read the story back to him and Yasch signed it. Then I told him what I thought was necessary to back up Yasch's story, how we had seen the LTD and disker from Bulchi Wiebe's plane, how we had found Yasch in the trunk, and had taken the LTD to try to catch the stolen '51 Ford. After I signed the statement Kowolchuk slipped it into a file folder.

"If you were after a '51 Ford, how come you were chasing a green LTD across that field?"

I stood there for a minute, trying to think. Kowolchuk looked like he thought I was lying through my teeth.

"I just wanted to ask if they had seen the '51 Ford."

"Do you know who was driving it?"

"No," I said, and that was the truth. It sure looked like Hilda Heinrichs but I really didn't believe a dead woman could drive a car.

"Well, I'll have to investigate this further, but I do think you could be charged with auto theft." Kowolchuk slipped the LTD keys into a plastic bag and stapled a card to it.

"You mean we can go?"

"For now."

"How're we supposed to get around without a car?"

Kowolchuk eyed me for a moment, then grinned, "Sometimes a detective has to walk the beat."

14

THE sunflowers faced the late afternoon sun. Near Simple Hein's bridge the sunflower cannon boomed and a flock of blackbirds flew up from the field. The cannon boomed again. The third boom was twice as loud and more birds rose from the sunflowers to join the flock circling and swooping to land again. I stumbled through the ditch and the cannon sounded twice more before I found it about ten rows into the field. The black metal barrel jerked as the cannon exploded and a half-second later a blast echoed from another spot near the Martens yard at the far end of the field. I stole through the sunflower rows, listening carefully to each cannon boom. Every third or fourth blast was followed by a boom from the Martens yard. When I got to the last row of sunflowers I hesitated, then stepped through and dashed across the strip of cultivated earth into the tall brome grass. I glimpsed the grey jeep through the willows as my ankles tripped on a wire. Shock shivered through my body. When I hit the ground an explosion stung my ears. It was not a sunflower cannon or a firecracker. I raised my head but another explosion pounded my ears. I ducked, thankful the electric fence caught on my foot wasn't very strong.

Everything was silent for a few minutes, then I heard the cannon in the field again. I raised my head and peered through the willows. The jeep was gone.

I slipped onto a small alfalfa field that looked like it had already gone through a second cutting. A burned smell drifted from four holes near the centre of the field. I tiptoed to the nearest hole. It was about as big around as an oil drum and two wires led away from it in the direction of a large machine shed at the end of the field. I looked around at the other holes but before I got a good look my foot caught on another wire and I was staring at a blue propane torch cylinder half buried in the ground with two wires coming out of it.

I galloped to the machine shed. The wires led under the padlocked double door. I thanked my correspondence locksmith course and had the door open just as the bomb went off.

I found the light switch. Five alarm clocks on the floor each had wires leading outside. I ripped the wires from the clocks and shuddered as I remembered bombs in TV shows.

The shed was like a war headquarters. Soldier posters hung on the walls, all kinds, army, navy, air force, mostly United States—*Soldier of Fortune* posters, posters that said "Be A Mercenary!" Guns were arranged on two tables made from sawhorses and sheets of plywood. At one end were toy guns, cap guns, water pistols, pop guns, suction cup guns and homemade wooden guns, guns for shooting rubber bands. Next, half a dozen Daisy BB guns, four rifles and two pistols, then a couple of old .22s, modified to look like machine guns. A sawed-off shotgun. Two Lee Enfield .303s with bayonets made from hay-mower knives. A four-inch pipe next to five darts made of hay-mower knives and bridge spikes looked like a crude rocket launcher.

Piles of *Soldier of Fortune* magazines littered the floor and a bunch of VHS war movie tapes were lined up on a little shelf nailed to the wall of a closet in the corner farthest from the door. The inside of the closet was lined with black tarpaper; trays, chemicals and photographic paper cluttered a work table. A Black Magic chocolate box contained old 620 negatives and black and white pictures with the Nazi flag in the background. Now I knew where the blackmail pictures had come from and I was pretty sure that the army bengel with the grey jeep was behind it all. I wondered where that bengel had gone with the jeep. Was he on his way to blow up Schmuggle Veens's States wife? Where had Schmuggle Veens gone? How had they gone when the RCMP had his car? Were they still driving Yasch and Oata's '51 Ford? Was Fleeda Shreeda helping them? Who was driving the doll woman's car? All these questions and nobody to tell me any answers.

I was putting the pictures back in the Black Magic box when I heard a plane. Its knocking engine told me it had to be Bulchi Wiebe. So I ran from the darkroom, almost speared myself on one of the hay-mower knife rifles, and pushed out of the machine shed door smack into Rosmack Rampel.

At least that's what I thought at first, until I figured out there were two of her, not friendly at all. The correspondence kung fu lessons hadn't taught me how to fight with two women, but these two had no such problem with me. One grabbed me by the shirt and the other tackled me by the pant legs and when I tried to use some Chinese foot fighting

Barbara Ball Bearing's loose pants pulled right off my legs. I toppled over the shirt-pulling girl and my head knocked the wind out of her, but my hands thought it was important to keep my loose shorts on and she scrambled out from under me. I turned over on my back and looked up into the mirror sunglasses of the five Indian girls I had seen at the auction sale. They were talking about me in a strange language and laughing, except for the one waving my pants. She wasn't laughing at all, not even smiling, and her mirror sunglasses hid all clues from me. I looked at each girl carefully to make sure none of them was Rosmack. I didn't know what to do and Barbara's shorts were quite air-conditioned and it is hard to have respect like that, but I tried. I cleared my throat and said, "I'm looking for Rose Rampel. Do you have any idea where she might be? She rides a Harley Davidson motorcycle and . . ."

Bulchi Wiebe's plane buzzed the yard and cut off my words. The girls ran for their LTD. The LTD made a U-ball and headed up the driveway. I sat up. My pants were waved out the car window and I waited for them to drop in the dust, but they disappeared back into the car. I sank back to the ground, listening to the airplane fade away. The yard became so still I could hear my heart beat. I tried to remember what was in my pockets. My wallet was in my pants, mostly ID and scraps of paper. I thought of the money belt but I remembered taking it off when we were emptying the Bibles. Had I put it back on? Those pants sure had pulled off easy. What could I do without my pants? And what were those girls up to? More and more people were infiltrating this story I had started when I picked up Oata's Bible at the graveyard and changed a tire for Hilda Heinrichs. My head started to swirl there on the Martens farmyard as the sun was setting and I got so confused inside my head I didn't notice the car until I heard a door close.

I lifted my head and saw another green LTD. Two men in long coats walked across the yard. Before I could sit up they bent over me. The older man had short blond hair and a dark coat; the younger had short black hair and a light coat. They looked freshly showered and dry-cleaned and I could smell Old Spice. The younger one in the light coat held an *Awake!* magazine in front of my face. The cover showed a black-hooded guy with a knife and the headline, "Satanism A Growing Menace." The older man in the dark coat said, "We ask seventy cents—to help with printing costs." I reached down to where my pocket should have been but I had no seventy cents there. The younger guy with the light coat said, "That's all right, we understand." He put the magazine in my hand and they straightened up, but before they turned away the older guy in the dark coat said, "We will pray that the Lord will give you pants." For just a second he looked me in the eye and I was wondering if he had ever come to bring magazines to our house because he looked like I had seen him before, but the sun was already going down. Then they were gone.

I wasn't really awake yet, though I hadn't been sleeping neither, and I had never read an *Awake!* magazine before. Mama usually just put them in the stove. But the cover was interesting so I started to read and there was stuff in there about dogs and cats getting killed in New York and how the police thought Satanists were responsible. Some pretty scary stuff, especially Satanists using the letters HH to mean Hitler who was really Satan, and I wondered if the murdered pigs and the initials in the zipper Bibles maybe had something to do with that. Had I stumbled on a Satanist headquarters? I read that before a coven meeting Satanists must rape a virgin, have a fiery holocaust, or a ritual murder of a person or animal. At least two of those three things had happened here, I thought, and I jumped up when it started to sink into me what Rosmack might be in for if the Satanists had her, and I wouldn't even let myself ask the question, was she or wasn't she? Pants or no pants, I had to do something about it.

The house door was unlocked. The kitchen table had dirty plates and peanut butter and jam jars on it. Crumbs covered the table and a spoon stuck in a jar of instant coffee. I walked through the empty dining room, into the living room, empty too, except for a torn wine-coloured sofa chair. I climbed the stairs, each creak making me shiver even though I didn't think anybody was up there, but where else could I look? Two closed doors faced me at the top of the stairs. I started to open the nearest one when a sound came from behind the other door. I froze against the wall, hearing my knocking heart. I reached for the doorknob, turned it gingerly and pushed. The door creaked as it swung open. I peered around the doorframe. In the dim room I saw a figure on a four-poster bed—Rosmack Rampel, tied up, a dirty sock stuffed in her mouth.

Well, of course, I'm not the kind of guy that carries a knife in my underpants, so it took me a few minutes to free Rosmack because those knots were pretty tight and she kept spitting after I pulled the sock out of her mouth. When I finally got her loose she tried to get up, but she fell against me, and I held her as she cried into my shoulder for a long time. Finally, she stopped shuddering and pushed her hand against my leg to sit up.

"Where are your pants?"

"A girl pulled them off," I said. "But how did you get here?"

"I don't know," Rosmack cried again. I took her in my arms and between sobs she told me how she had met Beitelkopp Blatz on her way home from the fire. "Beitelkopp he . . ."

"You were with Beitelkopp?"

"Yeah, on the road after I drove away from you I had a race with Beitelkopp, only he didn't tell me where we were going so I followed a little behind him and he led me all the way past Highway 75 on this road I had never gone on before and then all at once he turned his lights off so I turned mine off too and he turned onto a driveway and there we were in a graveyard. Beitelkopp took something out of his saddle bags and went over to a grave with a little white fence around it, though I couldn't see so good in the dark. Beitelkopp came back and gave me a zipper Bible and told me to put it in my saddle bag. Then he told me not to follow him back but I was supposed to meet him at Barbara Ball Bearing's place."

"Did he tell you what was in the Bible?"

"No, but he drove away as soon as he gave it to me. So I drove away as fast as I could and when I was past Highway 75 and knew better how the roads went I didn't go the same way we had come."

"And you drove to Barbara's?"

"I didn't get there. I was passing the yard where you said that woman had drowned and I thought I saw somebody with a flashlight there. I thought maybe it was you so I drove in the yard. I know I stopped and got off my bike, but then I don't know what happened. When I woke up I was here and it was so scary. I couldn't help it, I had to pee my pants.

And all the time there were these dunnasche big bangs and cars driving past and airplanes, it was like maybe a war had started. I tried to get loose, but I couldn't. I was too scared to try anything. I-I thought someone was going to kill me." Rosmack cried again and I held her for a long time.

Then she said she was very hungry. I remembered the peanut butter and jam on the table downstairs. But when we got down to the kitchen we looked into the barrel of a rifle. It was not a Daisy. The army bengel was holding it.

15

NOTHING in my life had prepared me for the terror I felt when I saw the rifle pointing at me. It was a real rifle, one of the .303s from the machine shed, and I had no doubt it was loaded. Nothing had prepared me for this, not my correspondence lessons, not the movies, not TV, not my history. As far as I knew there had been no Bergen in the *Martyrs' Mirror.* My family had come from Russia in 1874, before the Revolution. Nobody had shot at us; we just weren't allowed any land. My Bergens were conscientious objectors during the war. Papa had planted trees, dug ditches, not trenches. The Bergens never shot anyone, and were never shot at. That was why we lived in Canada, not in Russia or the States. We didn't shoot each other in Gutenthal. Even as a detective I had never carried a weapon. I had webbed feet. I was no good for war. Not even Rosmack's story had prepared me for this.

Yet here I was facing a rifle, the barrel wavering back and forth between me and Rosmack, my hands raised beside my ears, my knees trying to knock each other, Barbara Ball Bearing's loose shorts slipping lower with each shudder, and for once I wished I had a fat rear end.

The army bengel hadn't said anything yet. He just stood there pointing the gun. His mouth twisted from side to side and the rifle shook like the screens in a combine. That was the scariest part. He was shaking so much I was scared he might pull the trigger without even wanting to. Beside me Rosmack's stomach growled and I thought how hungry she must be, and the army bengel didn't say a word. The room got very dark, very dark. "Ask! Ask!" my father's voice said inside my head. "Find out. You have to ask to find out the truth. Help the bengel. Let him talk about it."

Against the grey light of the window, the bengel's face was just a shadow. He moved his head and I saw the flat top of his hair, the scoop ears, and I remembered a Sunday evening in the hayloft when I practised breaking old shingles with the edge of my hand, each crack sending ripples of pain up my arm, then Mama rising up the ladder through the hole in the floor, watching me. "Kjnals, we'll be late for evening church. Come put your Sunday pants on." No questions, no scolding, just Mama telling me it was time to stop playing. Mama didn't tell me to stop playing anymore.

A patch of light spread slowly across the wall, washed the bengel's face, and for a moment I was looking into a mirror, the face in front of me as terrified as mine. Then the light passed and I heard the soft pressing of tires in the dirt and the faint hum of a motor.

"Corny! It's time to go! Come or we'll be late!" The woman's voice was strong and clear, but she wasn't shouting.

In the darkness I heard the army bengel lean his rifle against the wall. He hurried outside. A door opened and slammed. Tires crackled as the car drove away.

"Neil, what's happening?"

"I don't know!" I groped along the wall for a light switch. When the light came on I saw Rosmack had wet her pants. In the movies they never show that when somebody is tied up for a whole day. I picked up the rifle and opened the chamber. There was a cartridge in it. I pulled it out. The shell casing was real, but the bullet had been carved out of wood. I wondered if there was gunpowder inside.

"Who was that?"

"Somebody called Corny," I said. "Somebody called Corny, who has a mother that makes him go places. But first I must get you home."

We had some luck. In the barn we found Rosmack's motorcycle, next to the grey jeep. I was saved from having to steal again.

I huddled behind Rosmack on the motorcycle, my bare legs freezing in the wind. I tried to gribble out what all of this could mean. Who was this Corny army bengel anyways? Who was the woman that picked him up? Could it have been the doll woman I thought was dead? If Hilda Heinrichs wasn't dead, was Yetta Hiebat dead? Was the army bengel behind the blackmail? I had thought so, but now the wooden bullet and the mother calling him made me wonder if I was wrong. Was all this a game? Was I just playing a game? But those Bibles with the money had been real, hadn't they? Had those been real thousand-dollar bills? They sure hadn't looked like play money. And what about Schmuggle Veens and his States wife? And Yasch Siemens in the trunk? That had been a real bump on his head. Where was Fleeda

Shreeda? Where was Beitelkopp Blatz? Hadn't there been real powder in the covers of those Bibles? And those had been real explosions and the girls I had wrestled with had been flesh and blood, and those had been real pants they stole from me, and hadn't those Witnesses who gave me the magazine been real? As I huddled against Rosmack's back I remembered Barbara Ball Bearing pressing against me so long ago that morning and that had been real, too. Barbara had put Rosmack's hairclip into my pocket, my pocket of those stolen pants, and in that pocket, too, was the swastika ankle bracelet—the only lead to who had ransacked my car. And I ran through everything that had happened since the brassieres had showed up on Yunges Yeeatze's washline, and even the funny things happening in the church before that, because I had to figure the story out of all this. That's what a detective has to do after he schneppas everything out, he has to make the story out of it, even if it isn't true. A detective has to make a story that makes sense, at least enough sense so he himself can believe it if he has to. Even a game isn't worth playing if you can't believe in it—only sometimes there is a mother who calls you out of the game to go to church and then your story has to be extra tough or it will fall apart. You can't have any loose pieces of binder twine for people to pull on. Only it's hard to know when you have enough ends of rope to tie the knot, and you have to decide if they all belong, or if some of them belong to another knot, and it helps to know what kind of a knot it is supposed to be, like a half hitch, or a granny knot, or a slip knot or a hangman's knot, or the Manitoba knot they used to tie sacks of grain in the olden days. I was dealing with a murder knot, a blackmail knot, a drug smuggling knot, a kidnapping knot, a double-cross knot, and somehow

I had to figure out if all these knots belonged to the same ball of twine.

But first I had to get Rosmack home, and I tried not to think about how it was going to look when Schneppa Kjnals without his pants on showed up on Rosmack's yard. I had to find out from Rape Rampel how come he had lied about Rosmack coming home. And I had to find out who that motorcycle driver was I had seen from the ventilator in the morning, so long ago.

It is hard to talk to someone when you're on a motorcycle driving along as fast as the loose gravel lets you, but there was a question bothering me and I wanted to ask it before we got to Rosmack Rampel's yard. So I leaned over to Rosmack's ear and said loudly, "Did they do anything to you?"

Rosmack didn't say anything till we had leaned around the second last corner before the home stretch. Then she turned her head and shouted, "Do you mean, did they rape me?"

"Yeah, I guess so!"

"No!"

We didn't say anything more, but I could feel her crying, and I felt covered in scum from Hauns Jaunzes' Fraunz's pond. I belonged on the manure pile like that prophet Preacher Janzen preached about one Sunday while I was in the basement snooping around the Sunday School rooms. We turned into Rape Rampel's yard and Mrs. Rape Rampel ran out of the house followed by the younger brothers, and there were so many tears and Rosmack almost fainted because she was so hungry, it was all I could do to find out Rape wasn't at home, that he had gone to some kind of meeting, and nobody even noticed I didn't have any pants on. They helped Rosmack into the house and left me shivering under the yardlight, pulling those loose shorts up.

16

HALF a mile from home Kowolchuk picked me up in the cruiser car. "You got caught peeking in a lady's window," he said. My legs were too cold for me to care what he said. "I think you're in trouble, boy. There's a bunch of farmers accusing you of blackmail." I had almost forgotten about the blackmail. Who was accusing me? How had they figured out that I had anything to do with it?

Kowolchuk turned into my yard. A.Dyck, Rape Rampel, Shaftich Shreeda, Holzyebock Hiebat, Bulchi Wiebe and Hein leaned against Bulchi's jeep. Bulchi and Hein must have talked. They were the only ones who knew what Fleeda and I had done.

I got out of the car and looked Rape Rampel in the eye. "Rosmack is home now!" I said. Rape's back stiffened. I continued, "How come you lied to me before and said she was home? I just brought her home now!" Rape coughed, but before he could try to give me an answer Mama called from the screen door, "Kjnals, shame yourself standing there with nothing on! Come in and pull some pants on and eat something." She called the others, too, to have some coffee, so I led them inside and went into my room to find some pants. When I came back into the kitchen Rape Rampel was trying to figure out how to use Mama's speakerphone. Mama showed him and as I sat down to eat fried potatoes mixed with eggs we listened to Rape talk with his wife. He didn't talk long, only enough to find out Rosmack was okay, and then he said he would be home as soon as he could.

When he hung up Rape asked, "Where did you find her?"

"At the old Martens place west of town." I told them Rosmack's story.

"Was she there alone?" Rape wanted to know.

"Yeah, she was tied up on a bed in the house."

"Tied up?"

"Yeah, tied up." This was getting a bit strange for everybody except Rape. He didn't seem that surprised. "That's where the Nazi pictures came from, too." I explained why I had gone there in the first place after remembering Hein's complaint about bombs close to his bridge and what Shusta Paul had told me about Martens the postman's photography hobby. "So I figure those Bibles and those blackmail notes came from the Martens farm."

"But who would do such a thing?" Shaftich Shreeda asked.

I described the army bengel and the old mail jeep. Their eyes got big when they heard about the propane cylinder bombs and the arsenal of guns in the machine shed. I said I figured the army bengel was involved, only I didn't think he had done it alone.

"Yeah," Holzyebock said. "We all got zipper Bibles with

pictures of us from the war when we went to that Nazi meeting in the school."

"Yeah, I got one about a month ago and then another one that asked for money," said Rape. "But I didn't do nothing about it till I got another note in a zipper Bible that said if I wanted to see Rosie again I better bring ten thousand to the disker at the auction sale."

"When did you get the note?" I wanted to know.

"Just before dinner-time today. We were all busy and we didn't notice nothing till we heard a motorcycle speed up on the road and for sure we all thought Rosie had come home and so we came running out. A zipper Bible was on the gatepost and a motorcycle was haeveling down the road on the way west. Carl and Canola tried to chase it but it disappeared. In the Bible was this note." Rape spread the note on the table. It was like the one Fleeda had showed me, the one Shaftich Shreeda had received, except for the words, "If you want to see Rosmack again," pasted with letters from a newspaper, and then, printed with a pencil, "Tell Kjnals Rosmack is home already."

"Who saw the note besides you?" I remembered Carl and Canola had been real surprised to hear that Rosmack was home.

"Nobody," Rape said. "I didn't want the others to worry so I just didn't say nothing. I phoned you to make sure you hadn't found her yet and went to the bank to get the money." He stopped for a minute. Nobody said anything. "But now Bulchi tells us that you and Fleeda and Hein got the money. Hein, where did you get money from to buy that combine anyways?"

Hein didn't sputter at all when he answered, "Find on road. Find zipper Bible on road. Ten tousand dollar on road. Finder keeper!"

"Where on the road did you find it?" I asked.

"On road close by bridge where I live before too much knowl."

"Close to the sunflowers?"

"Yeah, find close by knackzoat. Close by grass on the ditch."

"Did you see anyone around there?"

Hein picked his nose, scratched his head. "I saw green car stop there, then drive away."

"LTD?"

"Me I don't know cars so good. Never got driver licence," Hein frowned. "Green car. I think so same like Schmuggle Veens."

Kowolchuk smirked as he listened to all this but he didn't speak. He seemed to be waiting for me to hang myself. I thought about the Bible Oata had showed me in the cellar on Hein's bed, the one with the letters HH on the black end page. Hilda Heinrichs, the doll woman, must have lost it and I wondered to myself if maybe she had given the wrong Bible to Yetta and that was why I had found her body in the pond. Kowolchuk still smirked and I thought again about how the body hadn't been there when he showed up. And how a woman in a black dress had run from the waterhole hump to the green LTD and led me on a chase right into Kowolchuk's cruiser car. Another thing bothered me, too. Holzyebock Hiebat for sure wasn't acting like his wife had just died and I tried to think if anybody had said anything about Yetta Hiebat getting killed in that explosion at the trailer. But I had found bones in the ashes. Only the bones, too, had disappeared.

"So where is our money?" A.Dyck spoke for the first time. I didn't answer him. Instead I lifted my foot to the seat of my chair, pushed down my sock, and removed Hilda Heinrichs's ankle bracelet. "Did you ever see Yetta wearing a thing like this?" I asked Holzyebock.

"Yetta? What's she got to do with this?" I held it in front of his face. He stared at it, then said, "Yeah, I seen her wearing something like that on her ankle. Is that a Hitler hackenkjrietz hanging on there?"

"Yes," I said. "Did you find Yetta yet?"

"Y-Y-Yetta?" Holzyebock stammered. "Why should I have to find her?"

"How come you phoned me and said you couldn't find Yetta after the fire?"

"Me phone a schneppa naze like you? You maybe think I'm from the mental home?"

"You mean Yetta is at home?"

"That bothers you nothing!" Holzyebock got a little red in the face.

"Yetta is at home? Is she?"

"Well, no, not right now. . . ." Holzyebock got even redder, but Kowolchuk interrupted, "Maybe we should ask the *investigator* some questions." He stood up and pulled an ankle bracelet out of his pocket. "Found this in that LTD you stole."

"Say," A.Dyck said, "I saw Hilda wearing one of those when she came to pick Lawrence up."

"Who picked Lawrence up?" Rape asked.

"Hilda Heinrichs. They went to Niagara Falls to get married."

"Married? L.U.Dyck and Hilda Heinrichs are getting married?"

Mama spoke then. "Yeah, L.U.Dyck and Hilda were engaged once long time ago, only there was an accident with a pig. Her sister and her niece were killed and so they never got married."

Then Bulchi Wiebe added, "Oh yeah, Nita, I remember it now. Hilda's brother-in-law swerved on the loose gravel because A.Dyck's prize boar was on the road. The car rolled and his wife and daughter were killed. Yeah, I remember it now. That was your pig, wasn't it, Abe?"

A.Dyck looked very white, almost as white as the doll woman had looked in the moonlight. "It was mine," he said so quietly I almost couldn't hear him. Then I saw Mama put her hand over her mouth suddenly.

"But what's all this got to do with getting my ten thousand back?" asked Shaftich Shreeda. "Where is that money anyways, Kjnals?"

Everybody looked at me again. I didn't know how much I should tell them. Since Hein and Bulchi Wiebe must have said something about Fleeda, I said, "Well, I think Fleeda has it."

"Who is Fleeda?" Kowolchuk wanted to know.

"Shaftich Shreeda's daughter," I said. So I told the story of the double-cross and how Schmuggle Veens and his States wife had taken off with the disker and then Fleeda, who had the Bibles with the money, had asked Yasch Siemens to take her home in the '51 Ford. I described how Bulchi Wiebe and me and Hein had spotted the LTD from the plane and how Hein's shotgun shell clue had told us the '51 Ford had been there. I explained how we found Yasch Siemens in the trunk with a bump on his head.

"That's right, Kjnals," Bulchi Wiebe added. "Me and Hein flew all over Gutenthal and even over the Martens yard looking for the '51 Ford but we didn't see nothing until it was almost too dark to fly. Then we saw it along the States ditch.

It was on the States side, on that farmyard about five miles from here that has been empty for a few years because the farmer is getting paid from the government so he won't grow more wheat. It was too dark to land so I flew straight home and we came right away here but you weren't home, and then all the others came, so I didn't tell you this till now."

I got up from my chair. "We'd better go there right away. Who knows what kind of trouble Fleeda is in?" Or what kind of trouble she is cooking up with Schmuggle Veens and his States wife, I thought.

"Yeah! We better go!" Shaftich Shreeda turned to go out the door.

"Just a minute," Kowolchuk said slowly. His face looked like he was wondering how come he ever got transferred here among these crazy Flat Germans. "I don't know if I can believe a word of this. Are you all in this with Peeping Tom here?"

I had to think fast. I needed something to convince Kowolchuk there really was something going on. I turned to the blackmailed men. "When you got those Bibles with the pictures did you notice anything funny about them?"

"Those pictures weren't funny," Holzyebock said. "Specially not when you read the pieces of newspaper that were in it."

"I don't mean that, I mean, did you notice anything funny about the covers?"

Nobody had, but Bulchi Wiebe said, "Wait!" and hurried outside. In a minute he was back with a zipper Bible. I took it from him and unzipped it. Sure enough, the back cover felt funny. I took the butcher knife from the counter, slit open the back cover, and pulled out a plastic envelope full of white powder. I handed it to Kowolchuk. He would have to believe me now.

Kowolchuk slit a little hole in the plastic and poked his finger into the powder. When he touched his finger to his tongue he got a faraway look in his eyes. Very slowly he said, "I guess we'll have to check this out."

A few minutes later Kowolchuk and I were in the cruiser car leading a parade along the field road beside the boundary ditch. Kowolchuk wasn't saying anything. I saw two red reflectors ahead, then the white shape. "The Bible van! It's going to drive across to the States!"

17

I had never been in jail before. I hadn't even known they had a jail in the RCMP station in town. Even a detective doesn't know everything. But I was in a cell, a real cell with a real door made of bars, sitting on a bare mattress on an iron bed looking at a toilet with no seat. Stripped of shoelaces and belt, I was the first of my line of Bergens to be in jail.

Through the bars, resting on the corner of a small desk at the end of a hallway, I could see the sole of a shoe, a woman's shoe. Barbara Ball Bearing's shoe. That was something else I hadn't known before. I hadn't known that Barbara worked as a babysitter at the jail when the cops were too busy to guard their prisoners. All the times I had helped Barbara at her parties and she had never told me about this other job she had. I had been living in my head so much I had never even asked Barbara anything about herself. I had always only been watching, glutzing at her hair, or her tight sweater, or at the lines of her panties through her jeans when she bent to pick up a beer bottle, or at her long toes when she was barefoot. It started to seep into my head the way water on a tractor seat seeps through to the seat of knowledge—I had never taken a look at Barbara herself, the person inside all those curves. Why did she do what she did? Why was she always helping people? Why had she never found another boyfriend after that crashed '57 Chev? Ten years was a long time to keep such a fire burning. I thought how brave she was to treat McKay, the boy RCMP, like any other drunk at her parties when he actually was her boss. Something behind those curves was very strong, something the Hollywood School of Detection had never taught me how to find.

Barbara hadn't laughed when she saw she had to babysit me. She didn't even smirk. She just said, "Hi, Kjnals," and "Call me if you need anything." Then she had followed Kowolchuk down the hall and now I could see the sole of her shoe on the desk.

I didn't need anything except a kick in the pants. I had a story that wouldn't hold together. All the evidence was circumstantial, pointing the wrong way. And I was behind bars so I couldn't change the way the story was going. What had gone wrong?

Kowolchuk had stopped the Bible van as it tried to drive through the ditch to the States. But a search of the van and the short-haired Bible pedlar had turned up nothing illicit. A trumpet case under the seat had a trumpet in it. When the cop asked the guy why he was trying to cross the border where there was no crossing, the guy just said he was taking a shortcut. He was late for a religious meeting, and he thought just crossing to the farmhouse on the other side would be okay. Kowolchuk was not convinced. He arrested the Bible seller on suspicion of drug smuggling. The guy didn't put up any fuss as Kowolchuk handcuffed him and appointed Rape Rampel to guard him. He just shrugged as if we would find out soon enough that he was right. Kowolchuk talked on his police radio for a long time, then stared at the farmhouse lights gleaming through a row of planted trees. We couldn't see if there were any vehicles on the yard.

Kowolchuk was waiting for the States police to show up on the other side, though he said he had the okay to cross over if something happened that made him think it was necessary.

We didn't have to wait for long. Two motorcycles roared into the yard and cut their engines. A door slammed. "Don't think we should wait," Kowolchuk muttered. We followed him through the ditch, stumbled across the furrows of a ploughed field, and slipped between the planted trees. Two green LTDs and Knibble Thiessen's Thunderbird were parked under the yardlight. There was no sign of the '51 Ford. As we neared the house, we heard music—a hymn, "Amazing Grace."

Kowolchuk stepped up to the door and knocked. The music stopped, raggedly. The door opened. I thought I was seeing a ghost. A woman in a long black dress stood there, clasping a violin by the neck. She smiled at us and said, "Come on in!"

Her lacy black dress dragged on the floor as we followed her through a small kitchen. A black wedding dress, I thought. Could she have been the woman at the Heinrichs yard? When we entered the living room I figured she must be Knibble Thiessen's States patient because she sat down beside him and I caught a glimpse of her red high-heeled shoe. Knibble Thiessen was holding a cello between his knees, its little metal stand resting in a saucer on the floor. Beitelkopp Blatz sat behind a set of drums and Hova Jake leaned against the wall, kissing a saxophone. Five black-haired girls, also in long black dresses, knelt on the floor in a circle around a drum decorated with feathers. The soles of their running shoes poked out past the lacy hems. The Witness who had given me the *Awake!* magazine cradled an autoharp on his lap. When I looked at him it got through my thick head that the Bible van driver had been his older partner. I figured we had really stumbled onto something here.

But I had no thread to sew all these people into my story. They had their own story and it was more believable than mine. They had concrete evidence to support theirs. They were playing real music on real instruments with real strings and mouthpieces and they claimed to be rehearsing for the Cross Boundary Freedom Farmers' Orchestra Festival at the International Peace Gardens. One of the Festival rules was that each orchestra had to be a surprise—the players must never have played together in public before. That was why they were rehearsing in secret here at this farmhouse.

"Please, don't tell anyone," the woman in the black wedding dress said.

The orchestra story was pretty convincing—Knibble Thiessen even showed us a Festival brochure—but Kowolchuk wasn't quite satisfied; he couldn't be after all this sneaking around in the dark. He got out his notebook and asked for names, citizenship and time of entry into the States. The woman in the wedding dress said she was Inge Henkel and lived in the States right there on that farmyard. Knibble Thiessen had crossed over at 7:50 and Beitelkopp and Hova Jake said they had crossed over at 8:55. The Witness said he was Inge's son, Helmut, and he had come over at 8:30. The

Indian girls, who identified themselves as Madonna Smith, Juice McKay, Tina Mulroney, Carly Siemens and Luba Turner, said they had crossed over about 7:45. Inge didn't say when she had last crossed over the line, only I figured for sure now she must have been the one on the waterhole hump at the Heinrichs yard.

Another vehicle pulled up outside. The porch door opened. We heard footsteps in the kitchen. The army bengel squeezed a piano accordion between Bulchi Wiebe and Hein, who were in the doorway, and took up a position next to Hova Jake and his saxophone.

I glanced around the room. Just about everyone was there. Here was my big chance to take control. It was time to ask pointed questions, curved questions, slicing and peeling questions. Suddenly, it seemed to me this whole story was like an onion and I was holding it by that brown twist of the stem at last and if I could just slit the dry brown skin enough to insert the knife blade I would soon peel layer after juicy layer until the whole room would be in tears. "Ask! Ask!" my father's voice whispered in my head. The memory of Rosmack tied up on the bed with a sock in her mouth flashed through my mind. I had to seize the moment. Things were not what they seemed. Something was rotten between the States and Gutenthal. It was time to meet each guilty eye head-on.

I fixed my eye on the army bengel. "You're the blackmailer, aren't you? But somebody double-crossed you. I found your darkroom with the old pictures. I found your gun collection. I found your bombs!" I turned to Holzyebock Hiebat, though I continued to speak to the army bengel. "You blew up the trailer, didn't you? You blew up the trailer with Yetta Hiebat in it. Who hired you? Holzyebock?" Holzyebock started to protest but I turned to Beitelkopp Blatz. "Lots of zipper Bibles for your friends in jail, huh? Lots of zipper Bibles full of dope. And you, Hova Jake. What are you up to at the reserve anyway? Land claims or cocaine?" Hova Jake's eyes sparkled. He almost seemed amused, but I forged on. I swung to face Beitelkopp again. "Hoes on the beetfield arranged like a swastika. Was that a drop-off point for another zipper Bible full of dope? And Holzyebock, how come you gravelled the roads around Hauns Jaunses' Fraunz's farm so they looked like a swastika from the air? Is there a phoney crop duster dropping angel dust from the sky?" I bent and stared the phoney Jehovah's Witness straight in the eyes. "You drowned Hilda Heinrichs because she lost a zipper Bible with ten thousand cash in it! You committed murder for lousy drug money!" The phoney Witness just stared past my left ear. I looked at the Indian girls sitting around their drum. But they ignored me like I wasn't even there. They were all looking at the door.

I turned and my heart stopped. I heard A.Dyck say some of the dirtiest words in the Flat German language as he choked and turned purple. I thought I heard someone pluck the notes from an Easter song on a high string, and the words climbed a ladder in my head—"Up from the grave He arose!"—but it sure wasn't a triumph o'er my foes, no it was a defeat, an 'I surrender all' situation. Beside me A.Dyck tried to clear his throat of angst. My heart started again, beating like I had run a mile. In the kitchen doorway, holding a harp against the black belly of her long dress, a wooden harp like King David's in Bible story pictures, stood the doll woman, blinking her eyes at us through her big round glasses. She jerked her head back and tore a handkerchief out of her sleeve to catch a sneeze. From behind her Schmuggle Veens caught the harp just before it slipped out of her grasp and he cradled it while the doll woman blew her red nose like a trumpet. Then he helped her to a chair beside Knibble Thiessen and his cello. A harmonica stuck out of Schmuggle Veens's back pocket. When she sat down I saw the doll woman was wearing only one shoe. Her bare foot was black like she had walked across a field of summerfallow, and there was a cut along the edge of her foot just behind the little toe where the blood had run into the dirt. The ankle bracelet hung down over her black foot. My eyes flickered between the doll woman and Inge. At close range there was no way I could mix them up. Even their black dresses were quite different. The doll woman's was very wrinkled, like it might have been wet.

The telephone rang in the kitchen. The army bengel squeezed his accordion past Bulchi Wiebe and Hein again. I closed my mouth and swallowed hard. The army bengel called, "Hey fuzz, it's for you!"

Kowolchuk looked livid as he strode out. I tried to ask another question. I opened my mouth. I took a deep breath. But it was like trying to pump up a tire with a hole big as a zipper fly.

Kowolchuk's face was green when he came back. He glared at me, then with great effort apologized to the orchestra for the intrusion. He ordered the rest of us outside. The orchestra said we were welcome to stay and listen to the rehearsal but Kowolchuk insisted we had to leave. The musicians looked happy and pleased. They waved goodbye and accompanied our withdrawal with a spirited rendition of "Onward Christian Soldiers."

The first thing I saw outside was the eighteen-foot disker behind another green LTD. But Kowolchuk wouldn't let me go near it. "I've got five minutes to get you guys out of the States," he said, "and nobody's going to screw around with that!"

Back in Canada Kowolchuk took the handcuffs off the Bible van driver and apologized like he was trying not to wet his pants. The Bible van guy said it was okay, anybody can make a mistake, and he would pray for him. Kowolchuk even told him to wait until we were gone and then cross the border to join his orchestra.

I started toward Bulchi Wiebe's jeep. "You ride with me!" Kowolchuk ordered. So I got into the cruiser car, trying to stiffen myself against the earful I was going to get. And it's hard to stiffen yourself when drowned women show up sneezing. But Kowolchuk didn't say anything right away. He just drove and it seemed like he was working hard in his head to keep himself steady like they had taught him in RCMP school. His silence let my head get back to work, too, and I got in the first word.

"Drive to the Martens farm," I said, keeping my voice as steady as I could. "Something there you should see."

"You don't give up, do you?" he mumbled.

"My father used to say, 'The smart one gives in,' but I don't believe it."

Somebody had cleaned out the Martens place after Rosmack and I left. There were no guns, no bombs, no pictures, or any darkroom equipment. Even the .303 with the wooden bullets was gone from the house. I had to respect Kowolchuk for not blowing his RCMP cap right off his head. He just let the silence of the night say everything for him.

I was ready to give up. I asked him to drive me to my car at the auction yard in the village. He did it without argument. I thought he was glad to get rid of me at last. But when we got to my car he did blow his cap off and he arrested me right then and there. Because my Volkswagen was filled to over-flowing with guns, zipper Bibles, Nazi pictures, plastic bags of powder and six white brassieres. And I had no story to tell.

I hammered on the bars and called for Barbara. Her shoe disappeared off the desk and she walked toward me, her tight blue sweater pushing past the open zipper of the old hockey jacket with the Memphis name tag on the sleeve. She held her hand in front of her mouth and yawned.

"Good thing you called," she said, yawning again. "I was falling asleep."

"I couldn't reach the keys from here anyway," I said. I looked at her for a minute, looked at her blue eyes, tried to count her curled eyelashes, but she blinked when I got to nine.

"What's going on anyway?" I asked.

"I'm babysitting you. I do this off and on, only most of the time I just keep an eye on some drunks."

"I mean, what was going on at your place?"

"My place?" She was blinking her eyes more often.

"Yeah, tell me about the Bible van guy and Beitelkopp Blatz and Hova Jake. Tell me about Rosmack Rampel. Tell me how come you kissed me."

Barbara looked up and down the little hallway, then leaned against the bars.

"Dope," she whispered. "Those guys are dealing dope."

"I thought so, but what has that got to do with you and Rosmack?"

"They're forcing me to help them!"

"But how?"

Barbara pulled a piece of paper from inside the hockey jacket. It was the newspaper article about the woman getting killed for helping the Nazi war criminal.

"What's that got to do with you?"

"That woman was my aunt."

"Lena Bergen?"

"Yeah. How did you know?"

"I think she's related to me, too." Barbara bit her lip as if she was deciding if she should say any more.

"Mom and Dad are visiting down there."

"Your parents are in Paraguay?"

"Yeah, they have so many relatives there that they are visiting in Paraguay for a month already. The Bible van guy said if I didn't help them my parents would be wiped out!" Barbara could hardly speak the words. She turned away. "I can't talk to you anymore."

Barbara wouldn't come back to my cage after that even though I called her a few more times. Finally, I dozed off on the hard mattress, my head spinning with story parts that didn't want to fit together. When I woke up Barbara was gone and Kowolchuk's partner, McKay, was unlocking the door to bring me a red tray with coffee, toast and a jar of pickled herring. "You're really in a pickle," he said. "We even found the dope in your spare tire!"

At 10:00, Kowolchuk came to get me. He led me to a small room where Woarheit Wahl, the justice of the peace, sat behind a table with some file folders and a wooden hammer. His eyes got as big as pie apples when Kowolchuk read the charges: possession of narcotics for the purpose of trafficking, auto theft, operating a detective agency without a licence, possession of modified firearms, blackmail, creating a public nuisance, and attempted instigation of an international incident. The fact that I had saved his teenage son from drinking and driving many times didn't come into play at all. He set bail at a thousand dollars and advised me to seek legal counsel.

Back in my cell I tried to figure out what to do. I didn't have a thousand dollars, that's for sure. I hadn't had that kind of money since I worked up north. And I couldn't ask Mama. I didn't even want her to know I was in jail, though I figured it wouldn't take very long before the wind carried the news to her. As for legal counsel, the only lawyer I knew was Offkot O'Reiv, who had helped Mama figure out Papa's will, written in Flat German without any witnesses so it didn't mean anything anyways, and I somehow didn't think he would be able to help me if I couldn't make a story out of this.

So I lay there on the hard mattress giving myself a headache. From what Barbara had said there had to be some other people involved. People here and others in Paraguay. Aside from the Lena Bergen Bulchi Wiebe had told me about I didn't know if my family had any relatives down there. My family hadn't kept up any connections with the South Americans. All I could remember was that Papa looked down his nose at those Flat Germans who had sold their farms and moved away from this sinful country because they didn't want their children to go to English school, though he would also laugh and say that it had been good for him because he was able to buy a farm cheap. I heard him talking one time to Nobah Naze Needarp about how this family, in such a hurry to get to the promised land, had come back one year later and wanted Papa to sell the place back to them for the same price. I tried to remember the name of the family but I was very young when I picked up this story with my little ears.

But what bothered me more was the fact that somebody knew enough about me to pull a stunt like packing my car with all the evidence in this crazy story. That really was a problem. Somebody had given me all the evidence, only it told the wrong story, and I tried to claw through this in my mind. The Bibles, the guns, the pictures, the dope, even the brassieres I had returned to Mrs. Daughters Derksen on Sunday in time for church. Some shuzzel was playing games with me.

And the doll woman, Hilda Heinrichs, wasn't dead! How was a person supposed to know anymore if he was awake or dreaming? I made myself dream through that whole business with the Farmers' Orchestra, trying to figure out what had been really going on. Two women with black wedding dresses. I harrowed through my brain looking for all the times I had seen Hilda Heinrichs and I was just about remembering what kind of shoes she had been wearing to drown in when I heard McKay unlocking my cell. "You've made bail," he said. "Too bad."

Well, I was pretty mixed up about that. I hadn't even tried to get in touch with anybody, but I didn't argue. I followed McKay to the front of the station. Rosmack Rampel leaned against the counter, her hands on her white motor-cycle helmet.

I started to ask, "Did you . . . ?" but she cut me off.

"Pick up your belt and shoelaces."

I reached for the clear plastic evidence bag McKay had placed on the counter.

"Sign first," he said, pointing to a pen and a clipboard. I signed. At least a part of my life got buckled up and tied together though one shoelace snapped and I had to leave two eyelets empty.

"Need a lift?" Rosmack asked. She put on her helmet.

"Yeah, sure."

Rosmack refused to talk. She just said, "Not now," to my questions. So I climbed up behind her on the Harley and let myself enjoy the ride. It was sure warmer in the noonday sun with pants on than it had been the night before with bare legs. I tried not to think what Mama would be like when I got home after she had worried all night long. I just held onto Rosmack's waist and leaned my head into the black leather of her jacket as she took the shortest route out of town and opened up the throttle on the highway. For about twenty minutes I let myself think it was all over and wished I could stay there in the shelter of her leather jacket with the ends of her long black hair tickling my nose. I closed my eyes and leaned with Rosmack's body whenever she made a turn and I didn't even try to guess which corner we had reached and I didn't move even when the motorcycle stopped and Rosmack cut the engine.

"Are you sleeping, Kjnals?"

Against my desire I separated from Rosmack's back and left a spot of sweat from my cheek on the black leather. I stumbled a little as I swung my leg off the bike.

"Thanks," I said.

She grinned, "Any time, old man."

"Where'd you get the bail money anyway?"

"That's what Kowolchuk wanted to know. I wouldn't tell him either."

"But you've got to tell me what's going on!"

Rosmack hesitated. "I'm sorry, Neil, but I can't tell you right now. I just can't."

"But how can I figure this thing out if I don't know what's going on?"

"You've got to trust me. Don't try to figure anything out, okay? Just try to be normal and do what you usually do. Trust and obey." Rosmack smiled a little when she said that, but she got serious right away. "Please, Neil. We could all get hurt."

"But can't I help?" I thought I was the detective.

Rosmack leaned over and kissed me on the cheek. "Of course you can, but not yet."

By this time Mama was standing at the picket fence gate watching us. "Trust me, Neil," Rosmack repeated as she kickstarted her Harley. I suddenly thought of something. I grabbed Rosmack's handlebar and said, "If you see Simple Hein, ask him what happened to the Shinkuhbein lady's shoe. He'll know what I mean."

"Okay, Neil," she said. She revved her motor, then let it idle for a second. "Meet me at Hauns Jaunses' Fraunz's waterhole tonight, say 9:00?" She winked at me and roared off down the driveway.

18

W ELL, of course, Mama wanted to know what was
going on. Where had I been all night and was it true what
they said on the party line that I had been in jail?

"Yes," I said, then quickly got her mind onto other things
by telling her I was hungry. Once I was sitting at the table I
asked her about Lena Bergen.

Mama sat down across from me and stared into the coffee
cup in her hands. The cup's ear was broken off, but Mama
still liked to use it, except when neighbours were visiting. It
was her last wedding cup. Her fingers shook a little, so little
I almost didn't see it, but I did. I felt ashamed because I knew
what was happening with Mama. She really wanted to talk
about my being in jail. That bothered her like it should bother
any mother, I guess, if her son was in jail, and as she looked
into the broken cup thinking about my question, I thought
she must be deciding if she was going to talk about something

easy like Lena Bergen, or if she was going to try to get to the bottom of her prodigal son. She took quite a long time to make up her mind. I thought I saw something leak from her eye into her cup, but I wasn't exactly looking Mama straight in the face. I tried to eat the cold sausages as if all was well with the world. Then it seemed the war inside her heart was over. She lifted the cup to her lips with both hands and shlurpst some coffee to signal me it was time to perk my ears up and listen.

"This Lena Bergen," she started. I felt a little warmed that she had decided to have faith in me, then thought maybe Mama was smart enough to figure if I asked about Lena Bergen it probably had something to do with what was happening to me and she would find out more by telling me what I wanted to know than by trying to make me talk about something I didn't want to discuss. "This Lena Bergen, how you heard about her?"

"Bulchi Wiebe, I mean Bient, told me she was Papa's second cous . . ." I stopped. Mama deserved better than that. I got up from the table and went to my room. I had to admire Mama. She might wonder herself about what I was doing but she never schneppaed around in my room anymore. She didn't even go in to clean up so I wouldn't be able to find anything after that. I returned with the photograph and the newspaper clippings and passed them to Mama.

"These were in that zipper Bible the bengel in the army jeep brought."

Mama stared at the picture. "Your papa when he was young, he looked just like you. But that Hitler flag. Where did that come from? I never saw that before." Mama turned the picture over and read the words on the back. "Yes, your father was a CO, but for sure he never went with Hitler. Who sent this?"

"I don't know yet." I told Mama about the other men who had received such pictures and showed her the part in the newspaper clipping about the woman murdered in Paraguay. I told her what Bulchi had said, that the woman was Papa's relative, Lena Bergen. I told her Barbara Ball Bearing's parents were relatives with Lena Bergen, too, and were down in South America visiting. "Do you know anything more about this woman?"

Mama closed her eyes and bent her neck back so her face pointed up toward the ceiling light that wasn't switched on. She stayed that way for maybe five minutes. Then she tilted her head back down and opened her eyes. "I think Lena Bergen married a Blatz, but that was after . . . no wait, maybe it was Hilda who married a Blatz."

"Hilda?"

"Hilda Heinrichs, the one . . ." I kicked myself because my question had made her stop and think. "No, that couldn't be, you say Lena Bergen is dead."

"What do you mean?"

"Nothing, my head was just thinking dummheit."

"What do you mean, dummheit?"

"Ach, forget it, it was just a dummheit idea that came into my head, and if Lena Bergen is dead, then such a thing couldn't be." Mama looked away.

"What couldn't be?"

Mama looked back at me and I saw from the corners of her eyes that she was trying not to laugher herself, but she couldn't hold it in, and her breasts started waving up and down inside her brown flowered dress, her shoulders knocked against her neck, tears dripped down her cheeks, and she threw her head back and rolled her eyes and I reached out to steady the chair because I was scared she would tip over backwards. Never before in my life had I seen Mama laughing such a hah hah hah and I started laughing, too, it was so funny to see.

But she wouldn't tell me the joke. I begged and I pleaded and I offered to wash her swollen feet, but Mama wouldn't tell me the joke. And I didn't know if the joke was important or not. Finally, Mama calmed down enough to tell me other things, only every so often she interrupted herself with another apron flap of laughing.

"We were talking about the Blatzes," Mama said. "Now Barbara Buhler, the one you call Barbara Ball Bearing—such shoontich names you young people use—well her mother was a Blatz . . . now let me think which Blatzes it was from, oh, Papa would have known this but he never wanted to talk about those that went to Paraguay and Mexico. He thought they were people who figured just because the Lord rode on an esel into Jerusalem we should ride donkeys, too, so we could go to Heaven, and I remember now how he told me he bought this farm cheap from a family that went south— and then they came back a year later and wanted the farm again for the same price. Papa just laughed and told them to go ride their burros in South America where the bulchi brot would fall from the sky just like it had for the children of Israel. Oh, your Papa could sure make schpott with his mouth when he was young, but he was never like that with me, and he did all this before we got married. He made such a good deal for this farm when he was only nineteen, and then he never bought any more land. . . ." Mama's voice trailed off into silence.

"Yeah, I remember now," I said. "One time I asked him how come we didn't buy more land, because Hingst Heinrichs was always bragging about how much land his father had, and Papa looked at me and said, 'I have only one son and no daughters, and that one son likes to keep his nose in the *Reader's Digest* more than he likes to take care of the fields. So how much land do I need?' "

"Yes, your Papa's family came from Russia because there was no more land for the people and he sometimes talked about what his grandfather had told him when he was a young bengel. If there was going to be enough land for everybody, then nobody should have too much. Your Papa was interesting that way. He could sure make schpott about the donkey riders who sold their land cheap but still he never tried to buy more land after he got such a good start when he was so young. There were good chances, even my father would have given him a good deal, because my brothers weren't that interested in farming after they finished going to high school. But your father only said no to that. Sure, nowadays, the farms are getting bigger all the time, but look at us. We have only one quarter and that even we have rented out."

I felt myself get very red in the face and thought I should be shaming myself because I wasn't farming the bit of land Papa had left to us. Instead, I was playing dummheit games that had got me into a lot of trouble, and if I couldn't get myself out of that trouble with a story that made sense I could be sitting on a bare mattress in Headingley or Stony Mountain for a long time.

The problem with stories is that even if you haven't got them finished yet you have to believe in them or you can't finish them. Even if you lose your faith you have to pretend; you have to find some sincerity inside you someplace, like a country singer singing a song that can make you cry even when the singer feels like laughing, and so I tried to pull my loose ends together, at least enough to get this mother-son talk about my father back to the information I was trying to get.

"Do you remember which family it was that Papa bought his farm from?"

"It was a Blatz family, but my family lived close to Rosenfeld, and I was ten years younger than your father so these people that lived here then, I didn't know them, and there are so many Blatzes, I don't know which ones they were."

So there I had still more strings but no way of braiding them into something that would help me. I was also worried that Mama would ask again about my being in jail and for sure I didn't want to tell her about dope charges, so I was just about ready to slip outside while she was clearing the table when I thought about another thing.

"Do you know anything about Schmuggle Veens's wife?"

Mama stopped with the catsup bottle in her hand. "Schmuggle Veens? Veens's wife?"

"Yeah, the one they call Schmuggle Veens's States wife."

"Schmuggle Veens's States wife? Now let me think . . . I know, I will phone up Haustich Neefeld's mumchi and see if she knows. All these people are turned drall in my head, but Haustich Neefeld's mumchi knows all these things." But before Mama got the receiver off the hook the phone rang. It was Oata Siemens and she was complaining and worried. Yasch had never come home from the auction sale yet and Hein had come home real late with a story that Yasch had driven away with Fleeda Shreeda. I said I would come right away.

But it wasn't that simple. The police had my Volkswagen so how was I going to travel? I thought of calling Rosmack, but she had told me to be patient and check for broken fences and stuff like that. I didn't feel like pedalling the bicycle and the old Farmall tractor had a mulberry thorn in the single front tire. That left Marie, the old mare Papa had brought home from his last trip to the stockyards. I hadn't ridden her since one muddy day in the spring and I wondered if a horse could get lonely. I wondered why Papa had brought home the mare, a week before he got sick. Had Papa had some secret longing for a horse he decided to fulfil before he died? What made people do the things they did anyway? Why had someone tried to blackmail him for something he had done without thinking when he was only a teenager?

Marie raised her nose when I whistled and trotted over to the gate where I waited with the bridle. She stood patiently while I slipped the bridle over her head and crawled up on her bare back. Marie wasn't used to galloping so she was quite happy to be tied up to Yasch Siemens's gatepost when we got there.

Oata looked like she had been crying as she sat at the kitchen table feeding the baby with a little spoon. "Kjnals, Kjnals, where could Yasch be? Hein said such awful gruelich things. Is it true?"

I told Oata what I knew and she didn't say if my story matched Hein's or not. I tried to make her feel better by telling her I didn't think Yasch was with Fleeda Shreeda because he had been in town with me and I begged myself forgiveness for having forgotten all about him when I was finished at the RCMP station, and that for sure I should have watched out for him because he had had a klutz on the head. Then I asked if she had phoned the hospital.

"Oh yeah sure, I phoned to the hospital but he's not there and the polices don't know nothing neither."

"Where's Hein?" I wanted to know.

"He was hitchhiking to town to get his combine from the Consumers."

"Hitchhiking?"

"Yeah, his bicycle was stolen and he doesn't have licence to drive our truck."

"Say, did you ask Yasch's muttachi if she has seen him?"

"Now how come I didn't think of that myself? You know if Yasch got himself a klutz on the head maybe he went back to being a bengel living with his muttachi. For sure the mental home is full with such people. Yeah, I'll phone there right away." Oata handed me the baby spoon and stood up to turn the crank on the old farmer phone there on the wall beside the dial phone.

For once in this story I was right about something. Yes, Yasch was at his muttachi's place. He had come into the house at 1:00 in the morning and had gone upstairs to his bed just like he was still living at home. When Oata wanted to know if Yasch had been drinking his muttachi said no, but his hair had been wet like he'd been swimming. "Did Yasch drive there with the car?" Oata asked and I heard his muttachi say no, she thought he had come with foot. So Oata said she would come and get him home with the truck.

The sun warmed us as I set off on Marie's back down Oata's long driveway in no hurry to go anywhere. Insects and wires hummed, and a red-winged blackbird chirped from a fence post. A garter snake wiggled across the road close to Penzel Panna's place and I noticed a broken strand of wire in the fence. No livestock had escaped and since I didn't have any tools to fix the wire I rode into Penzel's yard to mention it. Penzel's daughter, Shirley, was hanging clothes on the line, but before I could say anything to her Penzel called from his tool shed, "What do you want here, Kjnals?"

So I rode a little closer and told him about the broken wire and he said, "Yeah, I know about it. I'm going to fix it right away." He turned back into the tool shed, thought of something, looked back at me and said, "Oh yeah, thanks, Kjnals," and closed the door behind him. As I rode away I noticed Shirley and her mother watching me through the screen door of the house. The clothes basket was still on the grass under the line, half full of clothes.

I tried to make sense of the way Penzel Panna had acted and before I knew it the store corner was in sight and I decided to pick up the mail. Quite a few vehicles were parked in front of the store and a glance at my watch told me the mail had just arrived. I urged Marie into a gentle trot and in a few minutes we stopped in front of the store. I slipped off and tied the reins to the one remaining post of the old hitching rail.

Everybody stopped talking when I stepped into the store. No sound except the hum of the baloney slicer, where Store Janzen's Willy paused before sliding the big sausage back against the blade again. I walked down the hardware aisle toward the post office wicket at the back. The talk started again, very quiet talk, almost a whisper, but loud enough so I heard, "Corny the Dope," and "Corny Coke," and from the back corner Fuchtich Froese's son said, "Bergen's Bargain Blackmail." At the wicket Barley King Barkman looked down to see if his fly was open. So quietly I almost couldn't hear him, he said, "I never use a Bible with a zipper," and hurried himself away.

I didn't have the mailbox key so I asked Jack Janzen, home from Bible College in the States, to give me the one piece of mail in our box, a black business-sized envelope with my name written on it in white ink. "You got black mail today, eh?" Jack said. I just put the envelope into my shirt pocket and turned away. I considered having a Pepsi from the cooler and listening for a while, but I sure didn't feel comfortable in the store.

When I stepped across the street into the credit union, Count Floyd right away put up his hands and said, "Sorry, no numbered accounts here!" I let it go by and filled out a withdrawal slip for a few dollars, pocketed the money without counting it, and walked over to Shusta Paul's shop. Willy Wahl's wife, Serena, was leaning against the counter in her nylon stocking feet, watching Shusta Paul smear glue on the spike heel of her left shoe on his last. After he put the glue on he picked up a little block of rubber and nailed it onto the heel with one nail. Then he handed it to Serena who bent to slip her foot into it. Shusta Paul put the other shoe on the last and pried the little rubber piece off the heel. I remembered my flat tire in Oata's yard. "Do those little black things sometimes come off by themselves?" I asked Serena.

"Yeah, it can happen," she said, straightening up a little and rubbing her stocking foot against the ankle of her other foot. "It happened to me once when I had to walk a mile on a dirt road because I had a flat."

Shusta Paul handed her the other shoe and as I watched her slip it on her foot I wondered me how women could even walk on shoes like that.

Shusta Paul still hadn't said a word. Even after Serena left, he didn't greet me the way he usually did. I watched him carefully roll a cigarette, light it, and place a jet boot on the last. He still didn't say a word.

"You were right," I said. "Somebody was asking for money." Shusta Paul didn't reply. "I don't think they will ask for more, but I haven't figured out for sure who is behind it all." The shoemaker pried the heel off the jet boot and blew a cloud of smoke out of the corner of his mouth, but he didn't speak. So I told him what had happened, told him about the blackmail notes and how Fleeda and I had intercepted the Bibles at the auction, how Schmuggle Veens had made off with the disker full of zipper Bibles, and how I had ended up in jail. Shusta Paul kept working, never even pausing to take the cigarette from his lips. I told him what Barbara had told me about the threat to her parents. I didn't tell him about Rosmack Rampel's promise to meet me at Jaunses' Fraunz's pond. I didn't mention any murders. Shusta Paul still didn't speak so I worried about what else I could tell him. I remembered my conversation with Mama, and I asked, "Which Blatzes had my father's place before he bought it?"

Shusta Paul put down his knife and butted out his cigarette in the sardine can. He rolled another one. When it was fired up, he finally looked at me. "Mrs. Buhler was a Blatz before she married. Her brother, Herman Blatz in Paraguay, sold his farm to your father. They are part of the Birkenhead Blatzes. What it means, I don't know. I don't know."

As I rode away I tore open the black envelope. Inside was one of my business cards. On the back of it someone had printed, "Drugs dope and dummheit." That didn't exactly brighten up my day.

The word dummheit started buzzing around in my brain like a mosquito on a hot summer night and I could hear again Mama's hah hah hah and how she had said over and over, "No, that couldn't be!" What couldn't be? It had something to do with Hilda Heinrichs and Lena Bergen. Only it couldn't be if Lena Bergen was dead. For sure it couldn't be so funny if someone was dead. But I had been sure the doll woman was dead, but now she was alive, playing harp in the Farmers' Orchestra, instead of marrying herself with A.Dyck's brother,

L.U.Dyck, in Niagara Falls. Dummheit. Who could explain this dummheit to me?

Then I remembered something else and I turned Marie around and galloped her back to Shusta Paul's shop. He was alone when I barged in.

"Who is Schmuggle Veens's States wife?" I panted.

"Schmuggle Veens's wife is Boyes' Leench."

"Boyes' Leench? You mean Lena Bergen?"

"Yes, Lena Bergen."

"Schmuggle Veens's wife is Lena Bergen? From Paraguay?"

"Yes, from Paraguay and Kansas and B.C. and wherever else Schmuggle Veens's slippery business takes him."

"So then Lena Bergen isn't dead?"

"Not Schmuggle Veens's Lena Bergen."

"If Lena Bergen isn't dead then Mama's joke could be!"

"Joke?"

"Yeah, what's the joke about Lena Bergen and Hilda Heinrichs?"

"Hilda Heinrichs and Lena Bergen? What's the joke?"

"Yeah, the joke that's so funny Mama almost laughers herself dead but she won't tell me."

"Well, Kjnals, I don't know what this would have to do with anything that is happening nowadays. I mean it's funny all right, but it's just a story that mightn't even be true, you know how things get braided from a few ends of binder twine into a whole rope, but it was a funny story, it even makes me laugh. It happened only a little while before the accident with the pig and so I don't really know if I should tell you such a thing. It is water under the bridge and dragging mud up from the bottom again, Kjnals, I don't know if it's a good idea, I mean, your Mama wouldn't tell you neither, but it sure was funny, even if A.Dyck and L.U.Dyck didn't think so at the time. . . ." And then Shusta Paul couldn't help himself either and he started laughing at the same time he took a big puff of his Player's roll-your-own and he started to cough and I thought for sure he was going to cough himself to death, only it's not that easy to kill an old smoker. But it was almost killing me, this not knowing what the hartsoft funny joke was that nobody wanted to tell me. A.Dyck and L.U.Dyck? Accident with the pig? Hilda Heinrichs and Lena Bergen?

Finally, Shusta Paul took off his little wire eyeglasses and wiped the tears from his eyes with a brown handkerchief. He put a black Sunday shoe on his last. "You see, Kjnals, at one time those two bachelors were real lover boys and L.U.Dyck was interested in Hilda Heinrichs. A.Dyck was after Lena Bergen. Hilda and Lena are cousins and they looked a little bit like each other, especially when they combed their hair the same way and Lena took off her glasses. So anyway, the two girls decided to see if they could fool the two brothers. See, A.Dyck used to wait behind the Bergens' beckhouse in the dark for Lena to come out. L.U.Dyck used to do the same at the Heinrichses' beckhouse. So the girls switched places, Hilda went to the Bergen beckhouse and Lena went to the Heinrichs beckhouse and the bachelors didn't notice the difference in the dark and the girls per-suaded the brothers to change wristwatches with them and the brothers agreed and then the next Sunday when they were going to the Sunday Night Christian Endeavour with the right girls each brother noticed that his girlfriend had his brother's watch on. So the two brothers almost had a fight right in the middle of the children's story at the Christian Endeavour. Then the next week the accident with the pig happened and Hilda Heinrichs wouldn't have anything more to do with L.U.Dyck because it was A.Dyck's pig."

"What happened to A.Dyck and Lena Bergen?"

"The Bergens moved to Paraguay and she married Schmuggle Veens."

"Would A.Dyck still recognize her?"

"Could be."

I brooded over all this as Marie followed her nose toward home. One minute I thought I had it all figured out, that I knew who was dead and who wasn't. Then the next minute I was thinking if that was Hilda, then the other one had to be Lena, only how could Lena be there when Hilda was supposed to be there and even then Yetta Hiebat was still dead without any bones. I had confused myself so much by the time we neared the church I decided to stop in at the graveyard. But my father's grave had no answers. I felt like I was cut off from him because I had been in jail. I felt a little angry with him, too, for having passed the snooping habit on to me, this habit that had caught me in behind the manure spreader again.

I left the horse tied to the tree at the back of the graveyard and wandered over to the church. Maybe I could find some clues to the dummheit that had been going on there. I always felt spooky when I entered the church alone. I didn't know why, after all it was just a building, but I guess it was because a person hardly ever went there alone. It was a place where there should be people. I walked through the double doors, down the aisle, looking for signs that something was amiss, but all the pews seemed normal, the pulpit held no surprises, the choir loft held only hymnbooks and a States quarter lay on the tenors' bench. The little ministers' room on one side of the front was almost bare—two chairs and a small table with some old church bulletins lying on it. I crossed over to the other side of the church and went down the back stairs to the basement. Nothing in the Sunday School rooms gave me a clue. I came up the front stairs, looked into the baby room on the women's side, looked in the mirror beside the men's coat rack and climbed to the balcony. Nothing. I sat down on one of the benches and let the feeling of gloom settle over me.

I must have dozed off, because I dreamed I was running over a suspension bridge and zipper Bibles were falling on me from the beams overhead. I awoke hearing footsteps below me. I peered over the edge of the balcony and saw Barbara Ball Bearing tiptoeing down the aisle. She had a zipper Bible in her hand and she placed it in the middle book rack on the back of the third pew. Then she tiptoed back up the aisle and I watched the jiggle of her breasts inside her tight sweater. She didn't look up, she didn't see me. When she passed underneath the balcony, I crept to the window. A moment later she hurried to her old Dodge pickup and drove away.

I felt even more depressed then, thinking whatever was going on was still going on. Barbara must still be helping the dope dealers. I wondered what new threat they had used on her. Then I thought a new threat wasn't necessary, the threat to her parents would be enough for anyone. I sat down on the balcony pew again, thinking somebody would come for the Bible Barbara had left. So I waited, thinking about Barbara, wishing I could throw my arms around her to keep her from harm, and myself from harm, wished I could rest in her softness, and then I was hiding in the willows beside the pond again and Rosmack and Barbara were swimming in the green water, naked, my eyes bulging as different patches of skin broke the surface of the water and then a voice behind me said, "Which are you, Schneppa Kjnals or Neil Bergen, Investigator?" and the doll woman stood there in her black wedding dress all dripping wet with green scum hanging down from her hair like a veil and her big brown eyes blinked through her round rimless glasses, blinked together like a doll, and she asked, "Where is my grandfather clock?" Before I could reply she raised the black lacy hems of her skirts and asked, "Where is my ankle bracelet?" I reached down to my ankle and remembered I had taken it off at home last night before Kowolchuk led us to the States. And the doll woman asked again, "Which are you, Schneppa Kjnals or Neil Bergen, Investigator?" And in my other ear my father's voice said, "Ask! Ask!" And then Rosmack and Barbara stepped out of the water, green scum clinging to their naked bodies, and they pointed their fingers at me and laughed, and for a second I saw myself from above, huddling in the willows with a stiff one in my pants, being laughed at by two naked girls, and then I heard footsteps in the church.

The inside of the church had grown dusky and as I peered over the edge of the balcony I made out a figure tiptoeing down the aisle toward the pew where Barbara had put the Bible, but I couldn't tell who it was. I tiptoed down from the balcony and crept to the double doors that led into the church and listened as the footsteps tiptoed nearer and nearer. As the door opened, the figure emerged and I embraced it. There was a gasp of surprise and then I realized I was hugging a struggling woman, a strong struggling woman, and it took all the power I had to wrestle her to the floor. Her Elvis Presley T-shirt rose and fell with her chest as she panted. I was sitting on Yetta Hiebat!

"You're not dead!"

"D-Dead?" Yetta tried to push me away. I was still holding down her shoulders. I quickly let go and got off her. She sat up. "A-A-Are you trying to kill me?"

"K-Kill you? Didn't you die in the fire at the trailer?"

"What are you talking about?"

"Well, when your husband's trailer burned down he couldn't find you when he got home, and in the morning when I looked through the ashes I found bones and I thought you had died in the fire."

"You thought wrong, Schneppa Kjnals. You thought wrong. I never even heard about the fire till I came home today. I wasn't ever in that trailer. So how could I die in it?"

I didn't know what to say to that, but Yetta wasn't finished talking. "What's loose with you anyways? I come into the church to get my Bible and I have to wrestle in the dark like Jacob, only it's no angel who throws me on the floor and sits on me. And then he tells me yet that I should be dead!"

"When did you forget that Bible in the church?"

Yetta started to reach for the Bible where it had fallen to the floor but I grabbed it first. "Give it to me!" she said, but I held it out of her reach and said again, "When did you forget this Bible in the church?"

"Well, of course, on Sunday!"

"Never saw you in church on Sunday."

"You don't see everything, Schneppa Kjnals!"

"On Sunday Hilda Heinrichs gave me a Bible to give to you. I put it in your hand at the Tax-Free Tuesday Toot. I gave it to you on the street."

"I don't know what you're talking about. I told you I forgot my Bible in the church on Sunday and I came to get it."

"How come you didn't get it sooner?"

"I told you I wasn't home till today. Don't you ever wash your corny ears?"

"Where were you till today?"

"None of your business."

"How come I saw Barbara Ball Bearing bring this Bible to the church only an hour ago?"

"You must have been dreaming it. Now give it here."

"I wasn't dreaming that. I saw Barbara put that Bible in the third bench from the front and now I saw you get that same Bible. So tell me what's going on!"

"Give it here, you schneppa naze!" She grabbed for the Bible again, but I reached for the wall and flicked on the lights. She took hold of the Bible but I pulled it from her hand and quickly zipped it open. A bundle started to fall out but I caught it and held it up high. It was a bundle of thousand-dollar bills tied with a charm bracelet with a swastika on it. Yetta's face was white. Her hand darted to the light switch and it was dark again. I could hear her breathing heavy. "Kjnals, this isn't funny. This is real dangerous, really dangerous."

19

I gripped the money in the darkness. The swastika chain pressed into the chicken drumstick part of my hand. Yetta was breathing heavily and I could smell a bit of old perfume mixed up with her sweat. I wished what she had said was true, that I had dreamed it, because then I could have awakened myself out of the dream, or willed the dream to do what I wanted it to without worrying about whether it was right or wrong or good or bad or if it might bother somebody. I could have stopped the dream, killed it, buried it in the sand and started fresh. I could have given up trying to make a story out of all these thousand-dollar bills and women who wrestled me in the dark. I could have pulled my nose out of where it wasn't supposed to go and stopped sniffing smells that couldn't be out of a dream. For a moment I thought I really could wake up, that I could just leave. Indeed, there was nothing making me keep on with this dummheit. Even Kowolchuk didn't care what I did and would probably drop the charges if I wet my pants for him a little. A whole manure spreader load of Damascus quality light hit me and I saw a way. I could just put the thousand-dollar bills into Yetta's hand, take one last noseful of perfume and sweat and walk outside to the graveyard, get on Marie's back, ride her all the way to the North Pole to play with myself and nobody would care if I ever made a story out of anything. Nobody would care. I was at a crossroad in a blizzard and all the farmers' yardlight bulbs had burned out. No matter which road I chose it would be the one less travelled by . . . only it suddenly seemed to me that that wasn't true either, that all the roads were untravelled by me and I was all alone in the blizzard. All alone.

Except for a noseful of perfume and sweat. Maybe it was a case of being led around by the nose but at least it was better than freezing at the crossroad. The chain with the swastika charm was in my hand. There was no ring in my nose, or on my finger either, and I had a problem men with rings on their fingers don't have—how do you get a woman to *start* talking? The only way I could figure this story out was if Yetta would tell me what she knew. I was no better off than a doctor who can't heal you if you don't tell him what's wrong with you—I mean, maybe even God has this problem, that even though He knows it all you still have to *tell* Him about it to make the story or why would there be such a thing as confession of sins, except maybe that isn't God's idea at all, only something invented by those who like to hear stories people don't want to tell. Of course, it's risky thinking such things in a church in the dark when you can smell the sweat and perfume of a woman you have just wrestled to the floor—another man's wife you thought was dead. You finally have to face it—you are just spinning your tires with thoughts that have nothing to do with putting bread on the table or getting on with the business of being a schneppa naze.

Well, Yetta figured I had been spinning my tires long enough, too, and I don't know what she was thinking all that time in the dark with me there, and I don't know if she could smell my sweat and the horse's sweat, or what she thought about having wrestled with me, Schneppa Kjnals, young enough to be her son. Not all women wait till they're a hundred like Abraham's wife in the Bible, so such a thing is possible, but if Yetta was wondering about stuff like that during the three days we stood there in the dark, she didn't tell me about it. Why should she confess to me? I wasn't a High Priest or even a Levite. Still, Yetta had her story and it was pressing her and it couldn't be held up much longer. Maybe that was the difference between us. I wanted to fit pieces into a puzzle and Yetta needed to move the story ahead. That seemed to be what was important, moving the story ahead. And since my nose was in the story, like it or not, I had to go along.

"Kjnals," she said. "We've got to get out of here. Give me the money and the Bible. I don't have much time!"

"Okay," I said. "But I'm coming with you!"

Yetta waited until the Bible was zipped up in her hand before she whispered, "Neil, it's more complicated than you think. Don't follow me. Go home." And as she was telling me this in her windy whisper her Bible-free hand pulled down my zipper and for a moment I couldn't follow her out of the church even in the dark. Who would have thought a Gutenthal woman could think of such a thing?

But for once the spirit was stronger than the flesh. I zipped after her and by the time Yetta was shifting the car into drive I was sitting beside her in the front seat of her LTD. She glared at me in the flash of dim light before I slammed the door, then she jerked the car forward, spun tires in the gravel and we shot out of the church yard.

"Should have left you in jail," she said as the speedometer needle jumped to sixty. She pulled out the headlight switch and I pushed at the floor with my right foot as the post road stop sign loomed in the sudden glare. Yetta slowed just enough to skid around the corner. The zipper Bible slammed over the speedometer hump into the corner of the windshield. The needle leaped back up to sixty. Yetta grabbed the zipper Bible. "Here, count the money. We could be dead if it's short!"

I zipped open the Bible. Yetta flicked on the interior light and watched me pull the bills from between the pages. I counted thirty bills, all thousands. "Thirty dollars," I said. Yetta almost jerked the car into a skid.

"Thirty thousand?"

"Yes." She got control of the car again.

"So tell me what's going on," I said.

"I can't tell you. It's too dangerous."

"This is drug money, isn't it?"

"Don't ask! I can't tell you!"

"Somebody is smuggling drugs to the reserve, right?"

"Please, it's none of your business."

"It is my business. I'm Schneppa Kjnals. And I've been charged with all kinds of offences because somebody planted drugs in my car, so it is my business."

"I know."

"So tell me, or I'll have to get tough."

"You're not so tough, not so tough as them."

I opened the window about an inch and peeled the top thousand-dollar bill from the stack. I held it near the window. "Should I let go?"

"No, don't, they'll kill me if any money is missing!"

"Who?"

"The ones who killed Hilda!"

"Hilda Heinrichs?"

"Yeah, they killed her when a Bible with money went missing."

"Who killed her?"

"The drug people, and they tried to kill me, too!"

"How did they kill her?"

"They drowned her in the pond. Supposed to look like suicide."

"Are you sure she's dead?"

"Yeah, I saw her body in the pond."

"When?"

"On Tuesday night. Right after you gave me the Bible in town."

At last I had a witness to back up my story. Somebody had drowned in that pond. But it hadn't been Hilda Heinrichs. I had seen her alive. Or had I? "How come you didn't say anything?"

"I was too scared. I had a delivery to make and I had just found out we weren't playing games anymore, and you really scared me when you gave me that Bible in town, and then I saw Hilda's car on the Heinrichs yard and I found her in the pond and I got so scared I just drove away as fast as I could and I was almost by Emerson before I remembered the delivery, but the trailer exploded before I got there."

"You were supposed to deliver something to the trailer?"

"Yeah, a zipper Bible full of dope. But the trailer blew up

before I got there and I drove away as fast as I could. I went home but before my husband came home from the fire they had contacted me and told me the trailer was a warning and then they told me what to do."

"Who?"

"I never saw any of them except Hilda."

"How did they contact you?"

"Phone."

"Was it a man or a woman?"

"Couldn't say. It was a young person anyways."

"What did he say?"

"Bible verse."

"Bible verse?"

"Yeah, they use Bible verses to send messages."

"So what was the verse?"

"Ephesians 5:12, 'For it is a shame even to speak of those things which are done of them in secret,' and Genesis 2:17, 'But of the tree of knowledge of good and evil, thou shalt not eat of it: for in the day that thou eatest thereof thou shalt surely die.'"

"So what did you do?"

"I drove as fast as I could to the yard in Blarney where Grandmother Blatz used to live and I put the zipper Bible under the apple tree in the garden there."

"How come you went there?"

"I just knew that was what I had to do."

"But how?"

Yetta hesitated. "It was the Garden of Eden to us kids. See, Hilda and me were cousins with the Blatzes and one time the boys found a snake in the garden and Ernst said it was the devil and then somebody said we should play Adam and Eve. Ernst and Hilda were bigger than me and Jakie so they made us be Adam and Eve with no clothes on and Hilda was holding the snake and playing like she was the devil and I had to pick a green apple from the tree and give some to Jakie to eat and then Ernst came with a willow stick and he chased us out of the garden because he was God and Grandmother almost saw us but we were hiding behind some raspberry bushes and Jakie pushed me into the bush so I got pickers into . . ." Yetta slammed on the brakes so suddenly that I almost bounced my head off the windshield.

"Oh you schneppa naze, you made me go the wrong way with all your questions! I'm supposed to take the Bible to the beetfield by Hauns Jaunses' Fraunz's waterhole!"

"How do you know that's the right place?" I asked as she turned the car around in three jerks.

"He leadeth me beside the still waters, stupid, you know, the place where you peek at Rosmack Rampel when she's swimming!"

"You know about that?"

"Yeah, that's how all this started."

"What started?"

"The jokes, the zipper Bibles, the brassieres."

"The red one, too?"

"Yeah, the red one, too. We stole it from Preacher Janzen's wife's line."

"And the blackmail notes, those are yours, too?"

"Blackmail notes? What you mean, blackmail notes?"

"Nazi pictures, zipper Bibles, CCIL diskers with seeder boxes, ten thousand dollars, auction sales."

"Don't know what you're talking about."

"Your husband was blackmailed. Brought ten thousand dollars in a zipper Bible to the auction sale in Neualtbergfeld. Him and five others."

"My husband? Ten thousand dollars? Zipper Bibles?"

The planks of the double dike bridge rattled as we passed over.

"Yeah. . . ."

"Shut up, we're almost there!" Yetta took her foot off the gas pedal and let the car coast to Hauns Jaunses' Fraunz's driveway. As she turned into the yard the headlights wiped over the old barn and the house and stopped on the shape of the '51 Ford. Yetta jerked the car to a stop. "That's where I'm supposed to leave the Bible," she whispered.

"In the '51 Ford?" I whispered back. "How do you know?"

"Joshua 2:7, 'And the men pursued after them the way to Jordan unto the fords,' " Yetta whispered. "I didn't know what it meant, but I do now."

"How do you know that's the right Ford?"

"See any other Ford? Give me the Bible."

"What are you going to do?"

"Take it to that car, dummkopp! Give it here."

"No, I'll take it. It's too dangerous for you."

"No, don't! If they find out you're here, too, they'll kill us!"

"Turn off your lights so I can see in the dark!"

"No, give it here . . . !" But her whisper died as I jumped out of the car and tiptoed toward the '51 Ford. Yetta's headlights washed over me as she swung her car around. I heard her tires spin behind me, heard her clunk the transmission as she shifted around the corner, heard the clitter of gravel as she sped away.

Moonlight glinted from the door handle on the woman's side of the car and I saw the hole where the shotgun shell had been. The window was rolled down. I peered into the car. It seemed empty. I reached in and lifted the lever handle. The door opened but the interior light didn't go on. I slipped into the front seat and closed the door. I rested the zipper Bible beside me on the seat and looked out the window on the driver's side. The shadow of the yard pole pointed toward the willows of the waterhole hump. Nothing stirred. I looked out all the windows. Not a light was moving.

It had been a long time since I had been inside a '51 Ford. In the moonlight I could make out the little triangle on the crossbar of the steering wheel that showed where to press to honk the horn. Behind the wheel, in the round speedometer I could see the needle indicator with the ring resting at zero. I leaned over to see how many miles this antique had on it and saw the keys were in the ignition on the left side of the wheel. Suddenly, I thought I had another chance to save myself and do something good at the same time. I had Yasch Siemens's car with the keys in it. I had a zipper Bible full of drug money. I could drive away and give the car back to Yasch. I could take the money to the cops and tell them about Yetta. They could pick her up and she could tell them what she told me. I mean, if Yetta and Hilda weren't murdered then I really just had to get myself out of the dope charges. Maybe it was Hilda in the pond, but she wasn't all the way drowned and my mouth to mouth really worked, only I didn't stay long enough to see her revive and that's how come she had a cold at the Farmers' Orchestra practice. So I slid over behind the wheel and reached for the ignition keys.

But before I could turn the key I heard laughing and then water splashing and more laughing, a woman and then a man laughing and talking and splashing in Flat German. I heard it sitting there in the dark '51 Ford with my hand on the keys and my head froze with a picture of Rosmack and Beitelkopp swimming naked, splashing and laughing naked in Flat German under the laughing full moon in Jaunses' Fraunz's laughing pond and I felt my blood pushing at the valves of my heart like frozen beer. Then I was blinded by the brightest headlights I had ever looked into and more headlights splashed over me from behind and I made out the Bible van in front of me and the grey army jeep behind me and over the mumbling of their motors I heard the rumble of a motorcycle and then I saw Rosmack's white helmet and her black hair flowing back and I heard the jerking sound of a rifle bolt behind me and I turned and saw the army bengel aiming a rifle over the hood of the jeep and I cried, "He's going to shoot Rosmack!" I jumped from the '51 Ford waving the zipper Bible and I ran toward Rosmack shouting, "Duck Rosmack! Duck!" A shot shattered the air and a streak of pain whipped my ass and as I tumbled forward I heard the splashing Flat German laughter for a second and then there were two seconds of remembering silence while I wished I had had two Gideon Testaments in my back pockets. I screamed the impossible scream, the scream you never hear when somebody is shot on TV. Shooting on TV is always such a clean, easy ending, such a peace-be-still solution. And I screamed again as I felt the seat of my pants getting wet and Rosmack Rampel knelt beside me, crying out, "Help! Help! Kjnals is shot!" And I heard the distant drone of an airplane and then more cars and motorcycles rumbled close to my ears and I heard doors opening and feet running and voices shouting.

"What's going on?"

"Holy shit, somebody's shot!"

A woman's voice, "We've got a first aid kit in the car!"

"I'll get it!"

Rosmack turned me over onto my back, trying to help me,

but when my rear touched the rough earth I screamed, "I'M
SHOT IN THE ASS!" Hands grabbed at me all over and turned
me back on my front.

"Jeez, look at the blood!"

"Pull off his pants. We've got to stop the bleeding!"

Hands grabbed my hipbones and raised me up while other
hands opened my belt buckle and unzipped me and still other
hands peeled the pants from my bloody posterior. I felt cool
fingers on my burning skin. "Hey, shine that flashlight here,"
said another woman's voice. "He's lucky, it just looks like a
graze. Doesn't look like any bones are hit." Then I felt gauze
being pressed down on my pain and tape stuck to my skin
and the same woman's voice saying, "Okay, we can pull his
pants up again."

Another woman said, "Wait. Let's give him those pants
we have in the car. They won't be so tight. Besides, those
are his anyway."

"Right," giggled another woman's voice, but then even my
whirling thoughts were drowned out by Bulchi Wiebe's
knocking airplane engine as he swooped over the yard. I felt
a drop of water on my head and I thought, oh no, it's going
to rain on top of everything yet, and I opened my eyes and
saw a pair of muddy bare feet joined to bare legs that
disappeared up into Fleeda Shreeda's dripping wet Africa
dress. Beside her stood Yasch Siemens, wearing a pair of
muddy high-top workboots on the wrong feet. There was a
rushing noise as the airplane touched down on the field road
and then the knocking engine got noisier and noisier as the
plane taxied into the yard, stirring up such a blast of dust and
gravel as it turned around I thought the bandage would blow
right off my ass. I closed my eyes against the wind but I
thought I felt Fleeda crouch down in her wet dress, then rise

quickly again, and I felt drops of water as if her skirt was shaking.

The plane's engine died and I forced my chin up onto my hands. I opened my eyes to see shadows climbing from the plane. Schmuggle Veens came charging into the light, waving a little leather folder with a picture ID card in it. The States wife was right behind, only she wasn't wearing short shorts this time. Instead she was wearing some shiny purple pants so tight they looked painted on and she had high heels on both feet. She looked like a dancer as she waved her leather folder. Bulchi Wiebe's belly came ploughing out of the shadows. Bulchi, too, waved a leather folder. Simple Hein galloped right after him, holding up the shotgun shell that belonged to the door of the '51 Ford. When Hein saw me he stopped, studied my behind, then bent to whisper in my ear, "Schinkuhfleisch don't look so good, Kjnals. Have to stand up in the beckhouse for a few days." I closed my eyes against the pain. Then Schmuggle Veens asked, "Where's Ernst Blatz?"

Somehow my father's spirit surged through me and all my nerves shifted their allegiance from the pain in my ass to my eardrums so I could clearly hear the babble of voices above me.

"Ernst Blatz?"

"That army kid's dad!"

"His dad?"

"Yeah, his dad, at least the army kid called him dad."

"It's Ernst who is doing all this?"

"Yeah," said the States wife. "Ernst Blatz was the one who sent the Bibles with the pictures."

"We didn't know who had sent those pictures," said Schmuggle Veens, "and we were a little bit scared and we even got the money ready but then we decided to see if we could get our money back by buying the disker. But we hadn't figured there would be any guns. And now someone is shot."

"Just doing my job, folks," said the voice of the Bible van salesman. "Agent Ernst Blatz, CIA Special War on Drugs Squad. And this is my son, Corny Blatz, Little Bush Eagle Explorer Scout, holder of thirty-seven merit badges including Firearm Safety and the NRA Right to Bear Arms Shield. You have the right to remain silent. . . ."

"Just a minute, Blatz," cut in Hova Jake. "You're in Canadian hot water here. Inspector Jack Harder, CSIS Undercover Anti-Contra, Anti-Sandinista, Anti-American Narcotics Division. You don't have the right to remain silent, but whatever you say will be used against you. I'm holding you for questioning."

"You're bluffing, Harder," answered Blatz. "I've got you red-handed with your drug operation and communist connections. I've got international authority as outlined in the secret agreement between the President and the Prime Minister."

"Secret agreement, my foot," answered Hova Jake. "You're the one smuggling the drugs into Canada. Pretty clever operation with your zipper Bibles."

"I think you guys are both drug dealers," said a woman's voice, the voice that had been in charge of bandaging my ass.

"Who are you?"

"Special Constable Madonna Smith, RCMP."

"Special Constable Tina Mulroney, RCMP."

"Special Constable Juice McKay, RCMP."

"Special Constable Carly Siemens, RCMP."

"Special Constable Luba Turner, RCMP."

"By the authority vested in us by the Wunnimin Band

Council and the Crown, I arrest you all on suspicion of trafficking illegal substances to the Wunnimin Reserve."

"Yeah," cut in Beitelkopp Blatz. "Sergeant Bernie Blatz, RCMP Narcotics, Prairie Division. I back these girls all the way. The jig is up, Jack."

"Since when did the RCMP let the Hell's Angels in?" Hova Jake challenged. "And who are all the rest of these people, your pushers?"

"Sam Weins," answered Schmuggle Veens. "International Joint Committee Civilian Spotter. And my wife, Lena, has credentials, too."

"Ben Wiebe," said Bulchi Wiebe. "International Joint Flying Farmers Civilian Spotter."

"Me?" said Hein. "I tell Bulchi Wiebe about dunnasche big bang close to the bridge. See, shotgun shell for '51 Ford."

I think I must have moaned or groaned or even screamed because suddenly Rosmack cried, "Can't you see Kjnals is shot and needs an ambulance? Doesn't even one of you fancy secret police have at least a cellular . . . ?"

Rosmack's words were cut off by a siren and blinking red lights and then Kowolchuk's voice boomed over a loudhailer and I will never again laugh at the moustache kids, even if I see them in their Smokey the Bear hats and their red tunics stretched over their beer bellies when the queen comes to visit. Kowolchuk and McKay had things under control very quickly. By the time the ambulance arrived the whole kit and kaboodle had been disarmed and handcuffed and loaded onto the Bible van.

Rosmack climbed into the back of the ambulance beside me and just before the door was slammed shut I heard Yetta Hiebat's voice shouting, "IF YOU ARE ALL POLICES, THEN HOW COME YOU HAD TO KILL HILDA?"

20

THEY say when a person is drowning his whole life flashes in front of him. But in the ambulance I wasn't worried about my flashing life. Not with Rosmack Rampel kneeling beside me holding my hand. The warmth of her hand made my pain seem just what it was—a pain in the ass. But my ears had other ideas. They rang with Yetta Hiebat's cry, "If you are all polices, then how come you had to kill Hilda?" I couldn't forget Hilda Heinrichs's cold cold body and how Yetta had found it, too. Had I really seen Hilda with the Farmers' Orchestra? And what about the bones after the explosion at the trailer just before Yetta got there? Had I really heard all those things while I was bleeding on the ground? Could it be true that everybody was a police trying to stop the drug smugglers? What kind of a story could it be if everybody was a good guy? I was in more of a blizzard than ever and all I could think of was that I had been made a fool of again. I mean, I was a good guy, I thought. I was the detective. So how come it was me that got shot? That wasn't how things were supposed to work. Why me? Was it so I wouldn't be in the way? What had I done to get in anybody's way? Then I wasn't so sure of myself anymore about whether I was that important for anything or if I was really just somebody who bungled things up that others were trying to do and I thought about Barbara and Rosmack and wondered if after this I would have any chance at all with a woman and I wondered if I would turn out like A.Dyck, all alone in his old age, or like Simple Hein somehow trying to get away from other people's simple-minded ideas about him and I wondered if he would have to return the combine once the dust settled, because the money he found in the zipper Bible on the road must have been part of all this somehow and I wondered if the men who had been blackmailed would get their money back right away or if the money would be seized as evidence and then be stuck in the court system till long after court was over and then I was thinking that my Volkswagen was in the same boat and how was I going to get money to buy some other transportation when it sure didn't seem like I would get much work with my good-neighbour-for-a-fee schneppa business after this was over. I thought again that if I had never picked up Oata Siemens's zipper Bible from her father's grave I wouldn't be in such a manure tank situation, when a marble shook itself loose in the vacuum cleaner bag of my head and then it was all I could do to stay there in the ambulance on the stretcher with Rosmack Rampel holding my hand.

When I woke up I was being loaded off from the ambulance at the hospital in town. In the operating room the doctor got the splinters from the army bengel's wooden .303

bullet out of my rear. I was lucky the bullet hadn't hit the bone. But I heard the doctor say I would have to stay in hospital for a few days because there could be leftover slivers from the wooden bullet that might cause infection. And of course I had to lie on my front the whole time.

So in between going in and out of the operating room and getting needles in the seat of knowledge and enemas and bed pans and tubes in and out of just about every place on my body, I got to hear the part of the story that I didn't know from all the visitors I had. Of course, Mama came and sat beside me the whole time and she even rented me a phone to use from the hospital, only they don't have party line in town anymore so I think Mama was a little disappointed that she couldn't listen in. Rosmack sat there most of the time, too, and when Mama wasn't looking she would hold my hand. We didn't talk much, at least the first two days when the nurses kept shooting me full of drugs to kill the pain. I couldn't think so good or talk either and besides I heard the nurse warn Mama and Rosmack that if they wanted to stay with me they shouldn't talk very much. Every once in a while it seemed like Constable Kowolchuk was sticking his head in the door, or other times it seemed like Hova Jake was looking in, and one time when Rosmack and the nurse were helping me to use the bed pan I was sure I saw Beitelkopp Blatz and one of the Special Constables, Madonna Smith or maybe Tina Mulroney, watching through a crack in the curtain the nurse had pulled around my bed. And sure enough, during visiting hours on the second day, Schmuggle Veens's States wife walked into my room all dressed up in a skirt that was maybe too short, but she had to show off the rhinestones on her nylons somehow. At least I thought it was the States wife, because who else would show off her legs like that, but before I could decide if it was worth the pain to turn enough to be able to look up to see her face, the matron had hurried her out of the room. That's when I decided I needed to talk to Rosmack alone.

Even Mama had to use the washroom sometime, so lucky for me this hospital was old enough not to have a toilet in the room. About five minutes after I heard on the loudspeaker that visiting hours were over, Mama got up from her chair and walked out.

"Rosmack," I whispered. Rosmack knelt by the bed and took my hand. I looked into her shiny black eyes. For a few seconds I just wanted to keep looking into her eyes until I could get enough nerves together to ask her the real important question about why she was spending all this time sitting with me in the hospital. But how can a person answer a question like that? And even if there is an answer maybe the truth would be something a person didn't really want to know. Besides, what use is a person in this world if he just melts like a snowman in May when he's looking into a woman's eyes, especially when she is only seventeen?

So I squeezed Rosmack's hand a little and whispered, "How come you wanted me to meet you at Jaunses' Fraunz's pond?"

Rosmack didn't say anything for a minute, then I whispered, "Mama will be back soon."

"W-w-well, you see Fleeda thought . . ."

"You mean Fleeda Shreeda is in this with you?"

"Well, not exactly, but . . ."

But Mama poked her head into the room just then and again I was kicking myself for interrupting, only somebody must have said some kind of prayer because Mama said, "I'm going to go to Wiebe's Little Hospital Store for a while. Maybe you can sleep."

I squeezed Rosmack's hand more tightly and whispered, "What did Fleeda think?"

"W-well, I don't know if I should tell you this but Fleeda said if you were out of jail, for sure you would mix something up and make trouble for the other guys."

"Other guys?"

"Yeah, Beitelkopp and Hova Jake. That's why she told me to bail you out with the money from the zipper Bible."

"You mean Beitelkopp's Bible from the graveyard at the reserve?"

"Yeah, it had two thousand dollars in it."

"And Fleeda told you to bail me out with that?"

"Yeah, see Beitelkopp was trying to set up Hova Jake in the church with a zipper Bible full of money."

"You mean those two aren't in this together?"

"Oh no. Each one was trying to catch the other one and Barbara was caught in the middle."

"You mean Hova Jake and Beitelkopp were both trying to get her on their side?"

"That's right, so Barbara told Fleeda she was making a drop at the church for Beitelkopp."

"And Hova Jake was supposed to pick this Bible up?"

"Yeah, I think so, only Fleeda got Yetta to switch the Bibles in the church."

"I know, I caught her there."

"That wasn't supposed to happen."

"Well, you bailed me out."

"I know."

"How did you know about the bail anyway?"

"Party line, Schneppa Kjnals, party line. Woarheit Wahl always phones his wife about everything that happens in court and Yetta Hiebat is on the same line."

"So Yetta was supposed to bring the Bible to Fraunz's yard. What was going to happen there?"

"I don't know exactly, but Fleeda said there might be lots of action and if you were there everything would get mixed up. She said you had a one-track mind and a guy who spies on women swimming in a pond can easily be manipulated."

"You mean Fleeda knew about that, too?"

"Sure, you're not so sneaky. Besides, a girl can always tell when a guy is pulling her out of her clothes with his eyes."

"B-b-but . . ."

A nurse came in with my supper then and even though I said I wasn't hungry, both Rosmack and the nurse insisted I had to eat, and Rosmack fed me with a spoon and didn't let me talk at all. And then Mama was back with some chocolate bars and another nurse came in with pills and a needle and my head started swirling with questions and the last thing I remembered was Rosmack telling Mama that she had to go home for the night and maybe she wouldn't come back till visiting hours tomorrow and Mama answered her back that she would stay for a few hours yet and then she would maybe phone Bulchi Wiebe to come and get her because there was so much work at home that wasn't getting done and it didn't look like I would die for a while yet.

In the morning the first thing the nurse did was pull all the tubes out of my body. She made me get up and she led me down the hall to the washroom. When we got back to my room my bed had been changed. The head end had been cranked up and there were pillows in the middle of the bed to take the weight off my seat. "You have to sit up today," the nurse said. "Lots of people want to talk to you."

Sure enough, I hardly had time to eat my breakfast before Constable Kowolchuk came in and sat down. After a few questions about how I was feeling, he took out his notebook and paged backwards in it till he found what he wanted. Then he started asking me questions about the woman I said had drowned in the pond. I wondered out loud to him why he hadn't believed me in the first place and Kowolchuk let himself go red for a second before he said, "Some new evidence has come up and we want to check out your story again."

"You mean Yetta Hiebat says she saw the body, too?"

"Something like that, only I can't give you any details at this time because that might jeopardize the investigation. I can say, though, that a woman named Hilda Heinrichs is definitely reported missing. Please cooperate and answer my questions."

So I answered Kowolchuk's questions and after he refused to listen to my opinion a few times I just answered his questions as straight as I could. I tried to read between the lines but he asked his questions too carefully for me to find answers in them. He didn't mention any names or places. He only asked for details about the body in the pond and the bones in the ashes. He didn't ask for any whys and he didn't throw me any curves which could have given me some clues. So after an hour Kowolchuk didn't get anything more out of me than I had given him last Tuesday evening in the cruiser car. I didn't know if he was satisfied but when I asked if the charges against me would be dropped, he gave me a funny look and said, "I wish things were that simple." Then he closed his notebook and walked out of the room.

Kowolchuk made one mistake, I think. He didn't guard me against other visitors. The other visitors weren't so careful about the questions they asked. By the time the evening visiting hours came and Rosmack arrived to hold my hand I was almost too tired to sit up anymore and my ass was throbbing between the pillows that had gone completely flat.

All the visitors pretended they were concerned about the condition my condition was in, even the army bengel, Corny Blatz, who had shot me with a wooden .303 bullet. When this Corny bengel, still wearing his camouflage army suit, came into my room with his father, Ernst Blatz, the Bible van guy and phoney Jehovah's Witness, I had to reach very deep down into myself to find any love for my enemy. Actually, if I had to affirm this in court I would have to admit I really didn't find any love at all for this Corny who should have been in jail for shooting me and kidnapping Rosmack, but at least I pulled enough cheek together to keep myself from attacking him with my bed pan. Maybe that is all the love that is necessary. Of all the visitors I had that day, facing the kid who had shot me was the hardest to take. It was too much like looking into a mirror, though exactly why I'm not sure because I never shot or kidnapped anybody, but that's how I felt when I looked at the bengel, like I was looking into a mirror.

Ernst Blatz apologized for his son, trying to make me understand the shooting had been a mistake, a misunderstanding, and I forced myself to bite my tongue on a joke in my head about the army bengel's great understanding—his size thirteen army boots. But Ernst Blatz had a way of talking that made a person listen, you know, the kind of talk a person uses who gives other people orders, so after a while I was half believing his story. He told me Hilda Heinrichs was his ex-wife and when she didn't come home on Tuesday night his son got worried and as the days went by he started getting desperate. Yes, Ernst Blatz told a pretty good story and his army bengel son had such a sad face with even a few tears leaking down the cheeks that hadn't ever been shaved yet and I listened with both ears trying to separate the wheat from the chaff. I mean, I have a little more than wind between the ears and I knew for sure this army bengel hadn't been worried about Hilda Heinrichs at the Farmers' Orchestra practice when I had outright accused somebody of drowning that woman in the pond. But I listened, trying to find out what they wanted from me. Ernst asked one question after another about the body I had found. He wanted to know why I had been at the Heinrichs yard and I said I was just passing by. I wouldn't admit to knowing anything about Hilda Heinrichs or even ever having seen her before. Ernst Blatz didn't seem too happy with that.

He was even less happy when I asked my one question. I wanted to know what the army bengel had been doing at the Heinrichs pond late on Tuesday night and why had he kidnapped Rosmack Rampel. Corny Blatz got very white in the face and he shook like he had when he was pointing the .303 at us in the Martens farmhouse. Ernst Blatz quickly said, "Don't know what you're talking about!" Then he led his shuddering son out of the room.

I only had a second to wonder if the army bengel was the way he was because Ernst Blatz and Hilda Heinrichs were first cousins before Hova Jake tiptoed in and pulled the visitor's chair up real close to the bed. He, too, was very concerned about my accident, as he called it, and said it was an unfortunate mistake. If I wanted to sue the United States of America he would support me all the way. For a few seconds I let myself think about how many millions my ass was worth, but then Hova Jake started asking about Hilda Heinrichs. He tried to wangle it out of me why I had been at the Heinrichs yard. He asked his questions like he was trying to figure out which side I was on, like maybe it was impossible to be totally innocent in this world. First he wanted to know if I was working for Ernst Blatz and then he wanted to know if I was working for the Heinrichs woman. When I wouldn't admit to that he thought I was working for the biker cop, Beitelkopp, or maybe his Special Constable harem from the Wunnimin Reserve. One thing he said told me how hard he was fishing and gave some weight to a thought I had had in the ambulance. Just before he left, Hova Jake almost lost his temper with me and said, "Come on, Kjnals, not everybody can be a drug agent. Somebody has to be smuggling those drugs!"

For sure, even in our keystone province with the Golden Boy running naked on top of the legislature, it didn't seem believable that cops could be so clumsy they would only be chasing each other, especially in Gutenthal where it's pretty hard to find a wild goose. It was time to sift through some of this alleged evidence. First, Rosmack had said Beitelkopp Blatz had been trying to set up Hova Jake. Hova Jake's questions gave weight to that idea. For sure, those two weren't on the same baseball team. Second, Fleeda Shreeda had gotten Yetta Hiebat to double-cross that scheme. Third, I had stuck a monkey wrench into the double-cross and got myself shot. Fourth, while I was dying on the ground everybody had tried to arrest everybody else, and then Kowolchuk had arrested them all. Only it all added up to the wrong answer—they were free to do as they pleased again while I was wounded in hospital. But why was everybody suddenly so interested in Hilda Heinrichs? How did she fit into all this? Was she dead, or was she alive?

Well, the five Special Constables seemed even more baffled than I was. They tiptoed in shyly, but quickly made themselves at home. They sat on the edges of the bed and I winced as the weight of each girl changed the pressure on my sore bum. The girls looked at me, waiting for me to speak. I didn't say anything. I just looked at each of the girls, noticing how different each was from Rosmack Rampel, how different the girls were from each other, how even their black hair came in different shades, and for a few seconds I wondered which shade Rosmack's was. Then the girl sitting closest to my head said, "I'm Madonna Smith, Special Constable. We are all Special Constables. We are trying to stop the flow of drugs onto the Wunnimin Reserve." She paused, then asked, "Who is this woman that's supposed to have drowned?"

I didn't say anything. I was afraid to say the wrong thing. There were ten dark eyes to look into and I heard Rosmack's words in my mind. *A guy who spies on women swimming in a pond can easily be manipulated.* Besides, this was the first curve I had been thrown. Kowolchuk, Ernst Blatz and Hova Jake had all asked about Hilda Heinrichs by name. These girls were asking who. I looked into each pair of eyes in turn and then asked, "Why?"

Madonna Smith glanced at the other girls, then bent toward me. "My brother tried to kill himself last month when he was high on drugs." She pointed to the girl behind her with her thumb. "Carly Siemens's brother beat up their mother to steal her money to buy drugs. Somebody's trafficking to the reserve. We thought it was Jack Harder, at least that's what Bernie Blatz tried to make us believe, but now it seems like everybody is claiming to be a cop, and we hear a woman has been drowned, but nobody wants to tell us anything. If you know anything that might help, please tell us."

There were no smirks on any of their faces. They might have pulled my pants off twice, but they had also bandaged my wounds. With all the dummheit going on after I was shot I could have bled to death if they hadn't patched me up. When I had first discovered the dope in the zipper Bible from the Bible van my better judgement had told me to go to the RCMP. Now they had come to me. It was time to talk.

So I told them what I thought I knew. I told them about the Bible with drugs I had bought from the Bible van. I told them about all the Bibles Beitelkopp had been buying.

"Beitelkopp?" asked the shortest Special Constable, who was sitting crosslegged at the foot of the bed. "Who is Beitelkopp?"

"Bernie Blatz," I said.

"Oh, you mean Sergeant Blatz."

"Yes." And I told them about finding Hilda in the pond, trying to save her, and then feeling the powder in the cover of the Bible Beitelkopp had had at Barbara Ball Bearing's place when I went for help. I told them about Hilda's body disappearing and how Kowolchuk thought I was crying wolf. I told them about the explosion and the bones that also disappeared. I told them about Rosmack's trip to the reserve graveyard with Beitelkopp and how he had exchanged Bibles there and that the Bible Beitelkopp had given Rosmack to carry had had enough cash in it to bail me out of jail. I told them about Rosmack's kidnapping and how I had been framed. I also told them as far as I was concerned the whole works of them were guilty of something and I was taking the rap for them.

The girls let me ramble on until I started to think I was talking too much, so much I might talk myself into a corner. So I stopped. I didn't tell them that maybe Hilda Heinrichs was dead, or maybe she was alive. Maybe I had found a body, maybe I had just dreamed it. I didn't say any more, but suddenly I had a picture in my head of the Cross Boundary Farmers' Orchestra and the doll woman's dirty foot.

Madonna Smith turned to the girl on the other side of the bed. "Show him, Tina."

Tina pulled a little chain out of her pocket and dangled it in front of my eyes. "Do you know anything about this?" she asked.

I reached for it and looked at the tiny swastika on the charm bracelet. I squinted at the tiny letters on the blades of the cross. I turned the swastika until the letters made some sense. The letters spelled the word MILK. That was the sense but it had no meaning. For a second I had a flash of a "MILK" bumper sticker but I didn't know if that connected with anything or not. I wondered what I should tell these girls. I decided to bargain. I said, "What were you up to at the auction sale?"

"Sergeant Blatz tipped us off that there was something going on with zipper Bibles at the auction. And you were involved. That's why we went there. He told us, too, that he thought there was something going on at the Martens farm, so when we ran into you there we had to take action, only we didn't want to get caught by the airplane because Sergeant Blatz had warned us about that, too."

"He warned you about the airplane, too?"

"Yeah, he said he thought drugs were being dropped from an airplane pretending to be a crop duster."

"Sounds like Beitelkopp knows an awful lot about this."

"Well, he's the sergeant, he should know," said the girl sitting on the far left edge of the bed. She was wearing a baseball cap with the word JUICE printed on the front.

"You think he could be the one doing the smuggling?" Madonna Smith asked.

"As I said before, I think all of you are probably in it up to your ears and you're trying to pin it on me. Tell me, what was really going on at that farmhouse?"

"You mean where we took your pants? We never even . . ."

"Not the Martens farm!" I cut Juice off. "The farmhouse in the States where you were pretending to be an orchestra. What was that really all about?"

"We were just playing music. It was Jack Harder's idea," said Madonna.

"Yeah, and Sergeant Bernie said we should go because then we could keep an eye on Jack," added Tina.

"Did you know the other people?"

"No, except for the woman that came in with the harp," said the small girl sitting at the end of the bed. "I remembered her."

"Yeah," said Tina. "She came to the reserve last year and had a meeting with women in the Mission Hall. I didn't go because that was the day before we went to Regina for training and we were too busy packing to go to a meeting."

"Do you remember what the meeting was about?"

"Something about the Third World," said Tina. "I don't think many women went because the priest was having bingo that night, too. Maybe Loretta went. She's interested in stuff like that."

"Loretta? You mean Rosmack Rampel's mother?"

"Rose Mack? You mean the girl from Gutenthal with the motorcycle is Loretta's daughter?"

"Well, I know her mother's name is Loretta. She lives in a house with a wrecked blue Dodge in the yard."

"Yes, she's the one. Maybe she'll remember something about this woman."

"You don't remember this woman's name?" I wanted to know.

"No. I only remember the woman because she was wearing the same black dress," said Luba from the end.

"So if the woman was wearing other clothes you wouldn't recognize her?"

"Probably not."

"And if another woman was wearing the same dress you wouldn't know the difference?"

"No, but I remember something else now. This woman was driving a green LTD like the one the Band got cheap at J.R. Friesen's for the Special Constables to use. I was going to ask to borrow it to get some stuff from my aunt's place, but I noticed this woman get out. Another thing was this car had a 'MILK' sticker on the bumper."

I thought for a second, then decided to share what I had figured out about the swastika charm. I handed it back to Tina and said, "Look at the letters on the blades of the cross. Those letters spell MILK."

"That's right," said Tina. "Take a look, Luba." Tina tossed the ankle bracelet to the crosslegged girl on the end.

Luba looked and then she said, "I remember something about that now. My sister stopped at the house on her way to the bingo and she said something about a meeting for mothers at the Mission Hall. A woman was going to talk about mothers, only I remember my sister said she knew all about it already and then she said the verse she made up in adult ed one time: 'A father for three seconds, a mother forever.'"

Madonna Smith was biting her lip. "What is all this supposed to mean, this woman? Who is she?"

"When I saw her come into the farmhouse," I said, "I

thought she was Hilda Heinrichs, the woman I pulled out of the pond. The woman I thought was drowned."

"You mean she's alive?" gasped Madonna.

"Somebody's alive," I answered. "Right now I don't know who is alive or dead."

"Now I'm really mixed up," said Luba.

I suddenly needed to go to the washroom really quick. I pressed the nurse button. A nurse came in right away and helped me out of bed and down the hall. When she led me back into the room, the Indian girls were gone. Schmuggle Veens was standing by the window looking out. His States wife was sitting on the chair next to the head of the bed. She wore a very short skirt and her nylons had rhinestones on them. She was lifting a cigarette to her pink lips, but she quickly stuck it behind her ear instead when she saw the nurse and remembered where she was. Then she reached into her purse and brought out a stick of chewing gum which she unwrapped and stuck in her mouth while the nurse helped me up onto the bed and fluffed up the pillows and positioned them to take the weight off my rear end. When I was comfortable, the nurse gave Schmuggle Veens and his States wife a disapproving look and told me to ring if I was getting tired of visitors.

"Thanks," I said. I was getting tired of visiting, but I wouldn't find out what was going on if I didn't hear what the visitors had to say. So I lay back and closed my eyes, waiting for the Veenses to start talking. Then I thought of something and opened my right eye and glanced at the States wife's ankles. The swastika bracelet dangled from the ankle of the leg crossed over the other one. I had forgotten to ask Tina where she had found the bracelet she had showed me just a few minutes ago. Now I couldn't think of how to get the

States wife to explain it to me. I heard Schmuggle Veens clear his throat. I racked through my brain. I felt I had to ask the first question. I needed to throw them off guard. Help me, Papa, I called in my head. I heard the States wife take a deep breath. I opened both eyes and stared into hers.

"So you aren't dead after all, Lena Bergen. Is anyone dead?" The States wife stared back into my eyes and uncrossed and recrossed her legs but I kept my focus on her eyes. "How did Bulchi Wiebe and Barbara Ball Bearing get the idea that you were killed for helping a Nazi war criminal in Paraguay?"

I heard Schmuggle Veens step closer to the bed. "Now Kjnals, it was just a story we fed to Ernst Blatz's family down there to mix him up, because his wife, I mean his ex-wife, Hilda Heinrichs, had it figured out that Ernst was smuggling drugs to Canada to raise money for the Contras."

"But I thought I heard Blatz say he was a CIA drug agent."

"Everybody is trying to use the war on drugs to cover up whatever else it is they are doing."

"And what are you trying to cover up?" I turned from Schmuggle Veens to his wife. "Didn't I hear you say you were drug agents, too?"

"Well, you see, Kjnals," she said, and her hand started to reach for the cigarette she had stuck behind her ear. Then she thought better of it and, leaning forward, put her hand on her knee and picked at a thread in her stocking and all of a sudden there was a ladder running all the way down her leg right beside the row of rhinestones. "You see," she continued, and I saw her move her foot so her heel came out of the shoe, "when Sam got caught smuggling Flat German Mexicans into Canada, the authorities made a deal with him. The deal was that Sam would use his connections in South

America to help stop Ernst Blatz. See, Ernst has been a mercenary ever since he retired from the army ten . . ." Suddenly, her hand dived into her purse at the same time as her head jerked back with the beginning of a sneeze. As her hand pulled out a pack of Kleenex, a pair of round eyeglasses tumbled onto her lap and then dropped to the floor as she ripped a tissue from the pack just in time to catch the sneeze. She barely had time to grab another tissue before she sneezed again and the violence of the sneeze jerked the loose shoe off her foot and it clattered down beside the round eyeglasses. Through the dark nylon of the stocking I saw the bandage along the edge of her foot behind the little toe.

As I waited for her to finish blowing her nose a parade of pictures marched through my mind and I sorted them into an answer. Then the answer broke up into questions. The woman sitting at my bedside slipped her foot into her fallen shoe, then crouched to pick up the round eyeglasses. I decided that was the moment to ask. "Who are you really, Lena Bergen or Hilda Heinrichs?"

She stayed crouched for a moment, looking at the eyeglasses, and I saw how the smoothness of her makeup gave way to wrinkles under her chin. I tried to picture the doll woman in my mind, the doll woman's face when I changed her flat tire and she gave me a zipper Bible to give to Yetta Hiebat. I tried to picture the face of the doll woman who had hired me to buy the grandfather clock at the auction sale. I tried to picture the face of the doll woman who had drowned. I tried to picture the face of the doll woman with the harp. I couldn't get a clear picture of any of them. All I could figure out was that the doll woman at the auction and the doll woman with the harp had been wearing round eyeglasses like the pair Schmuggle Veens's States wife was picking up beside my bed.

"Are you Lena Bergen or Hilda Heinrichs or both?" I asked again as she gripped the bedside table with wrinkled fingers to pull herself up. I figured I could braid enough of these threads together to say with only a very short shadow of a doubt that the doll woman with the harp had been the same woman who was in front of me now. She didn't answer as she sat on the chair again. Instead she pulled the cigarette from behind her ear and stuck it between her lips. She sucked on it and then held it unlit between her fingers as she rested her chin on her thumb. Schmuggle Veens came around the end of the bed and stood beside her. He was biting on the stem of his unlit pipe.

"Why would you ask such a thing?" he asked. "This is my wife, Lena. Everybody knows that." And he put his hand on her shoulder. His wife was sucking on the cigarette again and I decided I better get my questions rolling here before she would start a fire. I decided to start near the end and work backwards.

"How come you were wearing that black wedding dress to play harp with the Farmers' Orchestra?"

Lena flicked her finger as if she was trying to knock ashes off her unlit cigarette. "All of us women were wearing long black dresses for the orchestra," she said. "Didn't you see that? Inge Henkel, the Indian girls, me. We were all wearing long black dresses."

I had to accept that. The women had all been wearing long black dresses. "So it wasn't Hilda Heinrichs who walked into that farmhouse carrying a harp?"

"No, that was me."

"Yeah, " said Schmuggle. "Why would you think she was Hilda?"

I didn't answer him. Instead, I said, "You lost your

high-heeled shoe on the road where we found your car and
the disker."

"Yeah, that Corny Blatz was waving a machine gun at us
and he wouldn't let me stop to put it back on," Lena said.

"The army bengel's machine gun was just a BB gun," I said.

"A shot from a BB gun would still hurt," Schmuggle Veens
said. "And now they got away with the money."

"Who got away with the money?"

"Ernst Blatz and Corny."

"How did that happen?"

"Ernst cut us off with a '51 Ford and Corny cut us off with
the jeep," Lena said. "They both had guns. There was a guy
in the '51 Ford who was knocked out and Ernst made me
and Sam put him in the trunk of the LTD."

"You put Yasch Siemens into the trunk?"

"What could we do? They were pointing guns at us. And
you should know that Corny will pull the trigger, too. Then
Corny took the zipper Bibles out of the disker and made us
get in the jeep. That's when I lost my shoe."

"Was there anybody else in the '51 Ford?"

"Yeah, that woman with the big flowers on her dress,"
said Schmuggle.

"Fleeda Shreeda."

"Is that who it is? She wouldn't say nothing when we were
riding to the cop shop in the Bible van," added Lena.

"So what was Fleeda doing while you put Yasch Siemens
into the trunk?"

"Just sitting in the front seat looking straight ahead."

"She didn't do anything?"

"Not that I could see."

"Was she driving?"

"She was behind the wheel."

"So what happened after you got into the jeep?"

"Corny Blatz made me drive the jeep into the middle of a summerfallow field about a mile from A.Dyck and L.U.Dyck's place. There he made us get out."

"Did he say anything?"

"Not much. It didn't really make sense. While we were driving he was in the back seat all the time pushing his gun into my back. Then he started mumbling that if only the grandfather clock hadn't fallen in the pond he would have made both his mother and his father happy. I tried to ask him what he was talking about but he shot the gun off beside my ear. So I just did what he said."

"Yeah," said Lena. "When we stopped in the middle of the field, he pushed me out of the jeep and that's when I cut my foot."

"It sure was hard for Lena to walk over that summerfallow because it was a sunflower field the year before so there were all these old shtengels lying around. But we had some luck. We found Hilda's LTD parked in the willows behind A.Dyck and L.U.Dyck's yard. It had the keys in so we drove away with that."

"How did you know it was Hilda's?"

"She was parking it there while she and L.U.Dyck went on their honeymoon."

"So what A.Dyck said is true, that L.U.Dyck and Hilda went away to get married."

"Yeah."

"So where did you go then?"

"First we went back to the disker but our car was gone so we went to the Heinrichs yard to see if we could find the clock Corny had talked about."

"Was that the clock you hired me to buy for you?"

"Yes, how did Corny get it anyway?"

"If Corny had it he must have stolen it from my car. What was in it?"

"Nothing as far as I know."

"Why was I supposed to buy it for you then and meet you at the Heinrichs pond at 9:00 on Tuesday night?"

"We just wanted to make sure you wouldn't be at Jaunses' Fraunz's yard on Tuesday night. After Lena found you there swimming on Sunday after dinner we figured we couldn't take a chance that you would be around." Schmuggle stopped and pulled a lighter out of his pocket and flicked it, but remembered where he was before he set his pipe on fire.

"What was going on there anyway at the pond?"

"Inge Henkel's son was going to drop some drugs for Ernst Blatz from his crop duster plane."

"The crop duster plane is Inge Henkel's son?"

"Yeah, he works for the FBI, I think."

"So let me get this right," I said. "You hired me to buy the clock and told me to meet you at the Heinrichs pond on Tuesday night just to make sure I wouldn't be at Hauns Jaunses' Fraunz's pond when this crop duster made a drop?"

"Yeah, we decided we didn't want to take any chances."

"So then on Thursday afternoon when you found Hilda's car you drove to the Heinrichs yard to see if you could find the clock?"

"Yeah, and I wanted to see if you would remember our alternate meeting time."

"So when did you put on the black dress? Was that Hilda's?"

"Oh no, I put it on as soon as we were out of the village with the disker and Sam stopped long enough for me to jump off the disker and get in the car."

"So how did the dress get wet?"

"Wet?"

"It sure looked like it had been wet when you walked into the orchestra practice."

"I stepped too close to the water when I was looking for the clock and I fell in. That's how I got wet."

"Is that how Hilda fell in?"

"Hilda?"

"Yes, Hilda wearing a long black dress in the water face down. That's how I found her on Tuesday night at 9:00. Remember? I was supposed to meet you there at the exact same time. But I found Hilda instead, in a long black dress all cold and wet and drowned. She had a swastika ankle bracelet just like yours. I pulled her out and tried to revive her. When I couldn't I went to Barbara Ball Bearing's for help. Constable McKay was visiting there and called the cops. But by the time the cops got to the Heinrichs yard there was no body, no LTD, nothing to prove what I said was true. Kowolchuk almost arrested me for public mischief."

"So who would believe a schneppa naze like you anyways?" Schmuggle Veens said, looking down his nose at me.

"Just let me finish," I cut in. "Now Yetta Hiebat says she saw Hilda's body that night, too. That same night Holzyebock Hiebat's trailer blows up and Corny army bengel Blatz kidnaps Rosmack Rampel. The next morning I find bones in the ashes. But they disappear, too, before the cops get there. All this you did to make sure I wouldn't see a crop duster drop something at Jaunses' Fraunz's pond?"

"No, Kjnals," said Schmuggle. "We don't know nothing about Hilda drowning. As far as we know Hilda is off in Niagara Falls with L.U.Dyck."

"Then how come Yetta Hiebat thinks Hilda is dead, too?"

"Yetta Hiebat was always a little bit soft in the head."

"So who gave me a zipper Bible at church on Sunday to give to Yetta Hiebat?" I was starting to wonder if even there was such a person as Hilda Heinrichs. "Was it you, too, or is there really a Hilda Heinrichs?"

Lena sucked hard on her cold cigarette and when she pulled it out of her mouth the white filter tip was smeared with her pink lipstick. "I never gave you a zipper Bible to give to Yetta. Why would you think it was me?" She blew her nose hard.

"The woman had on a long black dress and looked like you except she didn't have glasses on. I thought she was the same person who hired me to buy the clock at the auction sale the next day."

"No, that wasn't me. It must have been Hilda. I wonder what she was up to. You say she gave you a zipper Bible to give to Yetta Hiebat?" Lena stuck her cigarette in her mouth and frowned as she put on the round eyeglasses for the first time.

"Yes, she asked me to give it to Yetta at A.Dyck and L.U.Dyck's auction sale because she had to go to Steinbach to visit a sick aunt. That's why I was so surprised when you were there in the black dress asking me to buy the clock for a thousand dollars."

"Hilda said she had to go to Steinbach? But she was there at the auction. She was in the house making the coffee." Schmuggle Veens waved his pipe. "Hilda was there, I mean she was the one that talked L.U.Dyck into selling the farm in the first place."

"Was Hilda wearing a long black dress?"

"No, she was wearing a pink pantsuit, actually," said Lena.

"But you know, I wonder if Hilda was wearing her wedding dress when she saw you at the church. See, when Hilda's sister was killed by A.Dyck's pig, Hilda took the wedding dress she had made to marry L.U.Dyck in and she dyed it black to wear to her sister's funeral. I wonder if she was wearing that dress."

"Did you break up with A.Dyck over that accident, too?" I asked, as I remembered what Shusta Paul had said.

Schmuggle Veens pointed his pipe at Lena and laughed, "You mean you used to go with A.Dyck?"

Lena turned a little red and sucked on her cigarette. "It was just a bit of dummheit Hilda and me cooked up to see if we could fool those brothers. I never broke up with A.Dyck. We just moved to Paraguay and I never saw him again till the auction sale."

"So who killed A.Dyck's pig?"

"Yeah, who did that anyways?" Schmuggle asked. "We heard about it, but wasn't us. We didn't stay long at the auction."

"Just long enough to make sure you bought the clock," Lena added.

"And the pig at the Neualtbergfeld auction?"

"We were gone with the disker before that happened, too."

"So you think Ernst and Corny Blatz got away with the money?"

"Yeah, sure," said Schmuggle Veens. "What else could it be? Don't you think that's what happened?"

Lena pulled out her lighter again and this time she lit her cigarette and sucked it so hard I thought smoke was going to puff out of her ears. Then she opened her mouth; words and smoke came out together. "You know, I bet Corny Blatz killed A.Dyck's pig for Hilda. Who else but that bengel would do such a thing?"

All I knew was I was tired from talking to them. "So what do you really want from me today?"

Schmuggle Veens and his States wife looked at each other. "Well, Kjnals," Schmuggle started. The orderly wheeled in the lunch cart and the States wife stood up and finished for her husband, "Have a good dinner and maybe I'll catch you swimming in the pond again sometime." Then she turned and hooked her arm around Schmuggle's elbow and walked out of the room with him. She might not be a spring chicken, I thought, but she looked all right in a short skirt, with the ankle bracelet flashing under the fluorescent hospital lights.

"Wait!" I called after them, but they didn't come back, and the kick in the pants I was giving myself inside my head almost ripped the stitches out of my ass. How could I have let the States wife get away without explaining what the swastika charm bracelets that spelled MILK were all about? I had a suspicious thought about the missing money, too. I hoped that Fleeda Shreeda would come to visit me. I had some questions for that missionary lady.

21

BUT Fleeda Shreeda didn't come to visit me with her flowered Africa dress. She didn't return the purloiner's drawers filled with zipper Bibles. She didn't return my money belt. And my head was filled with crouching shadows and bare feet and dripping dresses, and the needle the nurse gave me after I finished the lunch didn't clear anything up for me. I think I slept for a while and it seems like I had more visitors, only I can't have been much use to them with my head swirling around. I don't even know if I talked to them—I think Beitelkopp Blatz was there for a while and then later Bulchi Wiebe was there, too, I think, and both Beitelkopp and Bulchi were interested in Hilda Heinrichs, only it didn't seem like they cared if she had drowned or not. They were more concerned that there was a whole bunch of money missing. Nobody knew for sure what had happened to the blackmail money in the zipper Bibles and there was a lot of drug money unaccounted for. At least I think that was what they were saying, but I was drugged and I don't know if I told them anything. For sure I didn't know where the money was. I sure as hell didn't have it. All of a sudden I thought about the Bible Yetta Hiebat had picked up in the church and I wondered to myself, at least I hope I didn't say nothing to Beitelkopp and Bulchi about this, but I wondered what had happened to that Bible with thirty thousand dollars in it, the one I had been waving around when I got shot. The pain in my ass just flooded over all of my thinking so it had completely slipped from what was left of my mind. But if I was holding it when I was shot I must have dropped it when I fell down. And if I dropped it somebody must have picked it up. With so many people after that money somebody must have picked it up then in the dark and the confusion, or for sure it would have been found when Kowolchuk went back in daylight. So who picked it up? Who was getting all the money out of this bungled war on drugs, if that's what it really was? And who had murdered Hilda Heinrichs? I was still no closer to an answer to that than I had been when I pulled her body out of the pond and tried to breathe life back into those icy lips. Even there in the hospital bed, drinking herbal tea about as tasty as hot rain water, my lips could still remember that cold, cold, cold mouth. That woman just couldn't be still alive. Schmuggle Veens and his States wife might think Yetta Hiebat was soft in the head, and maybe Yetta's story was just another joke on me, but my instinct was to believe my lips.

Only Rosmack Rampel came for the evening visiting hours and she told me Mama had phoned her to say she had phoned to the doctor and the doctor had said I could go home the next day. I thought it was strange that the doctor would tell my Mama I was going home when he hadn't even come in to see me after he sewed up my bullet holes. It's not like I'm too young to have my own medicare number, but that's the way it is if you stay in Gutenthal—people keep you tied to your Mama's apron strings until you're ready to collect pension. Anyway it was good Mama decided not to come to visit because I needed to ask Rosmack to help me, to find some things out for me, and it was easier without Mama there.

My noon-time needle had worn off and I felt pretty clear-headed when Rosmack pulled the chair close to the side of the bed and took my hand. I had been on my back most of the day, so now I was lying on my front. I looked into Rosmack's black eyes, but black eyes are very hard to read, at least I never learned how and the Hollywood School of Detection didn't have a lesson on reading eyes and in the *Reader's Digest* I had read about Joe's nose and Jane's breast but never about Rosmack's eyes. Rosmack was wearing the beaded earrings and she had braided her hair into one thick shiny black braid that hung down her leather motorcycle jacket. I could smell a bit of perfume mixed up with the smell of oil and gasoline. The fingertips of her light brown hand were stained with grease.

"Change your oil today?" I said. I mean a guy can't come right out and say I love you to a girl when you aren't even smart enough to read her eyes.

"Yeah," she said. "Clean oil keeps my Harley happy." She spread all her fingers on the sheet, showing off the grease stains and broken nails. "You like fingers all shrivelled white from dishwater better?"

"I like your fingers any way as long as they're holding mine," I said, and I rolled myself onto my side with only a little shot of pain so I could hold her fingers in my hospital white hands. For a minute I thought I could hear our hearts beating together or maybe it was the clock on the wall and it made me think how much closer to pension I was than Rosmack was, and though it might not bother a hard-boiled detective, it made me feel uncomfortable. I guess I'm just a sunny-side-up kind of guy. Besides, I was in the middle of a murder investigation and Kowolchuk hadn't dropped the drug charges against me yet either.

And hard as it was for me to admit it, down in the cellar of my mind behind my right ear under a pile of brassieres, zipper Bibles and doll women's dripping wet dresses was the snake of an idea that Rosmack Rampel was maybe part of this joke Yetta Hiebat had said she and Hilda Heinrichs were playing on me. I mean, Rosmack had bailed me out because Fleeda had told her to, and she had told me to meet her at Jaunses' Fraunz's pond because Fleeda had told her to, and I started thinking, yeah, the first time I had seen Fleeda it was right after Rosmack was swimming in the pond that Sunday afternoon, and sure they had stopped to talk to each other on the road. And then at Knibble Thiessen's place Rosmack told me Fleeda Shreeda was home from Africa, and wasn't it funny that right after Rosmack called me in the middle of the night I almost ran over Fleeda on her bicycle and then that missionary stole my Volkswagen. And yes, it hurt, even more than the bullet holes in my hams, as I felt the yolks of my runny sunny-side-up eggs harden into rubber. At the same time the whole situation seemed too serious to be a joke. I mean, would Rosmack allow herself to be tied up with a dirty sock in her mouth just for a joke? Would she have pissed her pants if this was a joke? Would I have been shot? I had to get Rosmack to level with me.

"So tell me," I said. "Tell me what you and Fleeda are up to."

"What do you mean?" Rosmack pulled her fingers away from mine.

"Tell me what is going on."

"Well, I told you already, they're dealing drugs!"

"Who?"

"Well, Jack and Bernie and that army bengel and his dad."

"But they say they're all drug agents."

"So do you believe them?"

"Right now I don't believe anybody."

"Not even me?"

"Not yet. How can I believe you when you won't tell me everything? You told me to wait, to trust and obey, and what happens? I get shot in the ass."

"That wasn't supposed to happen."

"What *was* supposed to happen?"

"W-w-well." She stopped.

"Well what?"

"I don't know where to start."

"The beginning was good enough for the Bible—even a zipper Bible."

"I-I-I'm not sure what the beginning is."

"Well, which came first, Beitelkopp or Fleeda?"

"It was Fleeda."

"Where? When? What?"

"Only that wasn't the beginning."

"Fleeda wasn't the beginning? Then who was?"

"Yetta Hiebat and that Hilda Heinrichs you say is dead."

"That was the beginning? When? Where?"

"It was them that said you were peeking at me when I was swimming."

"Yetta and Hilda told you that?"

"Yeah. I had never thought you would do such a thing," Rosmack said, and her voice had such a sad, disappointed tone it wasn't easy for me to stay hard-boiled. "I thought you were my friend."

Even my hair felt like it was turning red when she said this. "So why didn't you do something to scare me away? Why were you still friendly to me?"

"I don't know for sure. It's not so simple." Rosmack crossed her legs and leaned back a little. "It made me nervous to know you were watching me swim. At the same time, a girl likes to be noticed. Besides, it was kind of funny to think you were there peeking, once the others had told me about it." Rosmack lifted her left ankle onto her right knee. Her ankle boot had a very scuffed toe. "It was like a game to see if I could keep you guessing." Rosmack stuck a finger inside her boot.

"So I'm a dirty old man," I said, "but there's lots more to this than playing jokes on a glutztupp. There's drugs and blackmail and shooting and maybe even murder. I could be in real trouble if I can't figure this out. Kowolchuk won't drop the charges against me yet and . . ." Rosmack had pulled her boot off and was rolling her white sock down over her ankle bone.

"Rosmack!" I cried. "You're wearing one, too!" A bracelet with a swastika charm dangled from her ankle.

"Of course, Kjnals." She scratched the impression the chain had made in her skin, then took her sock off altogether so she could scratch the whole instep of her foot.

"But why?" I couldn't believe my eyes and ears. "What do you want with the Nazis?"

"Nazis?"

"Yeah, you've heard of the Nazis, haven't you?"

"Sure, but this isn't about the Nazis."

"No? What is it about then?"

Rosmack unfastened the chain and dangled the swastika in front of my eyes. I saw the tiny letters on the blades of the cross. "Which way do the blades point?" she asked.

"To the right," I said. "So?"

"Hitler's swastika pointed to the left."

"So?" I repeated, and I reached for the charm. I turned its face around. "If you hold it the other way it points left, too. So what's the difference?"

"If it's pointing right it's a good sign. If it's pointing left it's a bad sign. It's like that all over the world, even among the Indians."

"And what does a swastika mean if it has little letters on the blades that spell MILK?" I passed the bracelet back to her. "And what does such a swastika mean when all of a sudden in Gutenthal there are women wearing such a thing around their ankles at the same time that roads get gravelled to look like swastikas from the air, pigs get murdered with swastika-shaped wounds, and then there's all this other stuff going on, including a woman that drowns with one of those around her ankle? What does it mean?"

Rosmack was staring at the tiny letters on the swastika. "I never noticed these letters before."

"Yeah, well, it takes a schneppa naze to see such a thing. Now tell me, what does this MILK mean?"

"I don't know, Kjnals. Honest, I don't know."

"Who gave it to you?"

"Fleeda."

"Why?"

"She said it was a secret sign of unity among a special group of women."

"And who are these special women?"

"I don't know really. I just saw Fleeda and Barbara with them. I thought it was just something Fleeda dreamed up for us."

"How come I never saw one on Fleeda's ankle? Or Barbara's?"

"Fleeda's ankle was too thick to get the bracelet around so she wore hers on another chain around her neck."

"Didn't look that thick to me."

"What would you know?"

"Let me get this straight," I said. "I have seen Hilda Heinrichs, Yetta Hiebat, Inge Henkel, Schmuggle Veens's States wife and you with swastika charm bracelets around your skinny ankles. Now you say Barbara Ball Bearing wears one and Fleeda Shreeda hangs one around her neck because her ankles are too thick."

"Right on," Rosmack said.

"Madonna Smith and her Special Constables from the reserve found a bracelet, too."

"So?"

"They say Hilda Heinrichs or somebody who looked like her was at the reserve last year to have a meeting with women in the Mission Hall. This woman had a 'MILK' sticker on her LTD bumper."

"So?"

"So I chased an LTD with a 'MILK' sticker from the Gutenthal store to Pracha Darp. That was the same day I first saw the Bible van."

"Bully for you."

"I bought a zipper Bible from the van after Beitelkopp Blatz bought three just like it. The Bible had drugs in it."

"Oh."

"That was the same day I had seen you from Bulchi Wiebe's airplane. You and two other bikers were driving towards the centre of a gravel road swastika on the section where Jaunses' Fraunz's pond is. The same pond where you swim, and Fleeda swims. Schmuggle Veens's States wife, who is really Lena Bergen, came there on a Sunday afternoon to pick up four hoes from the beetfield. The hoes had been arranged to look like a swastika. And come to think about it, that swastika pointed right, too."

"So it must be a good sign then."

"I should live so long. Schmuggle Veens and his States wife have admitted to me that field there by Jaunses' Fraunz's pond was a drug drop-off place for Inge Henkel's son in his crop duster. So I know these swastikas mean something. What are you women up to? Or do the men all have ankle chains with swastikas, too, hidden under their boots like you do?"

"I don't know, Kjnals. They never take their boots off when I'm around."

"Well, what about the women?"

"I only know what Fleeda said."

"But you said Hilda and Yetta had told you I was watching you swim."

"Yeah, that was maybe two, three weeks ago when they stopped me on the road after I had been swimming and they told me you were watching me swim. They didn't say anything else. So then I always knew you were watching when I went swimming. I even stayed underwater once with just my nose out for a long time to see if you would jump in to save me, but you didn't."

"I was ready to jump in but then you came up."

"Sure, a person could have drowned waiting for you."

"But what about Fleeda?"

"I didn't meet her until that afternoon at the pond."

"And she right away gave you a swastika charm bracelet?"

"No, it wasn't until Sunday night at Barbara's place."

"At Barbara's place."

"Yeah, Fleeda said she was going over to Barbara's place on Sunday evening and she asked me to come, too."

"So what happened there?"

"Fleeda talked about Uganda and all the things that had happened there and how her husband was killed. And then she took out these swastika anklets and gave them to us. She told us these anklets were a secret sign uniting women all over the earth who were trying to make a better world. She said in early times the swastika had been a secret cross for secret Christians and that women were using it as a secret sign now."

"Did she say what those little letters were supposed to mean?"

"No, like I said before, I didn't even notice the little letters. I just put the anklet on and forgot about it. No, Fleeda didn't say anything about it."

"So what kind of things do these swastika women do to make the world a better place?"

"I don't know. Before Fleeda could tell us about that, Bernie Blatz came on his motorcycle and I decided to go for a ride with him."

"So where did you go with Beitelkopp?"

"He just rode beside me till I got home."

"Now you said Fleeda came first. You first met Fleeda on Sunday at the pond. On Saturday night you were at Barbara's party with Beitelkopp Blatz. So how could Fleeda be first?"

"I didn't say I first met Fleeda on Sunday. On Sunday was the second time I saw her at the pond. The first time was maybe Tuesday or Wednesday. You were there, you should remember."

"I only saw Fleeda there on Sunday. So when did you meet Beitelkopp?"

"On Saturday night when I was on my way to Barbara's party."

"And you had never seen him before?"

"No."

"So how come you let him kiss you just like that?"

"Some guys don't wait till their beards are grey before they try to kiss a girl."

"So when did you see Fleeda again?"

"I didn't see Fleeda until Friday morning. I was on my way to your place when she flagged me down on the road. That's when I heard you were in jail. We found the money in the saddle bag and Fleeda thought we should bail you out."

"Was Fleeda driving the '51 Ford?"

" '51 Ford?"

"Yeah, Yasch and Oata's '51 Ford?"

"No, she was on her bicycle as always."

"And was Yasch with her?"

"No, what are you talking about?"

"You didn't see Fleeda from Sunday till Friday morning?"

"Yeah, that's right. I was kidnapped, remember."

"Was that Fleeda's idea, too?"

"You kidding, that was real!"

"Wait a minute. How could you phone me if you were tied up with a sock in your mouth?"

"I never phoned you!"

"No? You didn't phone in the middle of the night and say you were Rosie, Cozy Rosie?"

"No."

"You didn't say, 'Are you horny, Corny?' "

"To you?"

"You didn't say anything about barbed wire and ball bearings?"

"For sure not, you think I'm mental or . . ." Rosmack stopped, then said, "I wonder if Fleeda would have done such a thing."

"You mean Fleeda called me?"

"I don't know. I didn't see Fleeda till Friday morning."

"Yeah, you were kidnapped." The left side of my head started to ache. "So when did you see Fleeda next?"

"I didn't see her again till Fraunz's yard when you got shot."

"But you said Fleeda and Yetta were trying to double-cross Beitelkopp. Did Fleeda tell you all this on Friday morning?"

"Yes."

"Weren't you surprised that Fleeda and Barbara were involved in this drug thing?"

"Sure, but Bernie had involved me, too."

"And you didn't know that he was a cop?"

"No way did I know that. I mean, he even told me himself he was just released from Headingley Jail."

"What did you think when Fleeda told you Yetta was going to pick up that zipper Bible? Didn't it seem strange that Yetta Hiebat would be involved in something like this?"

"I don't know, Kjnals, what I thought. After a person's been kidnapped almost everything seems believable. I mean, I even believed that you were in jail. Who would have thought that?"

I saw by the clock on the wall the visiting hours were almost over and I didn't think they would let Rosmack stay overnight if Mama wasn't there. I combed through my brain trying to think of the best questions to ask.

"Did you see Hilda Heinrichs at all after she and Yetta told you I was watching you swim?"

"No, I never did. That was the only time I ever saw her."

"Was she wearing a black wedding dress that day?"

"No, the woman with Yetta Hiebat was wearing a pink pantsuit."

"And you didn't see this woman with the pink pantsuit at A.Dyck and L.U.Dyck's auction?"

"No."

"Was the woman in the pink pantsuit wearing round eyeglasses?"

"No."

"Could you mix that woman up with Schmuggle Veens's States wife?"

"I don't think Schmuggle Veens's States wife would ever wear a pink pantsuit. She doesn't look like that kind of woman to me."

"Say, have you seen L.U.Dyck around since that auction sale?"

"No, why?"

"Could you try to find out where he is?"

"Okay, Kjnals," Rosmack said, and she bent over and kissed me on the cheek and that was better for me than any nurse's needle could ever be, but the nurse gave me the needle anyway after Rosmack was gone, only an inch away from my stitches.

22

THREE things happened the morning I was to be released from the hospital. When I woke up a zipper Bible lay on the little cupboard beside the bed. It was Oata Siemens's Bible, the one with the inscription from Lawrence U. Dyck, the one that had contained A.Dyck's blackmail note. Only this time pages were marked with bobby pins and verses about swine were underlined with red ballpoint pen. One verse, Isaiah 65:4, had a box drawn around it:

> Which remain among the graves, and
> lodge in the monuments, which eat
> swine's flesh, and broth of abominable
> things is in their vessels.

Before I could read all the verses Susie Fehr, the nurse's aide, brought me breakfast and told me L.U.Dyck had been admitted into the hospital in the middle of the night. Simple

Hein found him wandering on the road talking crazy and brought him to the hospital because L.U.Dyck hadn't wanted to go home to A.Dyck's place. Susie didn't know for sure, but she thought L.U.Dyck had gone mental.

And before I could finish my breakfast Constable Kowolchuk came to see me. His face looked like two red suns setting over a field of burned stubble. He wasn't happy, for sure not happy enough to drop all those charges against me. He sat down, crossed his legs, and hung his police cap on his knee. I wondered if he would take off his boot and show me a swastika chain on his ankle.

He played with his cap without saying anything. Suddenly the skin around my stitches started to itch and ache. What else could happen to me yet? Kowolchuk just sat there dusting off his police cap for so long that the itch I was scared to scratch almost drove me crazy. Then he decided to talk.

"We can't locate Hilda Heinrichs-Blatz," he said. "The last time anyone saw her was on the Monday evening after the Dyck brothers' auction. Abe Dyck says Hilda and his brother, Lawrence, drove away from the Dyck yard with Niagara Falls as their destination." Kowolchuk stopped there, uncrossed his legs and lifted his right ankle to his left knee.

"Yeah, that's what A.Dyck was saying to us at Mama's on Thursday night, that Hilda and L.U.Dyck had gone away to get married," I said, wondering if Kowolchuk knew L.U.Dyck was in the hospital. He kept me wondering because he asked, "How come you refer to them as A.Dyck and L.U.Dyck?"

"Well, in Flat German, A.Dyck means vinegar, and L.U.Dyck means sourdock. So people have always called them that."

"I see," he said, trying not to roll his sore eyes. "Lawrence

Dyck was found wandering around late last night and brought into the hospital here."

"Yeah, the nurse's aide told me this morning."

"Did she tell you what he was saying?"

"Only that he didn't want to go home."

"When I tried to interview him he didn't say anything about that. But he kept repeating your name. S-n-eppa K-n-alls. Isn't that what people call you? He was mumbling something about you and a grandfather clock that Hilda had to find. McKay is checking the auctioneer's records right now, but we already have a number of witnesses who can swear you purchased a grandfather clock at the Dyck brothers' auction."

"Yeah, I did, but it was stolen from my car, when A.Dyck's pig was murdered." Kowolchuk took out his notebook and I told him the whole story of the clock, including Schmuggle Veens's States wife's part in it. I suspected the army bengel had stolen it from my car, but I couldn't explain why the clock was so important to him.

Kowolchuk scribbled furiously. I noticed how thick his fingers were and wondered if he would have to type all these notes by himself with two fingers the way Wojo does on "Barney Miller." Kowolchuk stopped writing and chewed on his pencil.

"You know, Neil Bergen, Investigator, all the crazy stories I have heard the last few days check out. All those people are who they say they are. They are all on one drug squad or another. And it looks like one big screw-up—a sting operation with no bad guys to sting. A perfect bungle in the jungle, except . . ." Kowolchuk paused and dusted off his hat for the tenth time. "Except for you."

"Me?"

"Yes, you. Now don't tell me you're working for the KGB

or MI5 or the French Foreign Legion, or is Interpol more your style? Crazy as it sounds, I checked into that possibility. No one has a record of you."

"So what are you trying to tell me?"

"Well, it's too early to say, but at this point in time I have to consider the possibility that you are an alleged suspect in an alleged homicide."

"Me? Homicide?"

"Like I said, it's too early to say for sure, but a policeman has to keep an open mind about such things. Truth is often a lot stranger than fiction. So for the time being, let me know before you leave town."

Well, I didn't know if I should scream or play dead. Me? Homicide? I was so bedutzed I couldn't even make Kowolchuk answer me some questions before he disappeared out the door. His footsteps echoing down the hall made me think of those footsteps in movie prisons and I shuddered as I thought of all those guys who have spent ten, twenty, thirty years behind bars for something they didn't do, only they can't prove their innocence and there is nobody left who cares enough to help them try. The thought scared me out of that bed. No way I could take this lying down.

Of course, my bloody pants had been seized by the police as evidence, underwear and all, and Mama must have taken my shoes and shirt home to wash like Mamas always have to do. So there I was, barefoot, wearing nothing but a bandage on my behind and a hospital gown too small to close in the back. For sure next time Pracha Platt came around to collect for the hospital I would give him something so they could buy some gowns big enough for a grown man.

But some good came out of all these dummheit thoughts. I sat down on the edge of the bed to plan my actions. It still hurt to sit down, but after a few minutes of sitting without moving, testing my strength against the itch and the pain, I figured the hospital clothes were an advantage for my first act.

It didn't take me long to find L.U.Dyck. Even with his hair dyed black and the curly perm some hairdresser had given him, he looked ten years older than he had at the auction sale. His face was so white it looked blue. If he hadn't opened his eyes when I tiptoed up close to his bed I'd have thought he was dead. At first I didn't think he recognized me. I asked him about Hilda and where he had been but he only stared at me with eyes opened so wide they looked like glass balls, big as balls on a pool table. He wouldn't answer me. I leaned over him and asked again, "Where is Hilda?"

Faster than lightning, he gripped my wrist in his hand, and the pain in my ass was nothing compared to the pain shooting up my arm from his terrible grip. He pulled me down, gripped my ear, and pulled it to his mouth. "Keep Abe away from Hilda," he whispered. He let my ear go, closed his eyes, and began to snore. I stood stunned by his request. Susie Fehr, the nurse's aide, found me shaking beside L.U.Dyck's bed and led me back to my room before anybody important noticed. She wanted to tell the head nurse something was wrong with me, but I managed to convince her I was okay, and I told her she had her hair combed nice and she went all red and hurried out of the room. No way I could afford to stay in the hospital any longer.

Rosmack Rampel and Mama came at noon. Mama had my Sunday suit.

"Are you planning to take me to the funeral home?" I teased.

"No, Kjnals," Mama said. "It's just time you tried to look like something."

So I left the hospital looking like I was on my way to church in my Sunday suit with Oata's zipper Bible in my hand. Rosmack opened the rear door of Rape Rampel's Chrysler for me and I was happy she hadn't come with the Harley. My schinkuhfleisch was still pretty sore. Of course, Mama insisted we go home right away, that I should stay in bed for a week at least, and no way would she let me go schneppa around anymore. It was high time I started farming the land the way Papa would have wanted and I should find myself a wife and grow up instead of trying to be a dummheit detective getting himself killed all the time. Rosmack's black braid hung down over the back of the seat and in the mirror I saw she was trying not to laugh. It had to be pretty funny for Rosmack to hear an old fortz like me getting bawled out by his mama like he was maybe thirteen years old. I tried not to listen to Mama, but looking into Rosmack's eyes in the mirror didn't help me either. It only made me think how right Mama was. I needed to grow up and find myself a wife, only it isn't so easy as all that, this finding a wife business. Parents never teach their sons how to do it, and in Sunday School for sure they don't tell you how to do it, and the Hollywood School of Detection has no checklist of how to find a wife. I mean, how do you get from glutzing at panty lines, or peeking through willow leaves, to a situation where you have something to hold onto? Those who have crossed that abyss think there is nothing to it but they never tell you how they did it and the older a person gets the harder it is to figure out.

Lucky for me Mama was so busy preaching about what was good for me she never thought to ask what kind of pickle I was in. Even luckier, when we got home Bulchi Wiebe's airplane was parked in the yard, and Mama forgot all about talking to me. I figured she must have forgiven Bulchi for wanting to borrow ten thousand dollars from her. For a second I thought I should ask Bulchi Wiebe for advice on how to get a woman, only he waited most of his life for my papa to die and that didn't seem like such a wonderful way to do things, but the thought of sitting in jail for the rest of my life waiting for a husband to die got me back on track and as soon as Mama and Bulchi Wiebe were inside the house I asked Rosmack to drive me over to see Shusta Paul.

Going to see Shusta Paul was a bit like crossing your legs to delay going to the beckhouse. I didn't think Paul could help me with my most pressing problem—the possible murder charge. L.U.Dyck's words were still rustling in my head. It was too late to fulfil his request, and I didn't know how to face what his request meant.

So I asked Rosmack what she had found out about L.U.Dyck.

"You know, it was the strangest thing," she said. "After I left you at the hospital, I drove right away to A.Dyck's place to ask if he could tell me where his brother was. When I got there all the lights were out. A.Dyck's car was in front of the house but his truck was gone. I knocked, but nobody came to the door, and when I turned away to go back to my bike I thought I heard something by an upstairs window. I looked up but I couldn't see anything. Then A.Dyck came home in his truck. I asked him where L.U.Dyck was. 'In Niagara Falls,' he said and hurried into the house and slammed the door after himself. You know, he didn't even switch any light on in the house, even after I drove away, because I looked back a few times to see if he would, but he never did."

"Maybe A.Dyck was just trying to save on his hydro bill," I said, though my mind was fitting pieces together into a whole different story now. L.U.Dyck's whispered words had put a twist on things I never would have thought of before. I had a chance not to be the only alleged suspect in this alleged homicide. My mind was noticing details that hadn't seemed important before. Some things were starting to make sense.

Shusta Paul had just lit up a new cigarette when we walked in and I took a deep breath of smoke and leather. When I leaned against his counter I realized I was still gripping Oata's zipper Bible. After satisfying Paul's questions about my health I got right down to the point. I wanted information.

I wanted to know about Ernst Blatz. I wanted to know how come Ernst Blatz was after this particular group of farmers for blackmailing. None of those farmers was all that well off. Others could have come up with more blackmail money faster. Well, Shusta Paul puffed his cigarette red hot before he told me, and at first he didn't want Rosmack to stay to listen to it, and I could see he shamed himself about something, at least that's the way it seemed to me. His hands shook as he rolled himself another smoke and the tobacco spilled out all over the table. He started a fresh one and this time he got it going. After he had smoked about half he began to talk.

"It happened the night before Ernst was to leave for the army and he already had his uniform with pointed army cap and everything. Ernst had been acting like a bigshot, showing off to some girls in Puggefeld, and we shuzzels were driving around with Shaftich Shreeda in his dad's Model T when we met Ernst walking along the road practising his stiff soldier walk and saluting the hydro poles. So we kidnapped him, pulled his uniform off and threw him into Buffalo Creek. Then we hung his clothes up on the washline by the Neualtbergfeld schoolyard where a bunch of teenage girls were sitting on the swings. It was just a prank then and for sure in the army Ernst went through lots worse but I guess he never forgave us because each one who was there that night got the blackmail note."

"How did Ernst get those pictures?"

"Well, Ernst Blatz's family was related to the Martenses and I guess that's how he found them. Maybe he had them all this time from the war years because he did come back for a short while after the war was over. It was only for a few days and I don't think we even thought about what we had done. Ernst never came near us. I think he was busy finding a girlfriend. He didn't bring home a war bride. He came home about the same time A.Dyck's pig caused that accident and now that I think about it, I think, yeah, when he left he took that Heinrichs girl with him, the one who had a sister killed in that accident."

"Ernst Blatz went away with Hilda Heinrichs, who was going to marry L.U.Dyck?"

"Yes, I think that's the way it was. It was a hard time for Lawrence and Abe, especially Abe. He almost committed suicide. Lawrence found him hanging in the hayloft and cut him down, and after that Abe wouldn't let his brother out of his sight. Sure, they were always arguing but they depended on each other for everything, especially after their parents died. I can't understand what is happening there now, how come they sold the farm so quickly."

"Abe told me they sold the farm so Lawrence could marry Hilda."

"Marry Hilda? You mean that woman has come back?"

"Yes, I've seen her a few times."

"You've seen her, here in Gutenthal?"

"Yes."

Shusta Paul opened a drawer and pulled out a leaflet with

a right-handed swastika on it. "This was in the second blackmail Bible I received." Letters on the blades spelled MILK. Underneath were the words *Mothers Initiating Loving Kindness. An Alternative Relief Agency.* "Is this the woman you saw?"

He opened the leaflet and pointed to a picture of the doll woman with a caption: MILK president Hilda Heinrichs-Blatz. I looked at it very closely to make sure it wasn't Lena Bergen. The woman wasn't wearing round eyeglasses. But in a list of names under the heading MILK Executive was the name Lena Bergen-Wiens, Fundraising Chairperson. I looked over the rest of the leaflet for Yetta Hiebat or Fleeda Shreeda, but I didn't see them. The leaflet didn't say exactly what MILK did, just that the organization was involved in projects in Africa. The leaflet didn't ask for donations.

Shaftich Shreeda and his wife pulled up in front of the credit union as we came out of the shoe repair shop. "Is Fleeda at home?" I called. Shreeda looked at me a little funny. He was wearing his Sunday suit, too.

"No, Kjnals, she's gone."

"Gone?"

"Gone back to Uganda."

"Back to Uganda?"

"Yes, we just took her to the airport, her and Barbara Buhler. Fleeda's agency just found funding to build an AIDS clinic."

"Barbara? AIDS clinic?"

"Yeah, Fleeda and Barbara joined a new agency, what was it called again?"

"MILK," Fleeda's mother said. "Like from a cow."

"And they just found funding?"

"Yeah, for an AIDS clinic. It's terrible how many people

have it in Uganda, Fleeda says. I pray to God she doesn't get it herself."

My head was making up a story out of this. Shaftich Shreeda started to back his car away when I saw his wife say something to him and he stuck his head out of the window. "Fleeda said if I saw you I should say thank you."

"That's all she said?"

"Yep, that's all she said. So long."

Shreeda drove away.

"Are you sure Fleeda never said anything to you about this MILK?" I asked Rosmack as we got into the car.

"MILK? No, but they sound like good people."

"Yeah, I guess so," I said. "They never asked you to go along to Uganda to help?"

"No way. If I wanted to help people there's lots in Canada that need help."

"Yeah, like me," I said. The itch and the pain were taking over my brain again. "Please take me home now. I have to take some pills."

Rosmack didn't say anything more till she turned into my driveway.

"Say Neil, there's a powwow at the reserve tomorrow. Would you come with me?"

For a moment I let myself swim in the pond with Rosmack after killing a buffalo, then I made myself look into her black eyes, made myself open the windows of my soul.

"Sure," I said. "I'll come with you."

Mama was out with Bulchi Wiebe visiting by Muttachi Siemens's place, so instead of taking a pill I made a phone call to the MILK office in Ottawa. I pretended I was a researcher for "The Fifth Estate" and got this secretary on the phone to tell me about Hilda Heinrichs-Blatz, and when I wanted to know if Blatz was Hilda's husband's name, the secretary told me that Blatz was Hilda's ex-husband's name and how Hilda had gone through a bitter divorce because her ex-husband was a mercenary soldier at total odds with the aims and objectives of an organization like MILK. But Hilda was over her personal problems. Right now she was on a very successful fundraising tour in southern Manitoba and plans for an AIDS clinic in Uganda were going full steam ahead. The line was suddenly disconnected, but I had heard enough. The bungled drug money was going to get laundered through an AIDS clinic in Uganda. Powdered MILK indeed. How would a hard-boiled detective deal with truth like that? What could I do with truth I couldn't prove? The truth that could make me free.

But something else bothered me more. I paged through the zipper Bible, trying to figure out who had given it to me. Fleeda had had this Bible last as far as I knew. I checked out another bobby pin. It marked a page in St. John. Chapter 19 verse 30 was boxed in red pen.

> When Jesus therefore had received the
> vinegar he said, 'It is finished': and he
> bowed his head, and gave up the ghost.

"A. Dyck," I said out loud. "Vinegar. But how would Fleeda know? Or could it be Yetta Hiebat?" I called Holzyebock Hiebat's place and he told me Yetta was visiting relatives in Toronto.

I made another phone call before I drove off on the old Farmall tractor, holding the zipper Bible against the steering wheel. On the vibrating tractor seat my wounds felt like a toothache you can't keep your tongue away from. The air smelled of ripening grain and tractor engine exhaust. For a few minutes I wiped my predicament from my mind and let myself dream of chasing buffalo on horseback with Rosmack at my side. A dream life as simple as a spaghetti western, black and white even in colour. But I couldn't shoot my way out of the dream I was really in. Even if I had a gun I wouldn't be sure which rings on the target were black and which were white. I had always thought a hard-boiled detective could separate the black from the white, but what colour was MILK? And what colour would I find when I finished this final investigation at the end of the tractor ride? The wrong answer could mean the black circle at the centre of the target was me.

A.Dyck didn't look up from the kitchen table when I came in. He was staring at a pile of old letters beside a wooden Japanese orange crate. I sat down across from him. He didn't move. I picked up a letter dated February 14, 1950 in Paraguay. It was addressed to Abe, in German script like we used to learn in school. The language was German, too, and I couldn't understand it very well. It seemed to be a love letter, quite a juicy one I thought, because the person talked about taking her coat off and washing her feet and something about her friend sticking his hand through a keyhole and making her insides tickle, and it didn't really say anything about happenings in Paraguay, only that she thought of Abe at night when she was reading the Song of Solomon. The letter was signed, "Liebe Lena Bergen."

I looked at a few more letters. They all seemed to be from "Liebe Lena Bergen."

"Dreck," A.Dyck said. "Those letters are all dreck. Lena never wrote them. Lena never wrote to me at all, just once, when she first moved to Paraguay with her family. Such dreck she never wrote to me though it hurt me just as much to hear she was going to have a baby and was marrying Schmuggle

Veens. It wasn't her fault, she was so young and I was so young and I didn't know how to do things, I was so shy and I wanted to tell her how much I loved her and that I wanted her to wait till I could marry her and get her from Paraguay. I was on my way to the Bergen yard, it was a Sunday evening, and I had made up my mind I would talk to her no matter how hard it was for me and as I'm getting close to the yard where the caragana hedge was just blooming with yellow flowers I see Lena behind the bushes with Blatz, Blatz in his army suit and that man he had no shame, I guess in the army you lose all your shame, and it was awful, just awful, like being in Hell I think but I couldn't turn away, even when he laid her on the ground, I couldn't turn away, and then Hilda spoke from behind me, and made shpott of me."

"Where is Hilda now?" I asked, putting the zipper Bible on the table in front of him. His face went white.

"Hilda?" A.Dyck's voice squeaked a little.

"Lawrence told me to keep you away from Hilda. Where is she now?"

"Now?"

"Where did you take her after the pond?"

"Pond?"

"Where did you take her after she drowned?"

"Drowned?"

"After you drowned her in the pond."

"I drowned Hilda?"

"You left her in the water. You thought she was drowned. I pulled her out and tried to revive her. I couldn't, so I went for help. When the police came she was gone. Where did you take her?"

"Take her, what are you saying, take her, drown her?"

"You took her to the trailer and set it on fire, right? You

burned the trailer to get rid of Hilda's body. But in the morning I found the bones. Then the bones disappeared. What did you do with the bones, Abe? What did you do with the bones?"

A.Dyck sat there and stared.

"How did she survive? You drowned her. You burned her. How come she was at that house with the orchestra? Is she still alive?"

"It wasn't Hilda!" A.Dyck cried in a voice like claws sliding off a steel granary roof.

"Who wasn't Hilda?"

"The woman with the harp!"

"Who was it?"

A.Dyck's face had no blood left in it. His eyes were almost clear like glass marbles. "It was Satan's ghost!"

"Ghost?"

"Oh Kjnals, it is such a grislich thing, Satan, when he takes you. How he can change his shape to anything he wants, sometimes Hilda, sometimes a zipper Bible with gruelich verses underlined!"

"But . . ."

"Lies, all lies like these letters. Always trying to mix me up. I thought Lawrence and Hilda were long gone to Niagara Falls. Then on Tuesday, the day they had a sale in town, I got the zipper Bible with the picture, and after you left I got out these letters and I was reading them and it fell me by that Lena never wrote these letters, and then the door opened, and there was Hilda in that black wedding dress, smiling like a woman that wants a man, and she had a cheque in one hand and a pen in the other and she came to the table and put the cheque in front of me. She wanted me to sign a cheque for all the money from the farm and the auction. She said it was a small price for a dead sister, that a pig couldn't even the score, and I saw Lawrence had signed, and Hilda said it would all go to missions, so I signed under Lawrence's name and for a second I felt like my soul was clean. But then I looked up at Hilda as she was putting the cheque in an envelope and I saw the shpott in her eyes and I-I-I couldn't let her do this to Lawrence, I-I could see it in her eyes th-that she would leave him as soon as she cashed the cheque, and it was just such a hartsoft gruelich thing to want for an accident that was maybe my pig's fault so long ago, and I couldn't let her break Lawrence's heart again. You know he tried to hang himself that time when she ran away with Ernst Blatz, oh Kjnals, so cold the blood got, so grislich cold, Schneppa Kjnals, and I could only think she was Satan herself, laughing in my face, and then my hands had her around the throat, oh Kjnals it happened so fast, so gruelich fast, Sodom and Gomorrah, it was too late to turn back. . . ."

A.Dyck looked at me and I felt my own blood get cold. "You know, Schneppa Kjnals, it was all so clear then, what I had to do, only you had to come before I could hide the car . . . and I saw you pull her out of the water, and then when you went away, I moved her so you would get mixed up and nobody would believe you, and I didn't think there would be bones left from the fire, only the next day you found them, and so I moved the bones, too, but the grislich thing about it was when I got home with the bones, I couldn't find the envelope with the cheque, and then Lawrence came home looking for Hilda, and Satan's ghosts started to bother me for money." A.Dyck covered his face with his hands.

"Where did you keep Lawrence?" I asked quietly. "Will he tell them in the hospital? Does Lawrence know what you did? Does he know? How did he get away?"

I asked more questions but A.Dyck never said another word. He just sat there, staring, breathing and staring, but he wouldn't react to me. I gave up. I couldn't badger the old man anymore. I got up and left the house, thinking I would go for a ride on the tractor and circle back and try again.

I idled for about two miles, my head whirling with thoughts, when I remembered what Shusta Paul had said about A.Dyck trying to commit suicide. A.Dyck had just told me L.U.Dyck had tried to kill himself. Who was right didn't matter. I raced back, the throttle lever pulled down past wide open, not caring how much the bouncing seat hurt my ass. A.Dyck was gone from the house, but he wasn't hard to find. A noisy engine was running in the barn. Not everything had been sold at the auction. A.Dyck was grinding feed.

Through the half-open door to the feed room I watched A.Dyck dump a scoop of oats into the grinder. Then he picked something black out of a ten-gallon cream can and threw it into the hopper. For a few seconds the sound of the grinding changed, then A.Dyck threw in another chunk. He added another scoop of oats, pulled a charred stick out of the can and tossed it in. Bones! The burned bones! I didn't think anymore. I barged into the feed room, grabbed the cream can. I had the bones! I had solid evidence. I had what I needed to finish my story. I had the kernel of truth. There really had been a murder in Gutenthal. A crime of passion. They would have to believe me now!

"Pig bones! Schneppa Kjnals, those are PIG BONES!" A.Dyck's hah hahs hammered through the feed room over the scraping of the empty grinder. Then his face went white and green and red and purple all at once. "Dunnaschet Gevitta!" he screamed. "Gott halp me! Hilda, best du nicht dout?"

In the doorway stood Schmuggle Veens's States wife in a

long black wedding dress, holding L.U.Dyck's hand. The couple wasn't smiling. She could have been Hilda Heinrichs crawled out of the grave. L.U.Dyck stared at the bones in the cream can and cried, "Abe, what have you done?"

It took a few days before I got my Volkswagen back. Even though the bones were still being tested in the RCMP lab, all the charges against me were dropped—except for the operating a detective agency without a licence charge. Woarheit Wahl gave me ninety days to apply for a licence.

Kowolchuk was out of sorts when he handed over my keys. He had a sore trigger finger from typing all those stories. He also wasn't happy because all this alleged money, government money if all the stories were true, was missing. I hadn't said anything about Fleeda and Barbara but the other drug bunglers had figured out what had happened, except how do you trace cash that wasn't supposed to exist in the first place? The farmers who had been blackmailed were planning to sue Ernst Blatz and the CIA. I thought of suing the army bengel but he couldn't even afford real bullets so what was the point. The scars on my rump might make for interesting conversation sometime.

The RCMP dragged the pond and found the grandfather clock. No one could find the envelope with A.Dyck's cheque in it. The army bengel had gone a bit crazy in the head after he heard his mother was really dead, and the hospital wouldn't let me question him to find out why he had stolen the clock from my car.

Schmuggle Veens's States wife was leaning against her green LTD when I came out of the cop shop. I thought she looked rather funny in her fluorescent spandex bicycle shorts. She was smoking an L&M cigarette, but there was no bracelet on her ankle. When she saw me coming, she got into her car. I hurried over and rested my elbows on the sill of her open window. Lena let a lungful of smoke drift from her nose and mouth.

"Thanks for coming when I called," I said. "You helped save my butt, what was left of it."

"It was the least I could do for Hilda," she said, inhaling another lungful of smoke.

"So what does your husband think of MILK?"

"He doesn't know."

"He doesn't know? But your name is right there on that leaflet."

"My dear Schmuggle Veens never learned how to read, so unless someone tells him, he'll never find out. Besides, the real Lena Bergen-Wiens lives in Ottawa. I don't believe in hyphenated names." She started her car. "So long, Schneppa Kjnals," she smiled as she began to back away.

"Wait!" I called. She stopped and I looked Schmuggle Veens's States wife in the eye. "When you took Hilda's LTD after Corny Blatz dropped you off, did you by any chance find an envelope in the car?"

"Well yes," she said. "I noticed an envelope under the seat. It was addressed to MILK in Ottawa. I figured Hilda had forgotten it so I put a stamp on it and was going to mail it."

"But you didn't?"

"No, and when I found out Hilda was really dead I opened it." She stopped and lit a cigarette. "I gave the cheque back to Lawrence."

"Was he pleased?"

"No, he put it back in the envelope and told me to mail it, so I did."

"Hope this MILK outfit has a charitable tax number."

"It sure does, Schneppa Kjnals, it sure does."

So I still had some loose ends and maybe they would stay loose. If I wrote to the AIDS clinic in Uganda, maybe Fleeda Shreeda would tell me how she knew it was A.Dyck and why she didn't go to the police straight out instead of marking verses in Oata's zipper Bible. Maybe when Yetta Hiebat came home from Toronto she could tell me about that Bible. Maybe A.Dyck was right. Maybe that zipper Bible was Satan's ghost changing his shape.

Rosmack Rampel stopped her motorcycle an inch away from my toe. "Race you home!" she said.

"Give me a minute to check if the RCMP siphoned the gas out of my tank."

Well, it wasn't exactly like chasing buffalo on horseback but it made me just as happy. For the next hour Rosmack and I chased each other down all the backroads to Gutenthal. Sure, there was an ache in my seat and an ache in my heart because I knew this joy wouldn't last, but for that hour I was full of dreams and plans and hopes. I felt really alive, and I could hardly wait for the evening when I would go with Rosmack to the powwow at the reserve. When we got to Rape Rampel's driveway, Rosmack leaned from her motorcycle and kissed me.

Then as I drove away on my rounds of Gutenthal I saw a self-propelled swather cutting down Penzel Panna's sweet clover. I knew for sure Penzel and his family had gone to the Black Hills for a week, so I floored that Volkswagen because I am Schneppa Kjnals. I am everywhere. I am the eyes at the back of your head. I see the world in a stepped-in cowpie. I am a good neighbour for a fee.

Photo: Jack Simpson

Armin Wiebe was born in Altona, Manitoba, and grew up in the Mennonite communities south of Winnipeg. He has worked as a beet weeder, peanut bagger, farm hand and teacher, and now lives and writes in Winnipeg. His first novel, *The Salvation of Yasch Siemens*, was shortlisted for the *Books in Canada* First Novel Award and the Leacock Medal for Humour.

His short stories have appeared in numerous journals, including *Canadian Short Story Magazine, Grain, The Fiddlehead, NeWest Review, Prairie Fire, The New Quarterly* and *Canadian Ethnic Studies.* He has also had stories anthologized in *Section Lines: A Manitoba Anthology, Liars and Rascals, Made in Manitoba: An Anthology of Short Fiction, Manitoba Stories* and *Good Humour Man.* A short story entitled "Mouse Lake" was selected for inclusion in the *Journey Prize Anthology* and was also a finalist in the Western Magazine Awards. Armin is currently at work on his third book, a "gothic" novel set on the shores of Lake Manitoba.